Cody Angel
by Joanne Whitfield

CODY ANGEL
by
Joanne Whitfield

New Victoria Publishers, Inc.

Copyright © 1991, by Joanne Whitfield
All rights reserved. No part of this work may be reproduced or transmitted in any form by any means, electronic or mechanical, without permission in writing from the publisher.

Published by New Victoria Publishers, Inc. A feminist literary and cultural organization, P.O. Box 27 Norwich, Vermont

ISBN 0-934678-28-6

Library of Congress Cataloging-in-Publication Data

Whitfield, Joanne, 1955–
   Cody angel / by Joanne Whitfield.
      p.   cm.
   ISBN 0-934678-28-6 : $8.75
   I. Title.
PS3573.H4884C6   1991
813'.54--dc20
                                                                                         90-26553
                                                                                              CIP

For my mother
Thea
and Evelyn
with love

CHAPTER 1

"They're so succulent," Karen had said.

Which was why Dana was looking in a freezer full of pale pink organic chickens. They looked like the ingredient for chicken a la triple rigor mortis, but she wanted to surprise Karen this weekend with organic chicken soup. It would be Karen's first visit to San Francisco since Karen asked her to leave Stockton six months ago. If everything went smoothly, perhaps she would ask Dana to come back.

Organic chicken in tow, Dana stepped into her baby-blue Pontiac, a gift from Daddy on her eighteenth, won by him in a poker game. She set the chicken down gently on the seat. A curly black-haired woman sauntered by—Jerri, her ex-lover as of two weeks ago. Dana felt ambushed. Her nerves stood at attention. She rushed a mildly shaking hand, shiny with nail polish, through her shoulder-length, light-brown hair, pushing bangs away from her large green eyes. As the woman entered the health food store, Dana realized it was not Jerri but another Jerri look-alike. Ever since Jerri broke up with her, the city has been teeming with Jerri look-alikes.

I really wish Jerri would call, Dana thought, swinging her car onto Mission Street. Mission Street was one big enchilada of five-and-dime department stores, discount furniture marts, thrift shops, burrito restaurants and Doggy Diners. She remembered they disconnected her phone yesterday for not paying that ninety dollars in calls to Karen. Perhaps Jerri tried to call but....

She fumbled in a small paper bag for an orange soda. It was a hot July day. Steering with one hand while easing the flip-top up, fizz shot into her eyes. The traffic blurred. Her Pontiac smacked into the Mercedes Benz she had been tailgating, causing soda to fountain out onto her white rayon blouse, run down her tight designer jeans, and trickle into the seat crease where various pizza crumbs lay lodged.

She was in a wreck—God, a real wreck.

And *blood*.

But she saw the wetness was only soda. Nerves tingling with electricity, she stepped cautiously from her injured Pontiac, leaving the orange soda dripping on her like a wound. Perhaps it would arouse pity in the Mercedes driver; perhaps innocent Dana would be forgiven, a victim of a can of orange soda.

A lowered black Lincoln Continental loaded with Hispanic teenagers loudly revved up behind her Pontiac, which now blocked traffic. Glancing uneasily at the Continental's contents, she heard a Southern voice tuba from the Mercedes, "Damn seat belt!"

Arms crossed, Dana nervously watched two stove-pipe-shaped legs struggling out of the Mercedes. Stockings and red pumps, accompanied by a silver poodle, descended.

The lady brushed wrinkles from her red dress-suit before making her debut to Dana, a cluster of blocked cars and two Goodwill drivers unloading a truck."Why'd you run into my Benz? I knew I shouldn't have come down into this part of town!"

Her eyes angrily darted at Dana, who suddenly felt more reduced than an amoeba. "I had to get to a pie shop down here and....." The woman looked flustered. "You turned my pie upside down!" Pausing to stress the seriousness of the situation, she said, "And it was a *meringue*!"

Fear rose in Dana. "I'm sorry." Even the lady's hair looked threatening: a large dyed red fist resting on a large skull.

The Lincoln honked. A cosmeticized teenage girl with a large red flower in her black hair leaned out the Lincoln's window. "Get out of the road! Move it!" The Lincoln let out a long honk.

"Ya'll can move on around us when this other lane clears," the lady snapped back. "Damn punks think they own the roads," she said to the Goodwill drivers.

The lady blasted out a sigh, heavy, thick, and accusing as tear gas. Her deliberating eyes glared too long at Dana, who felt as if she had been taken hostage. Then something strange happened: the lady's look softened somewhat. She began looking at Dana as if she was salvageable, appraising her; Dana imagined her conclusion: innocent face, vulnerable eyes, insecure stance, well-groomed appearance. "You should have been paying better attention to yer driving," she scolded in a motherly way. The lady looked closely at the damage: one badly dented bumper. "Looks like a hurricane hit it." The lady leaned over and touched the dent. "Poor Betsy." She looked at the Goodwill boys. "Looks like this little girl was trying to turn my car into a Mercedes Has Benz."

Chuckling, one of the truck drivers, beer-bellied and bald, said, "Kid just wasn't watching her driving."

Blushing, Dana wished she could disappear. This city had a conspiracy against her. Since coming here six months ago, she had been left by Jerri, her lover of almost six months, laid off from her lunch counter job last week, looted by the phone company. She felt landslided by life. And now the last straw—left to the mercy of a Mercedes Benz driver. Her eyes watered in self-pity.

The Lincoln jerked out around them. "Fat Bitchchhhhh!" Several other cars trailed quietly after the Lincoln.

Dana hoped the woman would not call the police. She hadn't called her a 'fat bitch.' She was just trying to open an orange soda on a hot day. The police would suspend her license for driving without insurance. She couldn't afford it. She couldn't even afford her rent. Her eyes fogged as she looked at the dented bumper much as she used to at a glass of spilled milk while Daddy scolded.

"I don't have time for this," the lady said. "I've got a one o'clock appointment."

"I'm sorry."

"Yer gonna pay for this. You better believe me, young lady. Yer gonna pay for every cotton pickin' cent of damage you did to this car. This is a brand new car!"

"I'm sorry." She could feel her face, Shirley Temple sweet, turn thoroughly pink.

Coughing, the woman whipped a gold-plated cigarette case from her watermelon-sized red purse, as if coughing reminded her to smoke. Dana was sure the lady would try to sue for thousands over the cruddy dented bumper. If only she were home in Cody, Wyoming, Daddy would take care of this.

She remembered high-tailing down the highway outside Cody, angry and hurt because Karen had said she was marrying Teddy. What had happened to their dream of living in New Orleans together after high school? Dana had slammed on the brakes for a jack rabbit. Spinning out, her Pontiac plunked into a road sign. Daddy had taken care of it at the gas station that he leased. He had hammered the dents out and put on a new tire. Then he had taken Dana, who only had a bruised elbow, out for a spare-rib dinner.

Dana considered how both accidents were Karen related. She felt like a martyr wounded in the line of duty, securing an organic chicken for Karen.

Fearing her non-responsive stance might provoke the lady past verbal violence, she slid her hands into her pockets and nervously said, "I'm really...I'm really sorry about this. It was an accident."

"Well, I hope you didn't do it on *purpose*."

"I'm sorry."

The lady's burning blue eyes pointed at Dana like machine guns waiting for the goods to be delivered.

"Don't worry. I'll pay for this. Uh, I'll take care of it."

The woman's pink almond-shaped lips formed an amused smirk as she sucked slowly, calculatingly off her cigarette. Dana avoided looking her in the eye. She would ask Daddy to wire money immediately. But no. She couldn't. Not after leaving him alone in Cody. She mustn't ask for anything.

"Could you ladies move your cars?" the bald Goodwill driver said with exaggerated politeness, rubbing his nose. "You got our truck trapped in here."

"We'll be done in just a moment, boys," the lady said. "Young lady, what's yer insurance company's name?"

Dana hesitated, thinking the woman would call the police if she found out she didn't have insurance. "Uh, I think it's...I don't really remember."

"You don't know who yer own insurance is with?! I want yer name, full name, address, and telephone number. I'd call the police but I'm running late as it is. I don't have time to bother with all this. I've got a beauty parlor appointment to get to. Now you write all that information down for me while I call the parlor to tell them I'm running late." She shook her head and handed Dana a leash attached to an overly trimmed poodle. "Hold Peach's leash." She stepped toward a pay phone then stopped. "You should calm down. Long as yer insurance pays for this trouble like you said it would there's no problem. Right?" Dana nodded up and down. This better not interfere with Karen's visit in any way. She felt angry at the woman as if she somehow caused the accident, as if Dana were her victim.

The woman's poodle sat by Dana's tan heels, whining and puddling the asphalt, while Dana worried whether all her savings, eighty-five dollars, would get her to the Mexican border before this lady learned that the only insurance she ever bought was for a dealer's twenty-one while playing blackjack in Reno with Karen once.

CHAPTER 2

"You gave me a phony phone number, young lady. But I reckon that's not news to you. What's going on here?!"

Dana would rather have found ten Jehovah's witnesses on her doorstep or a burglar picking her lock, than the large Southern woman with a new bouffant above her bulldog face, her nails manicured and painted red. God, help me, Dana thought.

"Soon as I was done at the parlor yesterday, and done dropping my car off at the dealer's," the woman said, punching the words out, "I rang you up to get the name of yer insurance company. Some assurance I got! A disconnected line's all I got." Her hand was fist-tight around the chain handle of her purse.

Like a cat licking itself when agitated, Dana tightened the tie on her bathrobe, pushed wet hair out of her eyes and inspected her fingernails. What was it she feared—a citizen's arrest—a subpoena—or just an address check as a preliminary to a post-midnight hired murder? "I've a mind to call the police."

"I'm sorry," Dana said quickly as if it was her motto, and genuflected her eyes to the ground. "That was my number. When I wrote it down for you I forgot it'd been disconnected yesterday." Looking past the woman she noticed a cab waiting. She hoped it would not have to wait long. She grew increasingly afraid that this woman might somehow ruin Karen's visit, just two days away.

"Yer phone's been disconnected?" Eyeing Dana suspiciously, the woman put a cigarette between her lips. Striking a match, she said coolly, "I think we'd better sit down and talk this matter over, don't you?"

She looked at Dana waiting for the yes which Dana could not help but offer. Dana opened the front door just as she would have for Jehovah's witnesses had they pushed. "Keep yer meter running, Honey," the woman yelled to the cab driver, tapping a gray spray of ashes on Dana's defenseless doorsteps.

Dana was glad her studio apartment blistered with mess—

perhaps it would perturb the woman, provoke a premature parting. Still soda-stained, her blouse and jeans hung on her painting easel by tall windows. Windows that looked three stories down onto Spray Craft Auto Painting, Sixteenth Street Quality Cleaners, the Graphics Center, and the Industrial Club for ex-alcoholics. The woman ran a critical eye around Dana's small studio, small enough to incite claustrophobia. It looked half-vacated, half-moved into. She hadn't had the money to furnish it fully yet. "How long you been living in *this place*?" the woman said, looking thoroughly out of her environment.

"Six months."

The woman eyed the easel. "You paint?"

Dana nodded.

"You got something I could sit down on?" Dana brought a chair in from the small kitchenette. Remembering the ashes on the porch, she handed the woman an ashtray, then sat down on her bed. Her heart beat like the drum roll before an execution.

"If you weren't so young I wouldn't be this patient with you. How old are you, young lady?"

"Twenty-one."

"You don't looked a day over eighteen. Where you from? You got an accent but I couldn't place it."

"Cody, Wyoming."

"Let's set one thing straight before we get down to business. You do agree this accident was entirely yer fault? One hundred percent yer fault?"

"My fault?" Dana faltered, feeling the orange soda, the organic chicken, Karen, the heat of the day, and the Mercedes had all conspired against her.

"Was there a thing I could a done to stop you from bumping into Betsy?" The woman sounded like a prosecuting attorney. Dana sat still, silent, a schoolgirl blushing without an answer, afraid to incriminate herself.

The woman took a quick angry suck off her cigarette. "What's yer explanation for what happened today?"

It all seemed somewhat unreal to Dana. She sat still for a second. "I was opening this can of orange soda. The fizz shot up into my eyes and I couldn't see the road and—"

The woman interrupted Dana with a laugh. "Maybe we should sue the orange soda people!" Her voice toughened. "I reckon they got insurance. What about you, young lady?"

Dana's bare toes, shiny with clear nail polish, bent and twisted. "I'd rather my insurance company didn't know about this. They'd raise my premiums. The rates are already so high. I can't afford any higher. Do you mind if we just settle this between me and you? I'll pay you anything I owe you."

"Six hundred and twenty-five dollars?! That's the estimate."

Dana hesitated, then nodded, a large lump in her throat. Six hundred and twenty-five dollars on top of the eight hundred Daddy had loaned her, three hundred Karen had loaned. The landlord, the phone company—it was overwhelming. She did not know what to do other than hold the woman at bay, lie if necessary, until some savior came along. Out of habit, she played the fair maiden.

"I'd hate to think I couldn't trust a sweet-looking girl like you. I want you to know nobody's ever gotten away with fooling with me. No one has. And no one will. That's the way it is." She punctuated her statement with silence. "When would you have the money for me? Six hundred and twenty-five dollars. I want a money order. Make it out to Mrs. Rosylyn Horstman."

"Monday. Come back on Monday for the money. The money order." Monday because Karen was coming this weekend. Karen would find a way to rescue her from this heartless woman. And if she didn't, at least Dana's last days would be spent with Karen.

"Tell me, young lady. Who's yer employer?"

"I'm between jobs. I was working on a lunch counter in the Financial District up until last week."

"You quit?"

"I was laid off."

"Me and my husband, *Mr. Horstman*...." She said his name as if it disturbed her. "We're in the restaurant business down South, selling wieners. You've probably heard of our chain, *Roz's Dogs*." Dana had not heard of it. "We seldom have to lay off any of our girls at our twenty-seven locations. Hard working and loyal those girls are." She eyed Dana suspiciously. "It isn't easy for an unemployed working girl to come up with six hundred and twenty-five dollars. An unemployed working girl living in a small place like this. You said they had disconnected yer phone. You behind in yer bills?"

"Just my phone bill."

"Just yer phone bill. I reckon yer planning to pay me with the money you don't have for yer phone bill?! You fooling with me now?"

"No."

"You sure?"

"No—I mean yes. I'm sure."

The lady rose out of her chair. Standing over Dana, she waved her cigarette like a conductor's baton. "Yes or no? I've a mind to call the police right now. I've got witnesses. Goodwill. And you'd be smart not to push my patience any further."

Feeling cornered, stampeded, Dana decided to throw herself at the rich woman's mercy, hoping to be saved by the grace of Southern hospitality. "I'm sorry," she said in a dejected voice. She did not look up. "Please understand. I hardly have any money. Just eighty-five dollars. I'll give it to you. But that's all the money I have. If I had more I'd give it to you. I would. I lost my job and I've barely got enough money for my rent and.... If I could I'd move back home to my Daddy's in Cody but I couldn't do that. I'm stuck out here with no money and I don't really know many people yet and I'm really sorry I hit your car. If there's anything I could do for you...."

"No insurance either?"

Dana shook her head.

"I've a mind to call the police. But...." She scrutinized Dana, helpless on the bed.

Between being rejected by Jerri, losing her job, and getting in a wreck with this woman standing over her like a Gestapo, Dana had no problem finding reasons for self-pity. She exuded self-pity, something the woman was apparently sympathetic to. In fact, she appeared to be delighted by it. "I reckon calling the police won't get me my money," the woman said, thinking aloud. "Don't you got a boyfriend who could loan you the money?"

"No."

"No boyfriend?"

"No."

She eyed a large portrait of a young woman with long, thick, strawberry-blonde hair on Dana's dresser. *All My Love, Karen* was scrawled on it. "Well, then, is there a girlfriend?"

If she finds out I'm gay, Dana thought self-protectively, she'll call the police for sure. "N-no," Dana faltered. The woman looked at her skeptically. "If there's anything I can do for you...."

"Perhaps you *can* help me."

Dana's nerves avalanched into her stomach. Perhaps the woman had been frigid with men and has heard the old cliche 'only a woman knows how to make love to a woman,' and would Dana please help her discover orgasmic bliss, pave the way for multiple orgasms. Or she was a closet case about to come out in her early sixties in Dana's studio. Dana, as eager to please and as well-mannered as the girl in the frilly white dresses, hair bows, and oxfords Grandma Wilkins and Daddy used to dress her in, said, "Perhaps I can."

CHAPTER 3

Three slices of pumpernickel with butter and orange marmalade. Three eggs sunny-side up. Salt and pepper. Two strips bacon. Coffee with two Tsp. sugar. Orange juice. Fresh fruit.

Dana reread the list once more before getting out of her Pontiac, parked near Mrs. Horstman's apartment complex on the Embarcadero near the water. The sun was just rising.

Mrs. Horstman had said, "Write this down so you won't forget. I like my breakfast in bed at eight a.m. sharp. Every morning yer to set a tray with three slices of pumpernickel with butter and...."

I have to do a good job on this breakfast, Dana thought. If she produced a good breakfast it would be a good omen. The other chores would follow suit. The woman would not fire her on day one, and Dana would last the fourteen days straight until she got, "...my maid, Georgia Anne, up here from Nashville. We've been together twenty years. I've been three weeks without her now, waiting for her to come, been having to pick up my own place. It doesn't look nearly as good as a maid would have it look. I don't function as well without a maid. So you work two weeks straight, picking up my place until Georgia Anne comes, and we'll call it even—you won't owe me a cent on Betsy." Hearing that offer, Dana had felt relieved, rescued.

"And I want you to start tomorrow morning." Then Dana had felt bitterly disappointed knowing that this meant Karen's visit would have to be postponed.

The doorman directed Dana to her destination. "Mrs. Rosylyn Horstman? Hummm. Oh yeah. New lady up in the pen. Top floor."

Dana, never even a maid in a sleazy motel, wondered at having become the maid of a hot dog aristocrat, with no experience. Her stomach shifted uneasily as the elevator stopped. She hesitated before stepping out. It all seemed unreal. She never considered the possible consequences of opening a can of orange soda.

"Good morning," the woman said, wearing a yellow quilted

bathrobe and red lipstick on smileless lips, still smoking. She motioned Dana into the grand plantation in the sky, and got right down to business. "You can put yer purse in the coat closet, Honey. Come on into the kitchen and I'll show you where everything is."

As she listened, Dana tried to look pleasant in spite of her discomfort. "After breakfast I want you to do the dishes. Then you can sweep the floor here. Broom closet's there. Follow me, Honey."

They walked into the living room. "I want you to vacuum the carpeting." Dana eyed the thick red carpeting, red crushed velvet sofa, glass coffee table, brass lamps, and large windows viewing the Bay Bridge in the distance. Karen would love it here, she thought, her mind slipping into a Karen fantasy as it often did. Just think if we lived in a plush place like this together. Heaven. There's even a balcony outside we could sit on together at dusk. She had hoped ever since Karen had asked her to leave Stockton that one day they would live together again. "It could use a good dusting too. When yer done in here, I'd like you to scrub down the tiles in the bathroom, and the toilet too. Polish the mirror, then tidy up my room. The bed's gonna need to be made everyday. I always say you can tell a good maid by how she makes a bed." She paused. "I've got a couple unpacked boxes still you can give me a hand with later before we get to fixin' supper. Now please get started on that breakfast. If you need anything I'll be in the bedroom, Honey." The whirlwind of words stopped, leaving Dana slightly disoriented. She was angry that she was trapped into doing this instead of being with Karen.

Nervously, Dana pulled eggs, bacon and butter out of the refrigerator, and melted two tablespoons of butter in a frying pan. She felt like someone learning to swim the hard way, dropped in the deep end. She hurried, worrying she would not get that gargantuan list of chores, staring at her from under a jar of orange marmalade, done today. She would surely be fired, then sued.

Quit thinking about flubbing up, she told herself. Think about something else. I miss Karen so much. And Jerri too. Dana hurriedly cracked three eggs and grabbed a spatula, wondering why Mr. Horstman wasn't here with Mrs. She grabbed for the marmalade, and knocked over an opened can of orange juice. Damn, orange juice on the penthouse floor. What if the woman saw this? Dana quickly grabbed paper towels. This is what I get instead of a visit from Karen, Dana thought. She rubbed up every last drop of orange juice, feeling as if the orange drinks of the world were out to get her.

At three minutes to eight, a black tray painted with red and yellow roses sat on Mrs. Rosylyn Horstman's lap. She set her San Francisco Chronicle aside and removed her pink horn-rimmed glasses, which had two rhinestones in the frame. She inspected the tray. "A crystal goblet for my orange juice? And my best china for bacon and eggs? A silk napkin? I must say, Honey, you serve one hell of an elegant looking tray." She laughed. The coffee and orange juice rocked about. Dana did not know if she was being complimented or criticized. She was just trying to do her best. She had assumed crystal and silver were the stoneware and stainless steel of the rich.

"Did you set yerself a plate in the kitchen?" Dana shook her head. "You didn't set yerself a tray? Well, Honey, get yourself some breakfast. Can't work on an empty stomach."

Sulking over a banana and buttered toast in the kitchen, Dana tried to time exactly how long it would take the woman to finish her breakfast, so she would know exactly when to go for the tray. She felt apprehensive of what the woman's verdict on the breakfast would be. It was crucial. She downed two cups of coffee to get up energy for the impossible load of chores, then went to the woman's bedroom. Her timing was perfect. Mrs. Horstman was dabbing her lips with the silk napkin and brushing crumbs off her hands. "Might I take your tray, Mrs. Horstman?"

"Yes, thank you," she said, glancing away from a portable color T.V. beside her dresser bureau on which the weather report blared. She looked as if she did not want to be distracted. "You cooked the eggs too long. Dried 'em out," she said looking intently at the T.V., listening to the forecast. "Don't like my eggs like that," she mumbled. "Gonna be a nice hot day for a change."

It was mid-afternoon and Dana was still not fired, despite the dried-out eggs. "Dana, Dana!" Mrs. Horstman yodeled. She was lying in a purple swimsuit on a yellow chaise lounge in the penthouse's patio garden, reading the *National Enquirer*. "Come here, Honey." She rolled onto her stomach. "Could you rub some of that suntan oil on my backside?" Dana set the broom she had been sweeping the patio with by the glass door leading into the woman's bedroom. All day the woman had improvised on the list of chores, adding new chores, deleting others for tomorrow.

Dana massaged the oil into her back. Small moans escaped from her. Dana's fingers felt lonely, thoroughly out of their environment. It was as if they had a memory of their own for Jerri and felt misplaced on this foreign turf.

It was eighty degrees and rising.

Dana felt slightly bored and tired, a state which left her mind prey to worries: And after working here two weeks where will you go? No money. No lover. No friends here. You'll get evicted for sure. Jobs are nearly impossible to find. You'll have no choice but to return to Cody and Lester will beat you up good. Just what are you going to do for the next forty years? A vacuous airy feeling edging on dread descended on Dana. Mrs. Horstman turned onto her back like a chicken rotating on a rotisserie. "That porch about swept up good?" Dana nodded and smiled like a beauty-pageant contestant at the judges. "I've always had a habit of sunbathing on Thursday mornings down South. Providing the weather was warm. Out here it's most always right for sunbathing on Thursdays. Why don't you take a break, Honey? You've been workin' hard five hours straight now. Why don't you put that towel down on the grass and lie down? Take in some sun. It's good for the nerves and complexion." Dana felt awkward. "What's the matter? Don't like the sun?"

"No, I just...," Dana said. "I don't have a swimsuit."

The woman laughed. "It's just me and you here, Honey. You can tan in yer panties and bra. No one's here to see you. Just me and you here." Dana did not want to offend the woman by refusing. She stood behind the chaise lounge where she could not be seen and stripped to her undergarments. Blushing, she placed the towel on the grass by the woman, who chuckled. "Where'd you get a pair of panties with tigers on them?"

"Stockton," Dana said, embarrassed. Karen had bought them for her.

"You got a real cute figure, Honey. Nice and slim." She ran an envious and appreciative eye up and down Dana's body. Dana wanted to cover her breasts—full breasts held in a tan, almost translucent nylon bra, through which her large, dark nipples were visible. She lay face down on the towel. "With a figure like that you should have no problem getting a boyfriend. Providing you show a little interest. Get 'em talking about themselves. That always does it," the woman said, chuckling.

Dana was quiet, uneasy.

The woman started softly humming, "*I'm Gonna Wash That Man Right Out of My Hair.*" Then she said, "What brought you to California, Honey?"

Memories bumped up in Dana's mind; ones she had tried to forget. Usually she was successful at that. She remembered four weeks ago with Jerri when she spewed out all the reasons why in a feast of talk which any therapist would have relished.

She had been lying satiated in the safety of Jerri's arms. Jerri had asked, "Do you ever feel like having sex with anyone else, Babe?"

"No. Why? Do you?"

"Yes." The word stung. It was dark in Jerri's room. The dresser, lamp, and mirror were faintly visible like colorless ghosts. "I've never been into monogamy much." Dana could barely see Jerri's black curly hair, cool blue eyes, full sensuous lips, high forehead and high cheekbones. "Dana, what do you think about us having sex with other women?"

Dana was quiet. Her heart ticked like a metronome gauged to Jerri's words, ticking faster and faster. She wished Jerri would take her arms from around her. She remembered Jerri once telling her that she had slept with over fifty women.

"Tell me," Jerri repeated, and leaned up on her elbow, hanging over Dana like a dragonfly. "Why are you ignoring my question? It's a legitimate question." In the dark, Dana could barely see the frustrated twist on Jerri's lips. "How do you feel about us having sex with other women?"

Dana felt frightened. She remembered Lester trying to force her to talk once. He had had that same frustrated look before sinking her face into the floorboard, then sitting back in his armchair and lighting a cigarette, naked but for an open blue work shirt and cowboy boots. "Why do you always clam up whenever I broach this subject?" Dana felt Jerri wanted to vandalize her voice box. "Talk to me." Silence. "Shit.... I'm feeling very angry...," she warned, her voice rising. Dana was scared silent. Jerri started shaking her shoulders, trying to shake the words out. "Talk!" she yelled. "Say something! Anything! Swear. Scream. Just talk!" Dana lay lifeless as a limp balloon. "I'm getting really angry!"

"What, what do you want me to say?"

"What do you mean what do I want you to say? Are you a puppet? You're so fucking passive. What do you want to say?"

"Nothing."

Jerri's hand whipped across her lips like a match striking a cover. It stunned her. "I'm sorry," Jerri said immediately. "I didn't mean to do that. I lost control. I'm really sorry, Babe." She stroked Dana's cheek tenderly, and kissed her forehead softly. "I'm sorry." She held Dana's head against her breasts. "I'll never do that again. I promise you." Dana had never seen Jerri so loving. Jerri was usually cool, aloof, only affectionate during sex—sometimes. She had only told Dana she loved her six times in their six months together. She continued rocking Dana against her breasts. Lester had never rocked her on his chest after any of their many fights. Lester had lit that cigarette and said, "Get the fuck out of my life. Slut. Dyke."

Dana felt guilty for getting Jerri so upset. Lately it seemed her silent nature was always pushing Jerri to the breaking point. She felt very fearful of losing her. Just last week they had had a fight like this one. Jerri had said that she needed more time alone, that she felt Dana was possessive and too serious about the relationship. She had asked Dana how she felt about that. Dana had been silent, hurt. Jerri had finally yelled, "God damn, I wish you'd tell me your feelings once in awhile. Tell me something besides 'I love you, Jerri' and 'I want to make love with you.'" Remembering that fight now, Dana felt doubly threatened.

She would make it all up to Jerri. She would be an avalanche of words pleasing Jerri, who she felt really deserved none of what had just happened. "I'm sorry," Dana said, "for getting you so mad. I just get like that sometimes. I get scared I guess."

"Of what?" She ran her fingers through Dana's hair.

"I don't know. I just do." She was quiet. "You had this look on your face like the one this old boyfriend of mine, Lester, had before beating me up once."

"Thanks. Just a second. I need a cigarette." She reached onto an antique night stand for one of her English cigarettes, lying next to a murder mystery and a fat law textbook.

"No. I don't mean it like that. I know you weren't going to beat me up."

"I didn't know you ever had a boyfriend." Jerri flicked on a small art nouveau brass lamp, causing Dana to squint.

"What's so weird about that?"

"Did I say it was weird? You know how many of the little darlings," she said facetiously, "I fucked...." She smiled, adding, "before seeing the light," and shook her head. "Anyway, who was the

15

guy? Why did you let him beat you up?"

"I didn't let him."

"No one can do anything to you without you allowing it to happen on some level. Just a second. Let me get some wine."

Lying alone, all five feet and five inches of her naked, Dana pulled a sheet up around herself, the thought of Lester causing an uncomfortable feeling of helplessness and vulnerability in her. She still feared him.

"Tell me about Lester," Jerri said, handing Dana a glass of wine.

"It's a long story."

"I'd like to hear you tell a long story. Believe it or not, I get tired of doing all the talking." Jerri stood by the bed, looking out the window onto Eighteenth Street, which was lined with Victorians, cars, and a smattering of gay men.

"Well, you know I told you about my friend, Karen, in Stockton?" she said, watching Jerri gaze out the window. Jerri always looked sophisticated, cool, seductive when she gazed out the window, smoking, one hand on her hip, completely at ease in the tall length of her tanned, toned body. A body Dana found herself always wanting to submit to.

"I remember you telling me about her. When I met you, you were a nervous wreck and really depressed because she'd just made you leave Stockton."

"Well, if I tell you about Lester I've got to start with Karen because it's all tied together. It all goes back to high school. We were really close and we planned to move to New Orleans and live together after graduating. Then one day she tells me she's going to marry Teddy, that's her husband now. She asked me to be the maid of honor. I was really—uh, I don't know. I didn't expect that." Dana envisioned Karen saying this, chewing gum, holding *Cosmopolitan*, her long hair about her shoulders, a turquoise cross necklace around her neck. "So I was her maid of honor." Dana remembered grating her fingers into the thatched handle of a plastic white basket full of carnations, trying to maintain a maid-of-honor smile, hoping if she cried the wedding guests would mistake it for tears of genuine wedding joy.

"By any chance," Jerri said, "you weren't one of those maids of honor dying to be where the groom was?"

Dana blushed. She had never told Jerri more than that she had a good friend named Karen who she had had a fight with. She was not one to talk about ex-lovers, especially when she still loved her ex much more and suspected she always would. She would drop Jerri in a second if Karen asked her to. Not that Jerri wasn't attractive, smart, fun, and not that Dana didn't need and love her—she just wasn't in love with her the way she was with Karen. "Yeah," she confessed.

"Tell me more. I never realized how little I knew about your past."

"Karen and Teddy moved to Stockton after the wedding. Teddy had a scholarship to the University there." Karen moving away had felt like falling into a black hole.

"The University of the Pacific." Jerri blew smoke rings as she lied on her back listening.

"I really missed Karen. She'd been around since I was fourteen. It was like she died.... Anyway, I immediately went to work at Daddy's gas station for distraction. That's how I met Lester, one week after Karen left. He'd come in for gas, just two dollars worth each visit, and say corny stuff like 'What's a cute girl like you doin' pumping gas?' Pumping gas wasn't exactly my dream job but it was something to do. My dream job's to be a famous painter. I just need to find some rich woman who wants to be my patron," Dana said, then laughed. She had often entertained the fantasy of a wealthy woman taking her under wing as an artist. "Anyway, Lester'd just got out of the Army. I don't know. I was really lonely and I was afraid of being alone without her. And he kept asking me out, so I finally said yes. That was a mistake. One date turned into a year and a half of misery."

"Was he the first person you ever had sex with?"

"Yeah." Dana remembered lying on Lester's soiled sheets in the little room he rented, feeling like a hot poker was searing into her, unhappily thinking so this is what it's like to lose your virginity. She caressed and caressed him so he would think she was good. "Anyway, Karen wrote me—we've always written each other two times a week—she wrote me that Teddy and her were having problems. I don't know why she married him. They've always fought. She's always said she's not in love with him really." Dana thought to herself, she's always said she loves me more than him even now. She's so afraid of being gay. "She wrote that he was neglecting her, getting all caught up in homework and classes. So one day she just up and took a bus back to Cody." Dana's voice faltered as if nearing a minefield. "She, she told me she wasn't going back to him...ever. I know it sounds really selfish, but I was glad. I've always felt jealous of Teddy. I used to go on dates with him and her in high school—Karen would always invite me—and I'd end up watching them kissing. I'd be in the backseat and they'd be in the front of this tiny Toyota. I had no choice but to watch. That's why when you brought up sleeping with other...." Dana stopped.

"Go on."

"I know what it's like to be jealous and I don't like feeling like that. You know what I mean?"

Jerri suddenly stood up. She poured herself some more burgundy. She pulled a joint out of a canister on her dresser. She lay back down on the bed, but further from Dana, and lit the joint. "I'm not the jealous type," she said solemnly, offering the joint to Dana, who shook her head. She never liked it that Jerri always either smoked marijuana, snorted cocaine, or drank wine as a matter of course before and after sex. "I don't let jealousy control me. People let it rule their lives too much. I don't." Jerri was quiet, holding the marijuana in her lungs. "So what you're trying to tell me is you just want us to have sex with each other?" Exhaling smoke, she shook her head disapprovingly.

"No, I didn't say that," Dana said quickly, feeling threatened that she would lose the relationship if she said the wrong thing. "I'm not trying to be possessive. You're free to do what you want. Do whatever you want." She said exactly what she knew Jerri wanted to hear, then changed the subject quickly. "Anyway, Karen came back to Cody." She was quiet a moment. "We were hanging around together all the time. Just like high school, but no Teddy. Lester was in Maryland because his dad was dying. Karen seduced me one day while Daddy was at the station." Dana tried to sound casual about it so as not to provoke any jealousy in Jerri. "We'd never done that before." She thought what she would not say: she adored Karen, and had since meeting her at fourteen. She could not imagine a more perfect love. She felt she could never love anyone as deeply as she did Karen. Those four months with Karen had been absolute heaven until.... "On my nineteenth birthday she took me to the rodeo in Cody. She bought me a pair of blue corduroy pants and a blue shirt with stencilled flowers on it. And this cowboy hat I wanted. I was wearing all that and we were sitting in the grand stand watching all these little kids chasing a calf trying to grab a red ribbon off it. And Karen said, 'I'm going back to Teddy. He's coming to drive me back.' She said she cared about him and he *was* her husband after all and she wanted to make it work. She said they'd started going to this Presbyterian Church in Stockton and she felt guilty about us. She said she would always be in love with me but.... So that was that. She said she wanted to lead a normal life and have children some day." It was painful for Dana to recall this.

"A normal life?" Jerri laughed.

"Lester started hounding me to marry him after his dad died. He even had a diamond engagement ring ready. It was good for my ego after Karen.... But he was always too hot or cold. Flowers and candy, all that, or else he'd be mean, bossy, getting jealous over anything, like if I just said hello to a stranger, some man passing on the street, he'd have a little fit."

"Did he know about you and Karen?"

"Just after she went back to Stockton we got to talking about her. He was being really sweet. He was saying, 'You miss her, don't you, Babe?' I said yes. I was upset, you know. I didn't have anybody to talk to about it really. I thought maybe I might be able to trust him. So I told him bits and pieces about how we'd planned to go to New Orleans and live together. He never knew I was in love with her. Maybe he knew. I don't know..."

"I didn't know until tonight.... But it's O.K...."

Dana did not know how to reply to that. "Lester started asking me why I never thought of living with him in New Orleans. It was crazy. He asked me if I'd like to go to New Orleans and live with him. I told him, 'Not really.' He got really uptight. 'What she got I ain't got? What I got to compete with some damned broad? You in love with her? That it?' He was acting crazy. And it was driving me crazy. So just to get him to shut up, I said 'yes.'"

"I bet that didn't shut him up."

"I wish it had. He got really serious. He said he could understand 'that kind of thing.' But that I'd grow out of it as soon as I grew up."

"Just a teenage phase, right?"

"Right. He acted real cool about it at first. Like he didn't care. But he was just baiting me and like a fool I fell for it. He asked me in a real sweet way, 'You ever slept with her, Babe? You can tell me. I'll understand. I won't hold it against you. I almost did it with this dude once when I was in the Army. He was a faggot. I was drunk.'"

"That's what they always say."

"You got to remember I was devastated over her leaving and I didn't have anybody to talk to about it, so I said that for the four months she'd been in Cody—and he went crazy. All of a sudden went crazy, saying, 'I don't know why I put up with you. You treat me like shit. Lie to me. Sneak around on me. Don't love me right. My old man's dying and you're out here fucking a girl. Hell, I wanted to marry you. Well, I ain't shit, Dana. You're shit.' He scared me to death. He was *really* mad. He pushed me to the floor and grabbed my breast. 'What'd she do to you? Did she do this to you? Did you like it? Like it more than what I do to you? Huh?' He bit my nipple hard and said, 'She bite your titties? What'd she do to you?' I didn't say a word. I hated him. He was yelling, 'Tell me what she did to you!' I wouldn't say anything. 'Tell me, bitch.' I wouldn't so he twisted my arm. I still wouldn't talk. So he forced me on my stomach and smashed the side of my face into the floor and kicked me in the butt."

"Oh God."

"I got up and ran out of there."

"That's good."

"Yeah, well, the next day he came over to my daddy's—my daddy was really mad at him for bruising up my face. It's a good thing he wasn't home or he'd probably have killed Lester. Lester was all full of apologies. He was crying. He said he'd never hurt me again. He asked me if it was all a lie about Karen to get him back for sleeping with this girl, Rosie, once. I was afraid of him. Afraid he'd beat me up if I didn't say what he wanted to hear. So I said yes. When he heard that you wouldn't believe how nice he was. He'd never been so sweet. He put that diamond ring on my finger and said, 'Pleasseee.' I didn't say anything. But I kept the ring on just to keep him sweet. Maybe he thought I was saying yes by keeping it on. I don't know. All I know was when I wore that ring he was a lot happier and nicer to me. So I kept it on, sort of used it to make him nicer. If he started acting mean, I'd start to slide the ring off and he'd see that and sweeten up. He was all apologetic about beating me up and made all these promises about treating me right.

"Anyway, I wrote Karen and told her what happened. She said that I had to get away from Lester, that he was Hitler reincarnated and she was worried about me.... She said I'd get trapped into marrying him or else get murdered by him. She asked me to move to Stockton. She said she'd talked Teddy into letting me come live with them. She said she really missed me and was still in love with me. I packed the next day...."

Dana was brought back to the present when Mrs. Horstman repeated, "What brought you out to California?" She fanned herself with the *National Enquirer*.

"I just wanted a change, I guess." Dana smiled and shrugged her shoulders. "What brought you here?"

"Change of climate." Mrs. Horstman looked uncomfortably quiet. "I reckon you came to the big city to find a man. A man with money. That's what I had in mind when I was yer age. And that's what I eventually got."

"No, I'm not looking for a man with money." It would be great, though, Dana thought, to find a woman with money.

"You hate men, Honey? You're awful young to be hating men." She rubbed suntan oil on her thighs.

"I don't hate them." She would like to say it's not that she hates men but that she loves women, but she feared Mrs. Horstman would fire any queer found polluting her precious premises.

Mrs. Horstman changed her tune to *There's Nothing Like a Dame*. Dana said, "What do you want me to clean now, Mrs. Horstman?"

"Honey, you asked me why I came to San Francisco. Well, I'll tell you. I came to get away. That's why I'm here. That's precisely why half the folks in this town are here. It's that type of town. I came here to get away from that damned husband of mine—excuse my language, Honey, but whenever I speak of him now I can't help myself. Get away from that damned George Horstman and all those Nashville busybodies." She flung her arms out in disgust.

"George Horstman, he's one hell of a.... Let me tell you, it took me twenty-eight years to find that out. Twenty-eight years. So you want to know what I'm doing in San Francisco, Honey? Well, let's just say I'm in a kind of exile. In exile for as long as it takes." Dana understood instantly, feeling in exile herself, in exile from Karen, missing her, fantasizing about her constantly, biding her time, hoping one day she would be hers. "Now I want you to run down to Safeway and get a pack of pork chops, potatoes, corn on the cob, strawberries, whipcream and half a gallon of gin. I'm gonna cook us a good supper, Honey. I love cooking. All you got to do is help me cook it and help me eat it. How's that?" She added with a laugh, "And clean up afterwards. Then maybe I'll treat you to a show. There's an old Fred Astaire musical playing. I love musicals."

CHAPTER 4

Dana, seven days a maid, was all Comet, Mop 'n Glow, Easy Off, Windex and Joy. She felt like a household appliance. Plug her in, turn her on, watch dirt and dust fall prey to the automated maid. Efficient. Obedient. Repentant. Subservient. Mrs. Horstman appeared to have taken a liking to her. "Honey, you've been doing a right nice job so far. Would you get me my red dress out of the closet? Peaches got a nine-thirty appointment at the poodle parlor. She's starting to look like Raggity Anne lately, you noticed? And get my red heels. With the gold buckles."

Dana nodded at Mrs. Horstman, in bed with her breakfast tray watching the morning news, and walked somnambulistically to the closet.

"You're acting queer this morning," Mrs. Horstman said. The possible insinuation, 'queer', shot a little adrenalin into Dana. The woman bit into pumpernickle toast. "You act like yer sleepwalking."

"I didn't sleep well last night." She had spent the night worrying over what would befall her after this job—jobs were so hard to find. She had worried, what if I end up selling jujubees at one of those sleazy Market Street porno theatres? Wind up working for an escort service? Working the streets? Never. I'd rather go back to Cody. But Lester would beat me up for sure for running away. If only Karen would let me move back to Stockton. If only Jerri would take me back. You would think Jerri would have cooled down by now. How can she blame me for being jealous over her sleeping with that girl within three days of deciding we should sleep with others. It wasn't fair, her calling me possessive and a pouter about it and getting mad at me because I didn't want to talk about it. Didn't want to hear the details. Why did she break up with me? I didn't cheat on her. I wish she would take me back. I'm scared. I wish I didn't need a lover so badly. Maybe Mrs. Horstman would let me stay here if worst came to worst. She's a nice woman, treated me to three movies and lunch once. No, she probably wouldn't want me staying here after her maid comes.... All night Dana's mind had been as frenzied as a scary ride on a midway.

"You should have taken some sleeping pills. I take a shot or two of whiskey but yer too young for that. Could you refill my coffee please, Honey?"

What had finally sent Dana to sleep was a scheme: she would be a tourist to Mrs. Horstman's life, photographing her in bed with breakfast watching *Good Morning America*, sitting at the beauty parlor, playing solitaire on the glass coffee table, watching *General Hospital*, sunning on the patio, walking Peaches downtown, reading *Reader's Digest* before her afternoon nap, drinking gin and orange juice, frying chicken and whipping potatoes, eating dinner, watching the evening sit-coms and eating her Saturday hot dog (she had a tradition of hot dogs for lunch every Saturday). Dana would paint the snapshots into a series called, *The Wonderful World of Mrs. Rosylyn Horstman*, or *A Day in the Life of a Hot Dog Millionaire*. Hopefully, Mrs. Horstman would purchase the series for a large sum. She had always wanted a patron for her art.

Remembering her scheme, Dana said, handing the refilled coffee cup to Mrs. Horstman, "Mrs. Horstman, would it be all right if I painted a series of portraits of you?"

She looked as if it was par for the course that someone would want to paint her portrait. She nodded perfunctorily, and was quiet a moment. "How'd you like that little green room as a studio for painting my portraits in?" Dana looked at her quizzically. "I've been thinking.... I've got an offer you'll like if you got any sense at all and I think you do. How'd you like to be hired on permanent?"

Dana's heart fluttered fast as hummingbird wings. "What about Georgia Anne?" she said, her lips parted with a reserved eagerness.

"I had to can Georgia Anne! Had to let her go last night long distance. She was fussing and fighting about not wanting to leave Tennessee. So I had to fire her." Mrs. Horstman shook her head, her lower lip pouted. "Twenty years together." She stared melancholily at her pink silky bedspread. "Now here's what you'll get and here's what I'll get, Honey."

Dana listened closely, cheer slowly lighting up her face, pinkening her cheeks, putting a twinkle to her sad eyes. Mrs. Horstman's eyes were glued on her as intensely as a losing gambler's on a possible win. "You'll get...what'd you get at that little lunch counter?"

"Eight hundred a month."

"You'll get eight hundred and fifty a month." She looked at Dana calculatingly. "And room and board." She paused. "You can have the blue bedroom as yours and that green one to paint my portraits in. I'll be yer patron. I'll make you famous," Mrs. Horstman said with a wink. "How's that sound, Honey?" Dana's nervous system felt as if it was sinking into a warm snug armchair. This was too good to be true—money and a patron and a penthouse to live in. "You'll get evenings off, of course, that is after yer done with the dishes, and Sundays off too. And I'll get a full-time, live-in maid to look after me. Now is that an offer you can turn down, Honey?"

"No, it's not. Thank you." Dana smiled. She felt very happy.

"You got my purse ready? Listen, after you do those breakfast dishes we'll get busy on moving you in here. As I recall you didn't have many things over at yer studio. It shouldn't take long to get you moved out. That's no place for a young girl to be living anyway. Even an igloo would be better than that," she said and laughed. "I'll call some movers. You'll like living here much better. And after I take Peaches to the parlor I'll stop by a uniform store and pick up a couple uniforms for you to wear when yer working." Mrs. Horstman had a fat smile on her face. "What size do you take? Dress and shoe. I'll pick you up a good pair of working shoes, too."

The Southern lady has taken care of everything. Dana looked at her gratefully as if she was some kind of savior. She thought it was ironic that her hitting the Mercedes has turned out to be a stroke of good luck, that orange soda, a blessing in disguise. She has a patron for her art.

"Could you hand me half a cup of milk?" Mrs. Horstman always delegated the peeling, chopping, mashing and measuring to Dana, saving the better tasks for herself like whipping potatoes with the electric beater, pulverizing pea soup in the blender, spooning meringue into peaks on lemon pie. She conducted the orchestration and Dana assisted like a nurse during surgery. "I like to know my maids. Here we're living under the same roof now, all yer things are moved in here, and I don't know more than a chicken's gizzard about you. I like to know my maids." Wearing a gold moo-moo and a plastic lei a "gorgeous little Polynesian girl put on me last month in Hawaii," Mrs. Horstman dunked a thumb into the mashed potatoes and then into her mouth. "Georgia Anne used to tell me everything. *Everything.* Told me more than I wanted to know really. Told me when she miscarried. When her man mishandled her. When the menopause was upon her." Mrs. Horstman suddenly got quiet, staring at the kitchen linoleum. Dana stood quietly by, wearing the maid's uniform with a lacy collar that Mrs. Horstman picked out for her today. "That Georgia Anne was my right hand. I don't know why she wouldn't move out here temporarily with me. She's probably got an irrational fear of earthquakes or AIDS. Her husband's been dead two years. At least she's loyal enough to not keep on with Mr. Horstman. She left him when I did, was as mad as I was—and am. We were so mad we could a set the Smoky Mountains a smokin' and burnin'. Hand me a quarter cube of butter for these potatoes. Tell me about yerself, Honey. You got any plans for the future?"

The question sounded like an insurance commercial to Dana. Plans for the future? "Not really," Dana said. For now, she was just trying to survive without Karen or Jerri. At her former lunch counter job, she had once been told by a co-worker who was an artist that San Francisco was becoming the graphic design center of the country, and that they both should get training in graphic arts. It was an idea Dana had entertained but not acted on. The intense competition in the art world had always been discouraging to her.

"My plan, my dream is to be the Colonel Sanders of the hot dog world," Rosylyn said with a laugh. Dana laughed too and made a mental note, Colonel Roz, and saw her holding a bucket of hot dogs. "I knew the Colonel when he was alive." Rosylyn asked again, "So what are yer plans?"

Dana said, lethargically, "I don't know what I'm going to do." Mrs. Horstman looked at her sympathetically like a high school counselor. "For now I plan to work for you as long as you need me, Mrs. Horstman."

"You can call me Rosylyn, Honey. Most folks do. Georgia Anne did." She watched the butter dissolve into the potatoes. "I can make you into a famous artist," she promised again. Then abruptly she asked, "You don't plan on marriage and children?"

"No." Her only plan for now was to pay off her debts and start saving money to create a buffer zone, some security of her own. And to paint Mrs. Horstman's portraits.

Mrs. Horstman looked at her skeptically. "Every young girl says that these days."

"I'm different."

Mrs. Horstman chuckled. "Every young girl says that too. I've been around long enough to learn no one's that different. Nothing's new under the sun. I'm getting to the point where nothing could surprise me. You can tell me anything, Honey. I've heard it all."

You haven't heard it all, Dana thought. You'd turn a somersault backwards if you knew your maid was a lesbian.

"Just today when I was out dropping Peaches off at the parlor off Polk Street I saw two homosexuals holding hands and a lot of others standing around staring at one another. Now I never saw the likes of that in Nashville but I wasn't surprised. Nothing under the sun's new to me. Nothing shocks me anymore. Let me tell you, Honey, the shock Mr. Horstman gave me knocked the chances of me ever being shocked again right out of me. Do you know when I was a young girl just married, a lesbian approached me? She was a nice enough girl. You would have never suspected...." She was quiet a moment. "Don't be afraid to tell me anything about yerself."

I'm never going to let her know I'm gay, Dana thought anxiously. She'd fire me for sure. This is the best paying job I've ever had and I don't want to lose it.

"You ever had a girl approach you like that?"

As if she didn't hear the question, Dana stammered, "I'd, I'd better get this food on the table before it starts getting cold." She could not answer yes. She could not answer no and deny Karen, deny Jerri, as if ashamed. Tensely, she set the table, wondering what Mrs. Horstman would do if she found out a homosexual was standing on her linoleum, touching her bowl of mashed potatoes, touching her butter, touching her precious china plates and even her sacred fried chicken. Would she be accused of molestation? She set the table so carefully, so perfectly, forks and knives at attention, rose saluting from a clear glass vase, that Mrs. Horstman would never suspect it was the work of a homosexual. The toilet bowls were too clean, the windows too clear, the chandeliers too sparkling for Mrs. Horstman to suspect anything at all.

Dana was anxious for dinner to start—homosexuality was not a subject Mrs. Horstman would find fit for her dinner table. Dana has learned that what the lady wanted from a supper was what Dana wanted from a night at the bar—to have her appetite so titillated that she could temporarily forget her worries. A good tasting chicken thigh, stringbeans, salted tomatoes, mashed potatoes, lemon meringue pie, could make Mrs. Horstman temporarily forget everything. Supper was a kind of drowning for her. Dana was congenial to this cause.

Sitting down at the table, Mrs. Horstman spooned herself a mound of mashed potatoes. "I saw the most gorgeous magnolia at the florist's today," she said, much to Dana's relief. "Of course they couldn't compare with ours in the South, but...." She led the conversation from magnolia blossoms to crock pots to the gourmet food on luxury liners to the ideal climate in San Francisco to the first apron her mother bought her as a child. "I've never heard you mention yer mama, Honey."

"She died in a car accident when I was four." Certain that death was one of the subjects blacklisted for supper smalltalk, Dana tried to make the subject as untragic as cotton candy. "Daddy raised me and never remarried," she tried to say in a lighthearted tone.

Mrs. Horstman did not look at all unhappy that Dana was motherless. "I bet you missed having a mama." Dana nodded. It was still painful. Even though it happened at age four, she still remembered her mother holding her in bed at night, comforting her when there was thunder and lightning. She remembered feeling loved all the time. Since then there had been an ache inside never filled.

"Were you an only child?"

Dana nodded, feeling like an orphan in Mrs. Horstman's eyes.

"I was an only child too," she said as if it was some kind of bond. "Never had any children of my own. Never any at all." Mrs. Horstman looked sad and inexplicably angry. "One would think you'd want to start a family of yer own so you wouldn't be so lonely as you were as an only child."

Dana mashed her string beans into her fork's bars, irritated.

"If you want a family yer gonna have to find yerself a husband first."

Dana pressed the stringbeaned fork into her mashed potatoes.

Mrs. Horstman glared at her rebellious fork. "Yer never gonna get a man with table manners like that. No mama's no excuse."

Dana put the fork in her mouth. Just a little revenge for incessantly slinging 'get a husband.' "You'd embarrass any man smashing up food like that in a restaurant."

It was open season on Dana, who decided to get out of there after the dishes, go dancing. Mrs. Horstman crunched down into a drumstick, her pink hornrimmed glasses roosting on her nose as she peered at Dana, grease waddling down her knuckles. "You never answered me in the kitchen, Honey. You ever been approached by one of them?" she said suspiciously.

The subject ambushed Dana, who didn't expect it at the dinner table. "One of what?"

"A homosexual."

Dana looked blankly at Mrs. Horstman, not knowing how to respond.

"Haven't you heard that word before?"

Dana was quiet. People were always pushing her to talk about things she didn't want to talk about. She clammed up self-protectively.

"Well, I reckon if you haven't heard about it yer better off not knowing. It's like liquor. If you don't know about it, then you won't be tempted by it." She winked at Dana protectively.

CHAPTER 5

What would Rosylyn think if she saw me now, Dana thought, climbing Calamity Jane's stairs to the second floor of the bar where there was a large dance floor. The population exploded with women—women everywhere, standing, drinking, sitting, dancing, twisting and shuffling on the dance floor to loud music. A bartender handed out drinks blackjack-dealer fast. An occasional man stood out like a mismatched button. Dana blended into a lineup of women standing along the dance floor's edge, waiting. The top three buttons of her blue silk shirt were carefully undone. She imagined Rosylyn in the future telling someone, "You never would have suspected she was one of them. She was such a nice girl." Dana looked around to see if Jerri was there.

She tried to looked nonchalant. She toyed with the gold chain necklace around her gardenia-perfumed neck, a gift from Jerri last Valentine's Day, accompanied by Godiva chocolates, roses, and a card that said, 'I love you.' She missed her. They had met in this bar at a special dance, 50's & 60's night. Dana glanced coyly at an attractive woman with immaculately trimmed short red hair and gold loop earrings, eyeing Dana. Her hair was the color of Karen's.

She played the bar like a slot machine. Her smiles and glances were like nickels invested, hoping for a jackpot. Jerri had been a jackpot hit her first week in the City. She had actually felt proud at that time that the longest she'd ever gone without a lover or Karen was only a week (now it was up to an unbearable four weeks). Jerri had approached her wearing aqua-blue sunglasses, a plastic headband, pedal pushers and bobby socks, dressed in the theme of the 50's. Chewing bubble gum, Jerri had said, "You look like you'd like to dance. Want to?" Dana had blushed completely. Had she looked that eager? Who was this woman? She had been gorgeous in spite of the costume. Dana had liked her bravado.

But usually Dana was less lucky. Some woman would ask her to dance a song or two, would smile periodically, then curtly say,

"Thanks," and move on to someone else, leaving Dana feeling rejected. On a bad night no one asked her to dance. She was too shy to ask anyone herself.

"Would you like to dance?" Dana turned and saw the woman with immaculately trimmed red hair standing almost on top of her. She had pale freckles, a vulnerable tough kid look.

Dana nodded. She never said no. Rosylyn's words suddenly seemed funny, "You ever been approached by one of them?" She imagined the look on Rosylyn's face had she replied, "Not as much as I would like."

The redhead flipped into rhythm, pulsating to the music's beat. Her pendulous breasts beat and bonged as if on a trampoline inside her sleeveless blue t-shirt. She wore white pants and white tennis shoes. Dana was careful not to dance too close. She moved her black high heels into her very best steps, turns and twists. "I like the way you dance," the redhead yelled over the music. Dana smiled. They exchanged names like business cards. Frankie. Dana. They danced well together, like salt and pepper on the shake, spicy.

Frankie took Dana's hand in the air and Dana twirled under it and saw Jerri. Their eyes stopped on each other like on a car wreck. The impact caused Dana's feet to falter, to forget how to move to music. She was thankful that Frankie was snapped up into the music, eyes closed, lips parted, as if in a catatonic dance trance, and did not see Dana's temporary loss of rhythm. Dana grabbed Frankie's free hand and moved closer to her. See this Jerri, Dana thought. Frankie's eyes opened and Dana gave her the biggest, sweetest smile. Frankie returned it graciously and chivalrously. Dana checked for Jerri's reaction but Jerri was gone. Dana anxiously looked around for her. She wondered if she had once again mistaken someone for Jerri.

The music changed to a slow rhythm. Frankie gallantly pulled Dana up close and wrapped her arms around her, leading them in a slow dance as if she was a slick dance pro. It reminded Dana of the musical Rosylyn had taken her to see. Grinning, she made a mental note, Frankie Astaire. Frankie's now tamed breasts rested against Dana's. "You come here often?" Dana hoped Jerri was watching this.

"Sort of," Dana said, feeling very non-committal. Her eyes were all over the bar looking for Jerri or the booby prize, her double. There, by the bar. She was smoking and talking to an attractive black woman. They looked chummy. It was definitely Jerri, who spent half her time looking at the woman and half at Dana. It unnerved Dana. Was that the one Jerri slept with? Why were they standing so close? "I'd like to get a beer," Frankie said. "Can I get you something?"

"A beer. Thanks." Dana followed Frankie, wanting to be by the bar, by Jerri and that woman. She would smile graciously at them. She would be polite and charming, all the while feigning a deep interest in Frankie, all the while trying to lure Jerri back. She would use whatever method she could to win her back. She felt like Custer making his last stand.

At the bar, Dana felt Jerri's hand on her elbow. "Dana," Jerri said. She looked at Jerri, that face she has missed so, and those well-kissed lips, half-Spanish, half-Italian. A blue scarf was loose around her neck. She hugged Dana, warmly. Jerri. Supple. Strong. Tall. Sensuous. Seductive. Always seductive. "I've tried calling," she whispered into her ear. "But your line's been disconnected and when I came by your studio they said you'd moved. You know I hate being curious." They both looked at Frankie standing awkwardly beside them with two clumsy beers in her hands. "Here's your beer."

"Thank you."

Jerri leaned back to Dana's ear and said, "I've missed you. Honestly. I wasn't expecting to. Listen, meet me outside in ten minutes." Without waiting for a response, she walked away, sure of herself. She disappeared into the crowd. Dana looked for her. But it was almost as if she was an apparition. Dana wanted to follow her now but this Frankie was a leash around her neck. She looked at her with pure disenchantment and watched her as she downed her beer in a machismo manner. Frankie was not Jerri. Her hair was not even really the color of Karen's. She was third-class Karen. Her rugged lips were so unappealing, square shaped. Frankie talked non-stop, mainly about her job as a parole officer; she had a know-it-all tone. Dana endured Frankiness for ten minutes, feeling under siege by Jerri. For the first time since landing the penthouse job, she felt on the verge of happiness. Jerri had said she missed her. Everything pointed to Jerri wanting her tonight, wanting her back. When Frankie asked to exchange telephone numbers, Dana gave hers quickly just to get herself off the hook, and to have an out should it not work with Jerri. She was a firm practitioner of always having an out. "Thanks for the beer," she said, smiling, then slowly, coolly, walked down the stairs as if in no hurry at all. She mustn't give Jerri the impression she was taking this too seriously.

Jerri was not outside. Dana looked around anxiously. Maybe Jerri got side-tracked with that woman. Maybe this was just a cruel joke to break her and Frankie up. Dana waited. She had always done a lot of waiting for Jerri.

"Hi." Jerri suddenly appeared, smiling. "What did you do with your cute friend upstairs?"

"Left her upstairs."

"Who is she?"

Dana knew exactly how to play this game with Jerri. "Someone I keep in my pocket for a rainy day."

"Really?" Jerri's eyebrows raised, amused.

Dana shrugged, leaning against the stone wall, trying to give off a relaxed and undemanding air.

Smiling, Jerri put her finger in the breast pocket of Dana's blue silk shirt, and pulled it out to peer in. "What else do you have hiding in there?" Dana smiled and blushed. Strangely enough, she felt shy as if meeting Jerri for the first time again. "Can I put my hand in there? Feel around, see what else you have hiding in there?"

Jerri leaned against the building, gazing out at the passing traffic. She lighted a cigarette quietly, looking as casual and cool as a cigarette ad. "Feels like we never split up, huh?" she said, turning to look at Dana. "Like we're just standing here like we used to on any old night." Dana nodded. "I mean what I said about having missed you. I *really* have missed you."

"I've missed you, too."

Jerri nodded as if she knew that. "Where are you living now?"

"I got a job as a maid for this rich woman in a penthouse. I get eight-hundred-fifty a month plus room and board and a room for painting."

"You're kidding."

"No. I'm her live-in maid. She wants to be my patron."

Jerri was quiet. "Is that all?" she said.

"What do you mean?"

"I love your naivete."

They were both quiet.

"I've been doing the same routine—law school, studying, jogging, going to the Feminist Lawyer's Coalition meetings. I could use a good vacation right now."

They were quiet again. It was all so matter-of-fact.

"You look pretty," Jerri said, eyeing Dana's silky streetlit hair, the pink of her clear complexion, her trusting green eyes that twinkled innocently—her parted lips, full of restraint and yearning. "But you always do." Her eyes dropped to Dana's full breasts, and played along her cleavage line. She looked up at Dana. "Well, do you want to come over to my place tonight?"

"Sure," Dana said in a tiny voice that sounded as if it was being swallowed.

A wild smile broke out across Jerri's lips like a wild horse gone galloping. The smile unsettled Dana—cool power laughing, a queen on high. "I've always liked that about you," Jerri said. "You don't ask questions. You let everything slide." She took Dana's hand and ran her finger in a spiral in Dana's palm, tracing her long lifeline. She looked at Dana calculatingly. "You know, I'm not making any promises." Dana's hand felt like a bird with a broken wing in the hand of a little girl who wanted to take it home.

It was late—and late made Dana's mind unwind. She forgot about getting back early to Rosylyn's. She forgot that Jerri and she were ever apart. Lateness, loud music, loneliness, liquor and lost love made her forget. Purgatory passed. She was Cinderella before midnight. Alice the other side of the looking glass. Jerri, the Queen of Hearts.

CHAPTER 6

At seven a.m., tiptoeing from the penthouse door to her bedroom, Dana felt uneasy. The glass and mirrors about her seemed cold and icy, a confusion of reflections. It nauseated her. Jerri shouldn't have given her so much to drink when she had to work in the morning. Perhaps a cold shower, a couple of cups of coffee and some Alka Seltzer would chase off this woozy bruised feeling. Rosylyn must not see her like this.

She heard something sounding like a chorus of rattlesnakes coming from her bedroom. She recognized the sound—the snoring of Mrs. Rosylyn Horstman, who was lying in her yellow quilted robe, horn rimmed glasses perched on her nose, on Dana's bed under a satin comforter. She lay on her back as if in state—in a state of expectation. Dana did not know why Rosylyn was on her bed. It frightened her. She stood still, staring as she would at a body in a casket. She watched the body to make sure it was still. When she was sure it was still, she tiptoed into her bedroom and stole her maid's uniform from her closet, slowly sliding open her dresser drawer and stealing nylons, white ped socks, and white underwear. The snoring stopped. Dana felt like someone yelled, "Put your hands up!" She turned to see if Rosylyn's pistol eyes were upon her. Relief, they were closed. The coast was clear. Dana left the bedroom so quietly that Rosylyn's breathing sounded like a windstorm.

In the bathroom, Dana took off her pants and shirt, preparing to shower. She felt like a mud pie in the all-white bathroom. The white was so bright, lit up by morning sun, that it seemed to stare at her accusingly. Like a drill sergeant, she inspected her naked body in the mirror. Rosylyn must not see her like this. Tired eyes—a little eye make-up should help. The hickey, thank God, was below her shoulders. But there were several small, light bruises on her arms as a result of Jerri's thrashing passion. How am I going to explain those, Dana worried. I could tell her they're from cleaning the oven yesterday. Dana looked at the hickey and bruises sentimentally. Jerri, she had Jerri. I love her, she thought. Dana's thinking was not all too clear about it but the marks proved something. She could not remember the night too clearly. All she remembered was a sensation of liveliness, liquor, lust and love.

The warm water of the shower washed over her, soothing her. She turned the water to cold so it would slap her awake. Her body pinkened, matching the color of the carnations which had been by Jerri's antique brass bed last night. Dana had not asked where they had come from. She briskly toweled herself dry, wrapped the towel around her hair and stepped from the shower—and saw Rosylyn standing there by the door, smoking. That woke her more than the cold shower. While Rosylyn sized her up in one quick head to toe glance, Dana grabbed a towel to cover herself. Taking a sharp suck off her cigarette, Rosylyn took it from her lips so briskly that ashes fell to the floor. "Where...have...," she said, punching each word out with controlled irritation, "you...been?"

Dumbfounded, Dana replied feebly, "I told you last night I was going out."

"Out where?" She took a slow puff off her cigarette. Her breathing was heavy. "I had you figured wrong."

Blushing, Dana felt as if a spotlight was on her. She remembered Daddy walking in on Karen and her making love when he was supposed to be at the gas station. He had looked completely bewildered. Angry, he had said, "I guess you're too old for spankings. And too old to let your daddy stop you from doing what you want. But don't be doing it in my house. And don't have me knowing about it." The subject was never mentioned again.

"Dana, you listen to me closely," Rosylyn said. "My maids do not, *do not*, sneak into my house at this hour of the morning with liquor on their breath, marks on 'em, worn out, looking like a wild cat in heat." Her speech quickened, gaining momentum. "I'm expecting a full day's worth of work out of you. That's what I'm payin' you for. I was damn worried about you, young lady. How was I to know you were all right? All's I knew was that you never came home. All kinds of killers and kooks run 'round this town at night. They even run 'round this town in the day—that's how bad things are here. How was I to know you were all right? You said you'd be in early. I laid up in yer bed waiting for you—fell asleep hoping you'd wake me up, coming in safely.

"You should have called to let me know you wouldn't be in. But I reckon you never stopped to think ol' Rosylyn might be worrying over you. What would you think if I went out alone and never came home?" Dana did not answer. Rosylyn was convincing her to feel guilty, inconsiderate. "Then you got the gall to show up for work looking hung-over. I'll be a son-of-a...if I'm gonna pay someone for this kind of behavior. Let this be a warning. Next time yer fired, Honey. And think about where you'll be then. Remember where you were before...." She spoke more slowly like a droning record losing electricity. "What do you got to say for yerself?"

"I'm sorry, Rosylyn."

"Why didn't you call?"

Dana shrugged. "You said I had evenings off...."

"And mornings on! I want you to clean out the refrigerator. Mop and wax the floors. The windows could use a shine and the toilets need to be sanitized. I'm gonna go to Sears Fine Foods for a good breakfast. Then I'm gonna go shopping and to a movie. I hope I feel better by the time I get back. I'll be back late this afternoon."

Clean the refrigerator, the floors, the toilets, the windows. Listening to the drill sergeant in her head, Dana downed four cups of coffee, hoping they would turn her into a roller coaster of energy. The phone rang. Jerri, Dana hoped. Jerri promised to call.

It was Frankie Astaire. "Of course I remember you," Dana said quickly, nervously. Frankie could not have called at a more inopportune time. "I really can't today," Dana said about a lunch invitation. "My boss was really mad because I came to work late with a hangover. She piled me up with work, then split for breakfast, mad. I'll probably get fired. There's no way I can get all this work done today."

"Listen. I can hop on my motorcycle and be right there. You'll never get it done alone."

"No, you don't have to do that."

"I want to. Please. What was the address?"

Dana hesitated. "Well, it's on the Embarcadero," she said, reciting the address.

Frankie was there in fifteen minutes, looking as clean-cut as a model in a Montgomery Ward catalogue, wearing jeans, polished tan boots and a brown and maroon plaid shirt. She smelled clean. Small diamond earrings sparkled on her ears. "Put me to work. I'm at your service. Where should I start? The place looks pretty clean already," she said looking about. "Are you sure it needs to be cleaned?"

"My boss likes her place a hundred and ten percent clean, no less," Dana said and laughed, sliding her hands into her maid uniform's pockets. "Excuse my looks. I'm a mess today."

"You look nice," Frankie said dotingly.

"You're sweet," Dana said, wondering if she should have Frankie sanitize the toilets. No, that would be rude. "Well, why don't we start on the refrigerator." Dana relayed Rosylyn's rules on refrigerator cleaning, beginning—all leftovers were to be thrown out after two days. Frankie listened too attentively, making Dana feel uncomfortable. She was like a doting pupil. Her attraction to Dana was too blatant, smeared across her cute freckled face like a billboard advertisement. You'd think from Frankie's expression that Dana was whispering words of love rather than leftovers.

"What about this mincemeat pie?" Frankie said flirtatiously. Dana did not comprehend how someone could ask that flirtatiously. What was sexy about mincemeat?

"We never throw out desserts," Dana said, careful not to look Frankie in the eye for fear she would read something into nothing—a simple look, or a mincemeat pie. "The reason being that they're never around long enough to reach the age of two days," Dana said with a smile. "But you can throw out this half a ham. It's a week old." Dana was surprised Frankie didn't say, "You throw out food when children are starving in India." Frankie was polite. Perhaps she feels guilty, Dana mused, as I have for throwing out food.

Dana offered the antidote to guilt, the rationalization Rosylyn had given her one day upon seeing Dana hesitate before the garbage can with a leftover roast. "My boss got an overdose of leftovers as a child. That's all she ever ate. Leftovers. And leftovers of leftovers. Her mother hated to cook. Whenever she did cook, she'd stretch the leftovers for at least a week, sometimes two, so she wouldn't have to cook again." The grimace on Frankie's face egged Dana on. "She got so lazy she even quit wrapping leftovers in foil or plastic. She'd just stick them in the refrigerator uncovered in a bowl. Then they'd sit like that all week before getting served." It was working—Frankie dropped the half-a-ham in the garbage as if it was merely soiled paper towels.

"Dana! Dana, Honey!" Rosylyn was in the penthouse.

"Hide," Dana whispered, shocked, shoving Frankie, who was pliable as bubble gum, into the broom closet, closing the door as Rosylyn's high heels hit the kitchen linoleum. Dana tried to act inconspicuous—what could be more innocent than a maid closing a broom closet?

Standing as still, righteous, and dominant as the Statue of Liberty, one arm poised in mid-air with a cigarette, the other hanging at her side holding her purse, Rosylyn said, "I got down to Sears Fine Foods and told the taxi driver to turn right around." She reeked of alcohol. "I was too hard on you. I forget yer still a young girl and don't have the sense of an older woman. When I was yer age I reckon I had my mama boiling mad many a night. But that doesn't mean I'm saying 'Come to work with a hangover, Honey, and God bless you.'" Dana's ears were tuned closely to the broom closet.

"Yer gonna have to tow the line if yer gonna last in my penthouse." She was pensive, quiet. "I don't reckon you'll let it happen again?" Her eyebrows rose and Dana nodded on cue. "A good maid is hard to find," Rosylyn said with a quick chuckle. "And yer as near good as I reckon I'll find here. I don't plan on being here forever and I don't want to spend the little time I'm here with no maid, looking for one.

"I didn't mean to be so harsh, Honey. You had me worried, that's all. That's why I acted the way I did. Why don't you come on down to Sears with me and I'll treat you to breakfast. Let's start the day off on a better foot."

Dana nodded politely, even though she was sure breakfast would nauseate her further, especially with Rosylyn's breath smelling like a brewery. But at least Frankie could escape while they're out. Dana felt that ever since she met Frankie she had managed to get in the way.

"Here, you'll like this," Rosylyn said, pausing as she opened the door to root in her purse. "Half a little fruit cupcake. Let's forget about this morning, Honey." She paused, and closed the door. "I forgot my keys." Then, she suddenly said, "What was that? I heard something. Did you?"

"No," Dana lied.

"I heard a noise," she said, "coming from the kitchen. Shhhhh." They stood still. "One of those apartments on the third floor was robbed last month. They even took their cat food." Rosylyn's lips were pursed and her breathing was short and fast. Dana had never seen her look afraid before. "I heard it again."

Rosylyn shut the front door and opened the hall closet door quietly, grabbed a baseball bat out of it. "Ever wonder what this was doing in here?" she said. Dana's heart raced. "Come on," Rosylyn said like a paratroop leader.

"I didn't hear anything. Let's go eat."

"Shhhhh!!!!"

As they tiptoed into the kitchen, the broom closet door edged open. Frankie, you fool, Dana thought. Raising the bat over her head, Rosylyn charged the closet, hitting the bat down on the door, closing it. God, she's drunk, Dana thought. Pushing all her weight against the door, Rosylyn yelled, "We got you. Don't try and get out. We got a gun on you. And we got a big bat. You try to get out of here and yer head's gonna be a baseball on the way to left field. You understand?" She whispered to Dana, "Hurry. Call the security guards."

Dana did not move.

"Why you just standing there?!" She continued pressing hard against the door. "Call the guards now, Dana. Hurry!"

Dana acted dumb as a fish in an aquarium, gaping with boulder-sized eyes.

"Am I gonna have to kick you to get you moving? This is no time to freeze up."

Like a cat taking on an air of ferocity to survive, Dana blurted out, "You call the guards!" If Rosylyn called, it would give Frankie time to escape unseen since the phone was in the living room.

Looking bewildered and angry, Rosylyn said, "You've lost yer head. Hold this door hard and I'll get the guards for heaven's sake. This is no time to get stubborn." With a worried wink, she added loudly, "Keep this gun aimed on the door."

A feeling of power stretched pleasurably into Dana as she pretended to push hard on the closet door. Rosylyn must be really drunk to think I can hold a burglar back alone, Dana thought incredulously.

"Hold that door. Hard!" Rosylyn said and took off like an ambulance into the living room.

Quietly and quickly, Dana opened the broom closet. Frankie, one foot in a plastic bucket, a feather duster in front of her face, moved the duster aside to reveal a co-conspirator's silly grin. Seeing Dana's sentenced-to-death look, she erased her grin. Dana made a feeble attempt at a polite isn't-this-funny smile but it only made her look more nervous. She whispered urgently, "Run, get out of here."

Stepping out, Frankie whispered, "I'm sorry I blew it. I thought you two had left. I heard the front door open and close and...."

"Don't worry about it—run!" Dana could hear Rosylyn talking to Security on the phone. "Rosylyn's so drunk, anyway, she doesn't know what's going on."

"I'll call you," Frankie said, looking as if this little adventure, brush with death, was now a bond linking them together. Then she ran off gallantly like Robin Hood into the forest.

Dana contemplated what to do. Should she lie on the floor face down with the bat resting by her head? Then drowsily come to consciousness when Rosylyn returned? No, Rosylyn might have a coronary or might call an ambulance for Dana. Better to play it cool. Dana heard Rosylyn still rat-a-tatting like a machine gun, talking to the guards.

Dana slammed the broom closet door closed and made a running noise, standing in place. Then she yelled, "Rosylyn! Hurry! Help!" Rosylyn was there immediately. "He got away. Pushed the door open. Knocked me down. A big guy. Had tattoos all over him. He ran out the front door. I'm sorry, Rosylyn. I couldn't hold him in. No one could have. He was huge...."

CHAPTER 7

She had not believed in Him until now. He was at her bedroom door. It had clicked and creaked, causing her heart to tap-dance with fear, remembering Rosylyn saying that Security said three more apartments had been robbed recently. She imagined him, huge and tattooed, peering through the darkness for his prey, his little morsel, just as vividly as she imagined him for Rosylyn, who during supper had interrogated her for a detailed description of the broom closet burglar.

"He had black hair, kind of oily," Dana had said at the dinner table, using a description of Lester for the imaginary burglar. The untouched lima beans, cranberries, mashed potatoes and stripsteak had sent up their scents, seducing her. But an unwritten rule of the penthouse was that Rosylyn served herself first, took the first bite, reached first for seconds, just as a Queen always entered a room first. It was a full five minutes before Rosylyn even started serving herself. Even then she didn't take a bite for minutes, captivated by the burglar.

"Describe that tattoo as good as you can."

"It was a jaguar. It was climbing his arm," Dana had said, describing Lester's tattoo. "There were little blood marks where the claws went in." She hated to lie, but felt cornered into it.

"Did he have scars anywhere?"

"No." Dana had felt tempted to bring in the pecan pie, a surefire temptress. It would surely snap Rosylyn's taste buds to attention.

Finally taking a bite, Rosylyn had said, "It's lukewarm. Here, Honey, slide all this food back in the oven for fifteen minutes." Fifteen more minutes of Rosylyn the Detective Stalks the Broom Closet Burglar. Starving, she had felt like throwing the mashed potatoes— plop—a bouffant on Rosylyn's head. She would fling the cranberries at her— a ring around her neck like those leis that 'gorgeous little Polynesian girl' had put on her; then the latest in fashion— shiny

42

lima beans slashed about her dress.

Now as the bedroom door creaked open at midnight, Dana imagined him, a little fat, black oily hair, a jaguar tattoo. Her back was turned toward him as she lay still as a cadaver, eyes closed. His breathing was deep and dark. Karen, I love you—she relayed her last words telepathically. Daddy, you too.

"You asleep?"

"Rosylyn?" It was as much a let down as a relief.

"Cover yer eyes, Honey." Rosylyn flicked on the light switch, muttering in a drunken slur, "I'm no competition for Rip Van Winkle tonight. Barely slept a wink. This place's noisy as a haunted house, a clickin' and creakin' and clackin'.... It's not safe the two of us sleeping alone in this big ol' place...burglar on the prowl. I read somewhere this city's got one of the highest crime rates in the country. One of us lying alone'd be a sitting duck. But two of us together might have a chance at fighting him off." The light struck Dana's eyes as she peeked out from under the covers at Rosylyn, who was wearing a fleshy, pink chiffon gown, holding the baseball bat and a phone. She set her artillery by the bed and crawled slowly into it like a large mammal coming ashore.

Dana scooted to the bed's edge. "We'll sleep better teamed up." Rosylyn smelled very heavily of gin and dusting powder, a smell which reminded Dana of Grandma Wilkins, who died five years back of cirrhosis of the liver. Feeling uneasy, penned in, far removed from Grandma's familiarity and warmth, Dana suddenly missed her. She used to bake twelve different kinds of cookies at Christmas and put them in a huge tupperware bowl for Dana and Daddy. Dana felt guilty for abandoning Grandma's portrait when she died—stuck in the closet next to several paintings of Karen and one of Lester, all unfinished due to romantic traumas. She remembered the one of Jerri abandoned after the break-up. "You got room enough there for yerself?"

"Sure," Dana said in a weak voice, worried she'd either fall off the bed's edge or roll downhill into Rosylyn.

"That burglar's a sly one. I couldn't imagine how he got in here without you knowing it. I'm afraid I'm getting nervous every time I pass the damn broom closet. I could wind up in a psychiatrist's office with a broom closet phobia," Rosylyn said and Dana stifled her laughter. "You been sleeping any?"

"No." But not because of the burglar. The only burglar that had been bothering Dana was worry stealing her sleep. She worried over whether it would work with Jerri this time. She worried that Rosylyn would be mad whenever she spent an entire night out. She wondered what Rosylyn meant earlier when she said she didn't plan to be here too long. What would become of her if Rosylyn left, taking her job, home and security away? Good paying jobs were impossible to find these days. Rents, frighteningly high. This was the first time she'd had a chance to pay off her debts to everyone, to live luxuriously, to get ahead, to have a patron.

She considered that maybe she needed something to fall back on, an out. Maybe graphic arts. Perhaps she could get trained in it somehow and get a job. That would be the next best thing to making a living as a painter, her dream job, which would only be possible if Rosylyn came through as her patron.

She worried that Karen still might be holding Teddy's lies against her. She replayed the whole ugly scenario of their Stockton split-up in her mind again, remembering Karen saying, "Please leave Stockton, Dana. I can't live here with you and Teddy after this. Please." The rims of Karen's eyes had been red. Her thin porcelain-pale hand was on her hip. "It hurts me too much."

"You don't even listen to my side," Dana had replied, her insides cracking, standing in her small pastel-colored bedroom just off Teddy and Karen's bedroom. She had just come home from work and was still wearing the white uniform that said 'Dana' on the right and 'Miley's Hot Dogs' on the left. Her hands were hidden in her pockets like small animals ducking down a hole.

"Teddy said it all."

"But it's not true. I never made a pass at him. He imagined it. He's the one who made passes! Believe me."

"Teddy made passes at you?"

Dana nodded. Twice when Karen was out Teddy had tried to get her into bed. 'What's your game, Dana?' he had said. 'You're always giving me a look like you'd like to, prancing around here in flimsy nightgowns with Karen. Then when I take you up on it you act all self-righteous and shocked. Shit!' he had muttered, shaking his head.

Karen's eyed watered up. She rubbed her palms on her blue and pink flowered apron, worn while making dinner, meat loaf, mashed potatoes and peanut butter cookies. "Why didn't you ever tell me 'til now that he made passes at you?! Why did you keep it from me? I don't understand."

"I was trying to protect you," Dana said, afraid, stepping closer to Karen. "I didn't want you to be hurt."

Karen stepped back. "God, it's been four years you and me and him have hung around each other. Has he been making passes at you for four years?"

"No, just recently."

Karen looked confused and hurt.

"Apart from his passes, it's just too confusing anyway," Karen said. "It just doesn't work us all living together. It would be best if you left. Please. It doesn't work."

Dana had thought it had worked wonderfully for the six months she had been in Stockton. She and Karen were together practically all the time. They cooked and cleaned together, laughed and shared good times. Dana accompanied Karen when she visited elderly shut-ins. She watched her tennis lessons. She joined a stained glass class with her. They were very happy together until Teddy made his accusation.

Then Teddy stepped into the hallway behind Karen, wearing a red-checkered flannel shirt and jeans. His dishwater blonde hair was trim and neat, his hands rough and callused. "Is she coming down hard on you?" he said, looking smugly at Dana.

"You're responsible for all this, Teddy. Don't deny you've made passes at her."

"Me? What about you, Karen? Ever since she moved in here it's been as if you two were married instead of us. You prance around together giving each other goo-goo eyes...."

She slapped him silent and yelled, "Teddy, leave! I want to talk to Dana alone." He rubbed his cheek and sullenly left the house.

"Come sit next to me," Karen said, sitting down on the couch. Her eyes were full of tears. She took Dana's hand. "I don't want it to be ugly and messy like this. I'm just confused. Teddy's jealous and doesn't want you here anymore. And it's hard on me you being here, happy as we've been together, Sweetheart. I feel really torn between you two. Teddy's right—I do feel as if you and I are married living here together. It just doesn't work. There's too much tension.... He's playing games with me and I'm getting all confused and even doubting you. It's no good. I hate to ask you to go. It's just too hard on me. I can't even touch you. Sometimes I wish I could just crawl in bed with you at night.... I feel so guilty and confused. I want this marriage to work and I know it won't with you here. I'm in love with you still. I've been praying to God to take these feelings from me, but they won't go away. As long as you're anywhere in Stockton, I'll want to be seeing you everyday. So go away where I can't get to you.... Please, Dana. For me."

Dana felt a horrible sucking fear. She was as silent as if someone had a gun on her.

"I'm doing this," Karen said slowly, squeezing and caressing Dana's hand, "because I love you *too much*. Please understand."

"I don't," Dana said in a low voice, severely hurt. "I feel you're rejecting me."

"What can I say?" Karen said. "I'm not. I love you more than anyone in the world."

"Then why are you telling me to leave instead of him?"

"I want kids. I want grandkids. All that. I want to be happily married. I want a normal life. You just don't understand, do you?"

Dana felt too devastated to understand.

"I love you," Karen said again and held Dana's hand against her closed lips. "It's just I'm confused. I'm scared. I don't want to be a lesbian."

"You talk about being confused. Well, I'm really confused. You say, 'I love you more than anyone but get the hell out of here.'" She started crying silently.

"This hurts me, too," Karen said. "More than you know. But we've got to start acting like friends and not lovers. I'm married. We can write, you know. Call each other. Visit. Like friends."

Well, at least she wasn't cutting her off totally.

She put her arms around Dana. They rocked each other for a long time. Then Karen kissed Dana's lips for the first time since their four month affair in Cody. It was a short kiss, sad and sweet, sensual and desirous, yet terribly restrained. Karen looked in Dana's eyes in a tortured way. "I'm thinking," she said, "I'm thinking, 'Why not?' I've wanted to for so long and I won't ever again." She leaned to Dana's lips and brushed hers against hers, sending deep ripples of pleasure and pain down Dana. She gave Dana a deep look of love and longing denied. Then she parted her lips and kissed Dana in a way she would never forget.

Knowing she couldn't return to Cody because of Lester, Dana had taken a Greyhound bus alone to San Francisco the next day, San Francisco because it was full of lesbians. And if she couldn't have Karen, she would find someone like her there. Someone unafraid to love her, she thought with a resentful vengeance. And San Francisco because it was just two hours from Stockton by car....

The horrible sucking fear gnawed on her for a week until she met Jerri, who took her to bed that same night, got her out of her roach-infested Tenderloin hotel, which she had temporarily holed up in, and into her Sixteenth Street studio. Jerri helped her find the lunch counter job, and made her feel desirable and attractive again. Knowing she couldn't have Karen, she decided to make a go of it with Jerri. She wanted to live with her, make a commitment. But Jerri said she "needed space" although she was "sexually infatuated" with Dana.

When Jerri broke up with her, that terrible fear had returned, until Rosylyn hired her on permanently.

Now lying in her own bed with Rosylyn, she expected her to request any second that the covers be straightened. Nightly at nine, Dana always pulled back the covers on Rosylyn's bed, fluffed her pillow, put her bathrobe in the closet, handed her her nightcap and stood by like a guard watching Rosylyn make it safely into bed. Then Rosylyn pointed here and there for Dana to give a tug, a pull, on the covers until they were all smooth and sleepable. The ritual completed, Dana was dismissed for the evening. An evening usually spent painting Rosylyn's portraits, bathing, reading one of Rosylyn's *Reader's Digests*, *National Enquirers* or *People* magazines, or writing Karen, sometimes Daddy. Now that she was back with Jerri, she planned to see her twice a week. (Jerri always limited it to twice a week, wanting "breathing room.")

Rosylyn rolled over and said, "Peaches gotten so damn lazy...doesn't bother barking no more. Ducks out under the nearest bed if she hears a thing. You'd think she was working on the burglar's side."

Once again, Rosylyn's speech was slurring under the effects of gin, causing Dana to wonder if she was an alcoholic, just like Grandma Wilkins and Daddy. Rosylyn slurred that Peaches was left on their doorstep in a lunch box of all things, and she never even placed once in fourteen dog shows, but she was a pleasant little dog, and next March twelfth was their tenth anniversary.... Dana gave up any hope of sleeping with this drunken train of talk taking off down the endlessly long track of night. She missed Jerri, and wished she were here instead of Rosylyn. "Who'd you say called earlier when I was putting on my nightclothes?"

"It was a wrong number."

"A wrong number." It had actually been Frankie, but Dana worried that revealing this might somehow trigger Rosylyn into remembering Dana's night out, seemingly forgotten under the more pressing life and death issue of the day, the burglar in the broom closet. "Get names on those wrong numbers. Get any information you can. Burglar could be calling, checking to see if we're home. I got a feeling we got a professional thief picking this penthouse. Not just some pickpocket up off the street." Rosylyn sounded proud she attracted only the best breed of burglar, with a doctorate in 'How to Unlock' and a taste for Bach.

"Let's not be up all night worrying about him," Rosylyn said, starting to slumber off. "You've been a good...little maid...all in all...." Dana was embarrassed that this made her feel good just like it used to when Daddy called her 'My good little Angel,' when Grandma Wilkins called her 'God's little blessing on me,' and when her sixth grade teacher, Mrs. Hornsbee, called her, 'a conscientious and well-mannered child.' "Yes, a good...little maid..." Rosylyn's hand patted Dana's back, then collapsed and fell asleep on it, making Dana very nervous as if a time bomb was resting on her. She did not budge. She kept her breathing even. She did not know what to make of that hand on her back.

Perhaps the excess of gin made her *too* comfortable. Perhaps Rosylyn was so weary she thought she was back in Nashville in bed with Mr. Horstman, Dana hoped. But why was Rosylyn so persistent in asking her if she'd ever been approached by a homosexual? Was that a prelude to a pass had Dana said yes? God, Dana, you're crazy. Crazy to think that. You really need some sleep. She's just a straight married lady with nothing like that on her mind. She's just in your bed because she's afraid there's a burglar loose. That's all. Poor Rosylyn, I really got her scared thinking a burglar was in that closet. She remembered how nervous Rosylyn looked coming into Dana's bedroom, remnants of peach lipstick smeared slightly over her lip, her bouffant hairdo tucked into a hair net, the pinkish-beige aging skin, the baseball bat, the liquor on her breath. Almost pathetic.

Dana felt a sudden desire to protect her. She was careful not to move and knock Rosylyn's hand off; she might awaken in a coronary thinking it was the burglar. Dana thought fondly, sleepily, she's really just a sweet lonely woman underneath it all. It if wasn't for her who knows where I'd be—jobless, no food, no money, forced to go back to Daddy's and Lester would....

Sleep, like an undertow, started pulling her down. She dreamed she walked anchored on warm sand while a vulture circled above. It landed on a rock and became Karen, fretting about Teddy and asking Dana to go to the New Orleans Mardi Gras with her this year. Karen became Jerri, naked from the waist up. Her breasts were tanned and full under the sun. "You're bold to go on the beach topless," Dana said.

"Bold?" Jerri said with a funny grin. "You're naive." She held up a piece of red glass, smoothed down by the sea. The sunlight made it glow. "Lick it, Dana. It's so soft. It's like a little heart." Lawnmower loud, Rosylyn's snoring rattled Dana out of the dream.

For a second she was confused as to where she was. Who was this with her? You're at Rosylyn's. She blushed realizing she was curled right up against her like a kitten against a mama cat. Rosylyn's body felt pudding soft and safe, vibrating with snores. A slight smell of sweat hovered over her. The smell reminded her again of Grandma Wilkins. If Rosylyn wakes up she'll think I'm a lesbian lying like this, Dana worried. She peeled herself away from Rosylyn. She indented the covers down between them like a safety divider on a freeway.

CHAPTER 8

"Teddy's going hunting the weekend of November fifteenth with Maurice. You know, the little French guy who's nuts about astrology?" Dana took the phone into the bathroom where she had been scrubbing the tiles to snow-glare whiteness. "They're going deer hunting someplace outside of Lassen. How would you like company that weekend?" Karen said, sounding excited.

"I'd, I'd love it!" Dana said. She had not seen Karen once in the three months she had been with Rosylyn. She had only seen her twice since being told to leave Stockton, a demand she still did not fully understand, yet one that hurt less with time. It was a rejection softened and sweetened by weekly letters from Karen expressing how much she missed and loved her, despite her original decree that they stick strictly to a Puritan-style friendship. When Dana visited, once last Easter and once to water ski with them on the Delta, Karen had been extremely attentive as if trying to atone for hurting her.

"I'll cancel with Jerri for that weekend," Dana said. During the two months she and Jerri had been back together, they had developed a pattern of spending every Saturday and Wednesday nights together, in bed. Dana always returned to Rosylyn's by eleven p.m., still afraid of being fired after that one time she stayed out all night. Although Jerri was becoming impatient with this set up—they routinely fought over it, Dana had managed to keep her pacified with sex, something Jerri always wanted. She repeatedly told Dana, "This is the best sex I've ever had. You're the only woman that can keep up with me. Most women lose interest after awhile." It's not that Dana was driven by the sex, but by the desire to keep the relationship. Sex was the hook to keep Jerri interested.

Karen didn't comment. "Would Rosylyn mind if I stayed with you at her place?"

"I'll ask her tonight."

"Good...I'm making carob mousse right now. You'd love it."

Dana remembered pretending to like the carob mousses, carob cookies and cakes Karen used to serve her in Stockton. And the tofu, which tasted like noodle-flavored jello. Ms. Pippins would sure be impressed, Dana thought. Ms. Pippins was their high school Home Ec teacher who got Karen hooked on health foods. After Home Ec class, Karen would usually say something like, "Ms. Pippins is so right. Look at her. Her hair, her figure, her skin, it's all so perfect. It makes sense to me to eat and exercise like that looking at her. Don't you think she's gorgeous?" Dana would shrug, jealous. Sulking, she felt she couldn't possibly compete with Ms. Pippins, especially when Karen baked her a triple-layered yogurt cake one Christmas, and Ms. Pippins gave her "Laurel's Kitchen," which Karen read cover to cover twice. Then she became Ms. Pippin's personal teacher's aide. Karen worshipped her.

"You still write Ms. Pippins?"

"What brought her up?" Karen said defensively.

"I don't know."

"No, we lost contact when she married that professional skier. Remember the one she fell for in Sun Valley? They're living in Switzerland now at his skiing school. She quit writing." She sounded dismayed.

"Can I ask you something about you and her?"

"Go ahead."

It seemed safe to ask now, insulated by the passage of time. "Were you in love with her?"

"No. I admired her but.... What gave you that idea?" Karen sounded affronted, accused. "You know I was going with Teddy," she said defensively. "You know I'm not gay." As if sensing Dana's thoughts, she added softly, "I mean what happened between us—those four months in Cody—was special, you know that. But...I don't know. I don't really think of you as a girl. You're just Dana to me. You know what I mean? I mean I didn't do that with you because you're a girl. I don't get that way about girls," she insisted. "And never Ms. Pippins. God no!" The line was uncomfortably quiet. "You know how confused I was over Teddy when we were separated. I just really needed to feel loved and wanted in a real way and you gave me what I needed.... But that doesn't make me a lesbian, you know?"

Hand wrench-tight on the receiver, Dana half-whispered, "You make it sound like you just used me."

"Dana! How can you think that?"

Dana felt like a discarded cigarette butt, picked up, relit, sucked on, discarded again. Used. She felt as if she was sitting in the Cody Rodeo again, Karen telling her she's going back to Teddy. The past whirlpooled up around Dana, who was surprised, stunned by this sudden resurrection of feelings that she thought had vanished. It was as if they tricked her, had only been hiding, then ambushed her. Pain, hurt, humiliation, rejection pushed up their nasty heads again. Her grip on the phone weakened. The feelings frightened her. She did not understand their intensity. It was as if they were a separate entity, a second personality hiding inside her.

She was in a time warp into the past. Now, like a dreamer hearing a distant voice call, 'Wake up,' Dana heard, "Did you mean that?" It got louder. "That really hurts that you'd think.... Do you really think that?"

The question struck through her fog of feelings. "No, I didn't mean that," Dana said. "I'm sorry..." She said slowly, cautiously, "You'll still come visit, won't you?"

"Of course. I'm very much looking forward to it."

Dana was silent, feeling too vulnerable to express affection right now.

"You know I love you very deeply," Karen said reassuringly. "I never mean to hurt you. But I seem to. I wish it wasn't so. Don't take things wrong. O.K., Sweetie?"

"O.K."

"I can't wait to see you again. You know Teddy's been a jealous tyrant about me seeing you. God, this will be our first time alone in almost ten months."

"It won't be as relaxed as if I had my own place...."

"Don't worry about it," Karen said.

"Oh, I've saved up three hundred dollars here to repay you. And I have another five hundred in my savings account. And I just bought a really nice color T.V. for my room. I'm doing really well financially."

"Good for you!"

Opening the toilet, Dana sprinkled Comet in. She watched the powder melt into the water, wondering what Rosylyn would say about Karen wanting to visit. She was as nervous contemplating this as she would be requesting a raise.

The phone rang again as Rosylyn came home from shopping in Union Square. "Dana? Is that you? Doesn't sound like you. This is Jerri. Sorry I didn't call back sooner. But Renee's up visiting from L.A., and I've been busy with school and entertaining her. In fact we're just on our way out the door now to see a Woody Allen film. I'd like to see you later tonight, but I really should hit the law books, you know? I've got all those exams coming up."

"Yeah." Plenty of time to see her ex-lover, Renee, but no time for me, Dana thought.

"How have you been?"

"Not too bad."

"Well, we'll get together for dinner some night this week. I'll treat you."

"Which night?"

"How's later in the week? This is such a busy week for me with exams, and Renee. How about Saturday?" What would Jerri be doing every night until Saturday with Renee there as her house guest? She only has one bed.

Dana said, "O.K., Saturday." There was an uncomfortable pause in the conversation. "I'm finishing the painting of you." This morning she had placed it back on her easel, deciding to finish it before continuing the series of Rosylyn. She wanted to make Jerri happy by finishing it.

"Good! I can't wait to see the finished piece. Anyway, Renee's getting impatient. I got to go. Be here Saturday at eightish. I'll be looking forward to seeing you...."

As Dana hung up, Rosylyn said, "Who was that?"

"It was a call for me."

"Oh," Rosylyn said curtly. "Tell me. Who was that up on yer easel?" Silence. "The girl floating in water on yer easel?"

"Oh, that. That's just an old painting I've been meaning to finish. It's no one. Just someone out of my head." Dana's face flushed red. Rosylyn didn't know Jerri existed. When Dana left to see her, she told Rosylyn she was going shopping, or visiting a fictitious old friend named Tom who supposedly had moved here from Cody, or visiting art galleries, or reading at a cafe in North Beach.

Rosylyn barked in a firm voice, "You better get busy on those tiles and get them finished."

Dana scrubbed the tiles until they were clean as a new Pamper. She scrubbed the toilet base and tank thoroughly. By the time she finished scrubbing down the bathroom, the only dirt in it was that on Rosylyn's heels as she stood on the tiles. Rosylyn leaned over and inspected the back of the base of the toilet. "Looks great, Honey. Great. You did a good job. Even got the back of the toilet looking brand new."

Sometimes Dana felt that she deserved a Nobel prize for housecleaning or at least a mention in the *Guinness Book of World Records* for cleaning more things than humanly imaginable. She had to clean the hands on the wall clock, polish the doorstop and even clean her cleaning equipment, such as the vacuum cleaner. Meaningless work had taken on a new meaning working for Rosylyn; it lapsed into a Twilight Zone beyond meaningless sometimes.

"Now I want you to do the doorknobs," Rosylyn ordered. "Brass polish is under the sink. Keep up yer good work and you'll be getting a raise," she said with a Mother Superior smile, her hand gently patting Dana's back. "I got us some tickets to a play, a musical, *The King and I*. You'll like that." Her hand continued patting Dana's back.

Hands pinkish-white from scouring with steel wool, back and neck sweating slightly, Dana blew upward to knock her bangs out of her eyes. She went for the brass polish as if it was a sweepstakes ticket, hoping to win a raise and a yes from Rosylyn when she asked her if Karen could visit.

Dana spent the evening shopping for art supplies and earrings for Jerri. She had a habit of buying gifts for Jerri. Upon returning home, she flicked on the light switch in her bedroom and was startled to find Rosylyn anchored in her bed, her new T.V. on. She hadn't slept in Dana's bed since that night over two months ago when she feared a burglar was on the loose.

"That you, Dana?" Rosylyn said, squinting her eyes from the sudden overdose of light. She looked at the alarm clock. Nine-thirty. "I was just dozinnnn off," Rosylyn slurred, drunk again. "You don't mind me sleeping in here, do you? I was watching yer T.V. It's a nicer set than mine." Dana glanced uneasily at the bottle of gin on her night stand, half-empty.

"No," she said reluctantly. Her worst fear was coming true: Rosylyn was trying to stake a claim to her bed and new T.V. She feared Rosylyn was going to be a nightly chaperone. I better look into some graphic arts programs, she thought quickly, and get some training so I can get a good job and get out of here before this gets too weird.

"Have fun shopping?"

Dana nodded. Then she turned away and put on her flowered flannel nightgown, her back to Rosylyn.

She felt those eyes on her. "I once had a gown like that.... We could a looked like a mother and daughter team...." Rosylyn yawned and smacked her lips. Dana tensely lay down on the edge of the bed. Gin pervaded the air as usual.

"I used to always wonder how I would a dressed a little girl of my own," Rosylyn said in a forlorn, sentimental voice. "But we never had any children. The doctors said it was my fault. But I never believed them until I found out Mr. Horstman had...," she said, stopping abruptly. "Would a liked to a had a little girl of my very own."

Dana was surprised and uneasy hearing Rosylyn talk so personally. She seldom mentioned anything more personal than what she liked to eat. Dana had come to see her as a creature without a past, without any feelings other than the desires to eat, sleep, drink, watch T.V. and boss Dana. Any inner life of Rosylyn's was as remote as the Antarctic. To hear Rosylyn lament the loss of a child she never could have stunned and embarrassed Dana. This was something she shouldn't hear. Rosylyn didn't talk like this during the day. She was different at night, all ginned up.

There was a perfect time to ask Daddy for favors, when he was sweet and sad. This was the perfect time to ask Rosylyn, sleepy, ginned up and gentler. "Rosylyn, I was wondering, I'd like to have my best friend, Karen—you know the girl who writes me all the letters from Stockton? I'd like to have her visit the weekend after next."

"She's married, isn't she?"

"Yes."

"Having trouble with her husband?"

"No."

"Then why's she coming out here without her husband? Always travelled with Mr. Horstman if...any travelling...to be done." She smacked her lips again.

"We're best friends."

"I haven't had a best girlfriend since grade school. Best girlfriend used to be Sue Anne.... Sue Anne something or other. Had the pinkest, palest skin and her mama always put her in frilly

55

dresses. We used to dress up as a bride and groom and parade down the street like we was in a wedding march when we were seven...we played house, dolls, doctor, played everything together. Sue Anne.... Haven't thought of her in years...." Dana blushed. Rosylyn wouldn't talk so personally if she hadn't drunk so much.

"Well," Dana said again, "can Karen come?" She needed an answer before losing her to sleep.

"Can Karen come?" Rosylyn said as if hearing the question for the first time. "I reckon so...if that's what you want...."

Dana was jubilant. Karen was coming. Dear, sweet, precious Karen. Coming.

Her enthusiasm was dampened when Rosylyn's arm suddenly slung heavily around her, and hung there matter-of-factly. A soft rattle of snores soon bubbled up out of her. She drinks too much after dinner, Dana thought, trying to explain why that arm was on her. She's not herself after drinking, she thought defensively, self-protectively.

CHAPTER 9

Scarves tied her ankles and wrists to the cold gold posts. Blindfolded, she felt like a maiden locked in a dark tower. What was her abductress up to? This was a precarious position to be left alone in. What if a rapist broke in? What if an earthquake occurred? How embarrassing to be shook out onto 18th Street, naked and blindfolded, tied open like an X on an antique brass bed.

She heard the floorboard squeak. But her abductress didn't speak. Dana felt her presence, however, like a sudden hot breeze. There was something almost holy about this silence, like the hush over an audience before the play begins. A smooth hand slid onto her breast and squeezed it playfully.

"Jerri?"

"No, this is Rosylyn."

"That's not funny."

"Then wipe that smile off your face," Jerri said, setting something down on the night stand. "I said wipe that smile off. Or if you prefer, I will." She sounded like Humphrey Bogart in falsetto. "I warned you...."

Her hand attacked Dana's lips with something that felt like cool mud. "That's not fair."

Straddling Dana's waist, Jerri slapped on another handful of the sludge. "Who said life's fair?" It tasted sweet. "I did invite you to dinner, didn't I? Open your mouth, Babe."

"Yeah, at a restaurant."

"Well, as I recall you haven't been too eager to leave for dinner since you've come. Come here, that is. Two hours and you haven't mentioned dinner, have you?"

Dana grinned.

Jerri licked and kissed Dana's lips clean of the sweet stuff she put on them. "Now hold still."

"Do I have much choice?" Dana said, illustrating her comment with a tug of the tied scarves she had willingly succumbed to earlier.

She let herself be Jerri's playground. She felt more sludge on her breasts. Something syrupy trickled down her cleavage. "I feel like a cake being frosted."

Untying Dana's blindfold, Jerri said, "Voila! A masterpiece of abstract art. A banana-tit split."

Dana quietly stared at her breasts as if they were two flying saucers just landed on her. Two maraschino cherries topped her nipples like stars on a Christmas tree. Her breasts were covered with new fallen snow, marshmallow cream. Was Jerri decorating early for Christmas? Spray-can whip cream encircled her breasts. Chocolate syrup scribbled out 'Eat' on one white breast and 'Me' on the other. If Rosylyn could see me now, Dana thought, grinning. She felt like a neon billboard on Broadway. Any second the cherries would begin to blink on and off. The 'Eat Me' would light up in fluorescent pink. Thank God the earthquake was safely sleeping tonight. Dana could not believe the things Jerri thought up—blindfolds, costumes, mirrors, whip cream, whips. Nor can she believe Jerri enticed her to go along with these wild sexual games, which she often found embarrassing. She would be happy just to have straightforward sex as she always had in the past. But she wanted to keep Jerri happy. And she cannot deny the fun and passion they had in bed.

"You are a true artist," Dana said, smiling at Jerri, amazed at her sexual imagination.

Jerri moved the maraschino cherries toward Dana's thighs.

"What are you up to?"

"Stocking stuffers."

"No, no," Dana said, laughing. "They'll get lost up in there."

"Won't the doctors be amused," Jerri said, holding a cherry threateningly close to Dana's upper thighs. "They'll think you're still a virgin. A good, sweet virgin with a candied cherry. A preserved cherry. You'll be a medical miracle!"

"No, thank you," Dana said, smiling. Jerri set the cherry in Dana's bellybutton. Then she slowly licked the sweets off until they were all gone.

"Where did you get all this sweet stuff?"

"Renee's birthday was yesterday. She likes banana splits. So I made her one with lit candles in it."

"Oh."

"Oh?" Jerri said. "What did 'oh' mean?"

"Oh, I didn't know it was her birthday." Dana's smile was gone.
"Yeah, it was her birthday. Her thirty-second. I took her out for omelets. Then we went for cappucino. Then she went to see some other friends and came back in the evening. I made banana splits and gave her some presents, a pair of opal earrings and Isadora Duncan's autobiography." Jerri's eyes were trained on Dana like a scientist's on a mouse under scientific experimentation. "And the only reason I'm telling you this is to see if you really get as uncomfortable hearing about Renee as I suspect. Do you realize how solemn and silent you get whenever I mention her?"

Dana shrugged. She no longer felt willing to be tied open naked on Jerri's bed. Especially with banana-tit splits. It was humiliating. "My wrists are starting to hurt. Could you please untie me?" she said, vulnerably.

"Oh, don't tell me your wrists are starting to hurt. Tell me what's really starting to hurt?" Jerri struck a match and lit a cigarette, sat on the edge of the bed naked, waiting for Dana to talk. "Well?"

"They are starting to get uncomfortable tied up like this."

"They never did before. Besides that's not what's making you feel uncomfortable. You're evading the issue," Jerri said in an even tone, letting out an impatient puff of smoke. "I'm not going to untie you until you tell me what's really the matter." She tossed her head back and ran her hand through her hair.

Dana's entire body tightened up. "Nothing." The idea of talking about Renee and Jerri and her jealous feelings about them while being tied up like a clown in a straitjacket made Dana feel totally powerless and frightened. "Please untie me, Jerri." She gave a frustrated tug on her ties. "This isn't fair."

Jerri talked with her back to Dana, pouring herself a glass of wine. "Neither are you. You keep things from me. You pout. You won't say what you feel ever. I'll tell you what you feel. You're afraid I had sex with Renee. In fact, you're probably worried I served her banana splits like yours."

Dana was quiet. "I'm just uncomfortable. My wrists. Don't you understand?"

"Of course I understand. But you don't understand how uncomfortable you're making me."

"What do you mean?"

Jerri's voice rose. "You make me feel all tied up inside. You try to punish me with your silences. You try to make me feel guilty." Her voice rose more. "I'm not guilty."

"I never said you were."

"You imply it somehow." Jerri turned her head sharply to face the open window. Her sudden movement caused ashes to jump off her cigarette and down her leg. "Shit." She set the cigarette in a cut-glass ashtray and brushed the ashes off her legs carefully. "O.K., you don't make me feel guilty. I make myself feel guilty. Isn't that how it goes?" She caught her reflection in the mirror and brushed a loose lock of black hair off her eyebrow. "I need a joint." She opened the canister atop her dresser.

Dana watched, expressionless, her insides turning somersaults. She closed her eyes. "Untie me," she said again, angrily.

Jerri didn't respond. Dana broke, yelling, "Jerri, untie me right now!" She had never yelled at Jerri before and she almost startled herself. "I'm not going to say a damned word to you like this," she said in a lower voice.

Jerri stared at the fake Persian rug on her hardwood floors. Her eyes darkened under her hard gaze. She untied Dana.

Dana went to the bathroom and took a quick shower to wash all the goop off. When she returned wearing the robe she kept at Jerri's, Jerri looked at her bitterly and said, "This isn't working. I think we should break up. I hoped things could be different, could work with us if we got back together. But they can't. I should stick to women my own age or older."

"Things can be different," Dana said, frightened.

"No, no." Jerri shook her head. "I see now that it can't work. You're too possessive. And I'm sick and tired of you never staying the night. It's been two months. This is ridiculous. And sometimes I feel like you learned to communicate in a prisoner of war interrogation camp." Jerri looked at her accusingly. "What makes you think things can change between us? We're at the 'Me, Tarzan, you, Jane' level of communicating. Besides, we're so different. There's such an intellectual gap between us. And we're from two different eras. You're thirteen years younger than me. Things that influenced me—the hippie era, Vietnam, the women's liberation movement—all that is not even in your frame of reference. I'm not criticizing you. You were just a kid out in Wyoming when it was all happening." She put her joint out. "You're no different than most others your age now. You're all a new breed. Less political. More materialistic."

Dana waited nervously for what this lecture was leading up to. "We're just...," Jerri shrugged. "Too different. What made you..., I mean how the hell do you think we can make it together?"

"I just think we can," Dana said. With love we can make it, she thought, but didn't say it, fearing Jerri would think that it was a corny idea, another difference in their 'eras.' Trying to think fast for the right words like a used car salesman on the verge of making or breaking a deal, Dana said, "I can give you what you want."

"You think so?" Jerri lit another cigarette.

"Sure," Dana said, feeling very vulnerable. She could feel that her cheeks were ruddy. "Just tell me what you want."

Jerri looked as if the question surprised her. Rubbing the back of her own neck, her head bent down, she said, "I don't know." She took a puff off her cigarette. "I want the good things we have. Like the fun we have together, you know?" Dana nodded. "The good sex. We really have great sex." Jerri rolled onto her back. She looked at the ceiling as she talked, blowing smoke rings. "I love sex with you. It becomes more and more evident to me that we're not cut out to be just friends, and I don't mean to degrade the word friend by prefixing it with just. Friends are as important as lovers, if not more. I'm just too physically attracted to you. We always end up in bed whenever we get together, you know?" Dana nodded, glad that Jerri didn't want her just as a friend.

Jerri went on. "And I suspect that we really don't have enough in common to build a good friendship. We're just really very different. That's not an insult, Dana. There's nothing wrong with not having a lot in common. I mean that's probably why I'm so sexually attracted to you. Because you're so different from me and my other friends. Being with you is like going away to a tropical island where everything is refreshing, different. I can get my head away from school and politics, from abstraction and just relax. Have fun. I need you for all that." Needed, Dana warmed up inside. "I just have such ambivalent feelings about it all." She kissed Dana quietly on the cheek. "I really missed you those four weeks we split up. I missed having sex with you." After reflecting, she said, "Things have to change between us for it to work."

"They can change," Dana said with a cheery nurse's tone.

"I want you to be more open with me about your feelings and your past. You only really talked to me once, that night you told me about Karen and your old boyfriend."

"O.K."

"And I want us to be nonmonogamous. Not be possessive. We have to trust each other's love and desire for one another. Not give in to jealousy. I want to be able to tell you if I ever have sex with someone else and I don't want you to fall apart over it. And vice versa. It's no big deal. O.K.?" Jerri said a little fiercely. Dana nodded her head up and down like a bouncing ball.

Jerri sat up, pleased. "I think we should see each other only once a week to give ourselves the space we need to work all this out. Besides I have so much studying to do, and I have so many friends to keep up on. I need my space.... Well, what do you think?"

"We'll do whatever you say," Dana said, wanting very much for Jerri to want the relationship and not leave her again.

With a funny grin, Jerri said, "We'll do whatever I say? Who am I? Svengali?" She moved slowly, putting her cigarette out. She stared at the ashes momentarily, her eyes at peace like a gambler's would be given the rare opportunity to go through the deck and pick the cards first. "You are a sweetheart," she said.

Dana was simultaneously relieved and apprehensive.

"And there's one more thing I want," Jerri said with a sweet smile. "I want to make love to you again." Their eyes hooked together longingly, but each with a different longing.

"No, no, that's too much to ask," Dana said, smiling.

"Who's asking?" Jerri said on all fours over Dana. She smiled mischievously. "Remember—we'll do whatever I say!"

Dana felt like a banana split—delicious, promising, sweet. But split.

At midnight, Dana said, "I should be back at Rosylyn's."

"Why?" Jerri said, lying on top of her, resting.

"I told her I'd be back by eleven."

"Did you tell her you were going out with me?"

"No. That would just cause a lot of trouble. She'd start asking questions. Maybe she'd catch on. I just said I was going over to Tom's."

"I don't believe this," Jerri said, rolling off Dana and onto her back. "Shit. This sounds like high school. I don't understand. I'm really sick of this set up. I've reached my breaking point with this nonsense. I don't like that woman. She's got ulterior motives."

Dana felt defensive. "She's not so bad. There's nothing wrong with Rosylyn. God, she's offered to be my patron. How often does someone do that?"

"Patron my ass." Jerri was sullen. "Don't you want to spend the night?"

"Yes." They have had this conversation dozens of times in the past.

"What business is it of Rosylyn's anyway?"

"You don't know Rosylyn."

Shaking her head, Jerri said, "What a set up you've fallen into. Not only her maid, but her dinner and theater companion. What next?" She lit another cigarette. She always chain smoked when agitated. "I don't understand."

"There's nothing to understand," Dana said defensively. "I'm just a live-in maid, paid to clean this rich lady's place and keep her company somewhat. It's a job like any job. She expects me to be to work on time, do my work well, and not let my social life interfere with my job. And a lot of employers, even in San Francisco, still get really upset if they find out a lesbian works for them. I think that's why Mr. Bartizal laid me off from the lunch counter job, even though he didn't admit to it. He saw me holding your hand that one time down on the Marina. I could get fired at Rosylyn's."

"That would be a blessing."

"It's a good-paying job. I don't want to get fired."

"Fired for what you do on your time off?! This is ludicrous. Don't go to Rosylyn's, Dana. Stand up for yourself. What am I, someone you're ashamed of? Your mistress you have to sneak off to see? Will we ever be able to spend a night together again? This is asinine. Dana, why not just be a kept woman?! You'd get your own maid then."

"I don't want to get fired." Dana's arms were crossed tightly across her chest, holding herself protectively.

"So what if you do. You worry too much. You can find another job."

"Good jobs are really hard to find here. I don't know how to type. I'm not smart like you, Jerri. I didn't go to college. There's not much I can do, besides paint. I've been considering studying graphic arts because there's more jobs in that than painting. But for now I have to take what I can get, and if it pays real good like Rosylyn's, then I'm not going to just let go of it that easily. Besides I'd have to find a place to live, and rents are so high. I can't afford it. I'm working to get enough saved for a studio apartment. I need first, last and a security deposit, at least fifteen hundred dollars to get in."

"It's too bad you ever gave up your studio."

"The penthouse is much nicer. It's really nice...."

"That's not what I meant. I meant for your independence. For us."

"We weren't together when I gave up my studio, remember?" Dana said.

"Why couldn't you just have worked for her days?"

"Rosylyn needs a live-in maid. Try to be patient. I'm saving for my own apartment."

Jerri said, "*Needs*? Why does she *need* a live-in maid?"

"She's lonely, I guess. She doesn't know anybody here. She's used to being looked after by her husband and live-in maid in Nashville." Dana looked at the clock and Jerri looked at Dana looking at the clock.

"Well, you know what I think," Jerri said. "It's your decision whether to stay or go. But if we're going to make it together, we need entire nights together."

Dana felt cornered and without a choice in the matter. Jerri threatened to break up with her tonight. She hadn't done that since they got back together. Jerri would be furious if she left. Jerri would think it didn't work between them. Jerri might....

"I'll stay."

The next morning she told Rosylyn she fell asleep at her friend Tom's while watching a movie. Dana was surprised at how calm and matter of fact Rosylyn was, as if she had expected Dana to stay away for the night again and had pre-planned the reprimand. "I'll have to put you on two weeks probation. I need a dependable maid. One I can count on. One I don't have to worry over. I know you need a private life, time to have fun, but you mustn't let it interfere with your job responsibilities. Two weeks probation. And today I want you to do all the woodwork."

Dana did the woodwork so thoroughly a doctor could operate on it. She cleaned as if all prior cleanings were rehearsal for this probationary period. And on her face whenever Rosylyn approached, a salute of a smile. She would try her hardest to keep on with Rosylyn. And with Jerri.

CHAPTER 10

After tooting twice before Jerri's blue and white Victorian flat, Dana checked herself in the wobbly rear-view mirror, loose from over use. Her face had the timidity of a fawn's; her taut and agile body had a 'ready to bolt' look. She smoothed Vaseline on her lips, lit one of the cigarettes she always kept for Jerri, hoping that would make her feel tougher. She hoped Jerri wouldn't notice she had lip gloss, mascara, and blush on, knowing Jerri regarded make-up as "War paint, developed for the war between the sexes. Also used on clown's faces." She turned the radio to the jazz station Jerri liked. She brushed her hair, shiny under the street light. She felt guilty for feigning cramps in order to get out of having to accompany Rosylyn to the play tonight.

She saw Renee sauntering down Jerri's steps. Away with the comb, up with the rear-view mirror. Dana, reposing in her Pontiac, listening to a jazz station, smoking, coolly said, "Hi, Renee."

"Dana! It's good to see you again!" Renee said enthusiastically, tossing her long black hair over her shoulders and leaning down to Dana's window, causing Dana to worry Renee was coming in for a crash landing. Renee was big on hugs—pasted them on everybody. A whale of a smile alighted on her lips, a whale of a smell, spicy musk, enveloped her. Dana's senses felt assaulted. Renee always came on like a Hollywood movie lighting up. "How have you been?"

"I've been fine. How about you?" Dana said, a strung up smile strapped to her face, worrying that Jerri wanted to bring Renee along tonight.

"Just great!" She stepped back and like a peacock fanning up, straightened the long cloth belt that caressed her purple, Indian-style flowing blouse. A blouse which covered a slender, sleepy, dreamy body with legs veiled in silky light-purple pants. Six thin chains glistened at her neck. Dana wondered which were from Jerri—probably all six. She felt accosted by the chains, bracelets, perfume, beautiful long hair, silky pants, exotic sensuousness. Jerri had said Renee was 'half French, half Egyptian.' Dana felt as common and dull as pavement next to Renee. At least, she thought, she's not really pretty. Renee's face would be classically beautiful but for a slight crookedness to it; her nose and mouth looked as if they were diving in different directions. Dana pretended to watch a kid cycling by with 'no hands.' She tried to remember how Jerri described Renee's face—unique, different, unusual? No. Interesting.

"Jerri'll be down in a second," Renee said, and brushed her hair over her shoulders again. "She's feeding and watering the cat. Do you have a spare cigarette? You've tempted me," she said with an uncanny grin and funny look in her eyes. She paused before adding, "With your cigarette. I've been trying to quit."

Dana handed over a cigarette quickly, a slight tremor to her hand, which she felt Renee had spotlighted. The 'You've tempted me ...' confused her. Did she imagine the innuendo? She managed a polite, "How are things in L.A.?"

"Great! I finally got my own dance studio. I have twenty students. The energy's incredible. But...," she said with a sigh, "money's still tight. I've been cocktailing on the side. At a straight bar. Good tips." She lighted the cigarette and stepped away from the Pontiac to exhale a puff of smoke. Holding the cigarette, she gazed up at the night sky, looking graceful, stylish. Dana felt like a weasel.

Dana smiled politely, glancing quickly at Renee's body, toned and firm from dancing, smooth and sensuous. "I'll run up and rush Jerri on down," Renee said.

"No, you don't have to do that. She'll be down any second. She's always late. I'm used to it." I'd rather wait here with you, Dana thought, than sit here with you two up there alone. She felt like a shadow creature, reeking of vile emotions, sitting in the darkness of her Pontiac. She scratched a loose thread on the upholstery, feeling Renee was obtrusive.

"That's not a good thing to get used to," Renee said. "Don't wait on Jerri. In any way. Don't be subservient to her. She's in denial about a lot of things. She won't own up to anything. She just gets angry if I try to confront her." She stopped. She shrugged. "I guess that's not my place to be saying this." Dana listened to Renee's words as she would those of an enemy crossing the line to sabotage her, trying to turn her against her own compatriot with fancy logic.

Sabotage. In reaction, she felt loyal to Jerri. Renee was trying to put a wedge between them as Teddy tried to do with Karen and her. That *was* a pass, that "You've tempted me...," Dana decided.

Flustered, not knowing how to respond, Dana said, "You have a good tan."

"Thank you," Renee said, leaning her lovely brown body against Dana's car. "The gym I go to has a tanning room."

Jerri finally came out. Dana was a boxing bag of emotions—relief, resentment, loyalty, love, distrust. Jerri smiled like a favorite child. "What idle gossip have you two been swapping about me? Whatever it is, it's all true."

"I hope not!" Renee said, smiling.

"Oh?" Jerri said with a taunting smile.

"Dana was just commenting on my tan."

"I'm always telling her," Jerri said to Dana, who felt lost in left field, "that she's gonna get skin cancer from broiling her skin."

"And I tell her," Renee said to Dana, "that she ought to be nicer to a dying lady."

They sounded to Dana like an old couple at their silver anniversary reminiscing and spatting fondly. Her body tensed up more.

"Well," Jerri said, "we'd better get going before Cost Plus closes. Have fun at Maggie and Betty's. What time do you think you'll be back?"

"Elevenish."

They hugged good-bye and exchanged short kisses. "Bye, Sweetheart," Renee said. They're sleeping together, Dana thought angrily, leaning over to fling the passenger door open.

"Sorry I took so long," Jerri said, watching Renee walk off. She pressed Dana's hand, and kissed her quickly. She tucked her red shirt, rolled up to her elbows, into her tight black jeans. Silver loop earrings glistened against her black hair.

Dana steered her Pontiac down Market Street. "You sure are quiet," Jerri said, lighting a cigarette and unrolling the window. "Something bothering you?"

"No." Dana slammed on the brakes, slowing the car before a red light. Jerri buckled her seat belt.

"Renee thinks you're cute." Jerri wore an amused grin. "She'd sleep with you if she could. But she knows I'd kill her. I get jealous if my lovers sleep together. There's plenty of other women they can sleep with." Dana fumed under her poker face. Lovers?! How many are in the harem? "Slow down! This isn't the Grand Prix." Dana let up on the gas. "What's eating you tonight?"

"Nothing." What's been eating you, Dana thought. She boomeranged the Pontiac around onto Van Ness Avenue, nearly knocking Jerri off balance.

"You ever thought of being a taxi driver in Mexico City?" Jerri said. "You'd fit right in. Give me a break." Dana braked suddenly at a yellow light. "You should have speeded up and made that light!"

"Speed up, slow down, which do you want?!"

"Don't raise your voice."

"I didn't raise it."

"I can tell we're in for fun tonight." Jerri bounced her cigarette butt up and down in the ash tray. Lighting another cigarette right away, she said, "You've got me on edge now. I feel like I'm in a driver's training car."

"I drive fine. I've never had a ticket. I drive defensively. I watch out for other cars."

"You're defensive all right."

They sat as silently as two grave markers. The jealousy spread to every cell in Dana's body, twisting and igniting them, making them feel like bricks breaking. She felt all jammed up. Her throat tightened. The steering wheel was moist where she clasped it. She realized her jealousy was jeopardizing their relationship. I have to be nice, she thought, or she'll dump me. Dana felt her whole life was on probation. She didn't know how she could be nice when her insides were in a bloody civil war with her wanting to break out and bash something on the outside—the window, the steering wheel, the door. She was a saint of self-control. Calm down, Dana, she told herself. Watch out for that car. You don't even know for sure if she slept with Renee. "When you're done at Cost Plus, is there any place else you need to go?" she tried to say sweetly, obligingly. Jerri shook her head.

"Did it bother you seeing Renee?"

Quickly, Dana said, "No. Not at all. She's always really friendly to me."

"She likes you. Don't look at me while you drive. Watch the road."

"Sorry."

"Turn on Geary," Jerri said. "I know why you're mad. Because I didn't call you all week." Dana didn't answer, remembering waiting all week for the call that Jerri had promised to make that last night when she had risked sleeping over. "I didn't forget. I was just wrapped up in other things."

Dana thought resentfully, yeah, in Renee's arms.

"Law books mainly. I was going to call you but you called me before I.... Shit, Dana, what is this—bumper cars? One more inch and we'll be in the trunk of that BMW."

"Do you want to drive?" Dana immediately felt guilty for saying it so snottily.

Jerri was solemn. "What time is Rosylyn expecting you in tonight?"

"I want to be in at ten-thirty before she gets back from a play."

Jerri didn't protest. Dana was jealous, thinking that Jerri was not protesting because she wanted Dana gone by eleven when Renee returned. Feeling a little spiteful, Dana said, initially having wanted to conceal it from Jerri, "Rosylyn put me on two weeks probation for staying out that night."

"Shit. This really is like high school. Reminds me of being grounded." She shook her head. "Maybe it would be better if you just didn't talk about Rosylyn to me. O.K.?" She was silent. "Tell me one thing, though. Does she have you so afraid you won't ever spend a night with me again for fear of being fired?"

"I don't know."

"You don't know! Damn! This frustrates me." Jerri crossed her arms. "It's like you're her lover and sneaking out to some sordid affair with me. It puts me in a very awkward position that I don't want to be in. You can't really blame me if I have sex with someone else.... I'm sorry, Dana. I didn't mean that. That was a low blow." Jerri was quiet. "Listen, Dana, do you want me to tell you if I have sex with someone else? I want to know if you do."

"Just tell me," Dana said, wanting Jerri to get it over with quickly, tell her she fucked goddamned Renee and they had seventeen orgasms in one night, setting a world record.

Geary Street was dizzy with people and cars, congested. The lights fell sharply on Dana's eyes. She concentrated on the back of the car in front of her, not looking at Jerri.

"You already know, don't you?" Jerri said.

Dana looked past Jerri at the sidewalk scenery. Well-dressed men and women were walking by. There were ticket takers, and billboard play ads. Dana noticed the letters, *A.C.T.* Her heart took off like the speed of light as she thought, Rosylyn is here somewhere, this is the theatre she's going to tonight. She glanced about nervously.

"Ever since Renee and I broke up three years ago we've slept together now and then. As friends. It's purely recreational. It's no big deal with us. And it needn't be with you either. Don't look so upset."

Dana was trapped in traffic on the front lines. Her impulse was to run out of the car and hide before Rosylyn saw her and opened fire. "Goddamn red light—change!" Dana blurted out. Rosylyn would kill her seeing her out with another woman when she was supposed to be home sick with cramps.

"Calm down, Babe," Jerri said gently.

"Damned traffic," Dana muttered and looked in the rearview mirror for Rosylyn. She was nowhere in sight which only made Dana more nervous. Perhaps Rosylyn saw her without being seen herself. She totally blanked Jerri out, developed one effective case of emotional amnesia toward her, wishing the cars ahead would clear out.

"What are you doing?!" Jerri yelled.

"What are you doing?!" Dana yelled back at her, losing control.

"Why not just drive up over the tops of the cars?!"

The traffic slowly started to move and Dana pounced the car forward, all the while glancing around for Rosylyn as if Rosylyn was about to swallow the car whole.

Sounding disgusted, Jerri said, "Let me out. Let me drive." She opened the passenger door to come around to the driver's side. Dana had an impulse to drive off, leave the treacherous whore on the streets where she belonged. She slid to the passenger's seat and slumped down really low in it so Rosylyn could not see her.

Jerri got in the driver's seat and glanced uneasily at Dana. "You've really lost it," she said under her breath, putting the car in gear and pressing the gas slowly. "I can understand you being upset if I said I'd fallen madly in love with someone else, but shit, Dana, I only slept with Renee a couple of times and it was no big deal. Really, believe me. It's nothing worth trying to smash us into other cars over. You know I want you still even if I slept with Renee."

Did she have to keep repeating 'I slept with Renee?' Dana

wished she could just dissolve and disappear. She wanted to cry.

"Where are we?" she said.

"You know where we are. Snap out of it."

"Where are we?"

"We're by the Hyatt on Union Square," Jerri said, irritated.

"Can you see *A.C.T.* from here?"

"No. Why? Did you want to try out for a part? You seem to have a natural aptitude for dramatics."

"No. That's where Rosylyn is. At *A.C.T.*"

"Oh," Jerri said with a groan. "So you were afraid Rosylyn had spotted you out with the internationally known lesbian, Jerri Lavenderface. Is that why you're slouching down so low?"

Dana attempted to make light of it. "You were ready to drive me to psych emergency, weren't you?"

"Almost," Jerri chided. "I thought you had literally gone 'insane with jealousy.'"

Dana sat up. Her insides still felt as if they were being shoveled up.

"Are you all right?" Jerri said softly, watching the traffic and taking Dana's hand.

I've got to be nice, Dana thought, felting very threatened by Rosylyn, by Renee, by her own emotions. She had a terrible fantasy, momentarily, of Jerri saying, "I'm moving back to L.A. to get away from you and be with Renee."

"How do you feel about me having sex with Renee?" Jerri pushed.

Dana felt as if she was holding her breath under water. If I tell her how I really feel, she'll break up with me for sure. She's upset enough already about me not spending nights with her so freely anymore, upset about me working for Rosylyn. If I act really cool when she makes love with Renee or whoever, she thought resentfully, it'll make her like me more and want me more. Not many women would put up with that. "Didn't you hear me the other night when I said you could have sex with other women?" I'd like to shoot Renee, she thought.

"Yeah," Jerri said. "But I wasn't sure. I know it's a sensitive subject and you try hard to accommodate me."

"You're free to do what you want." And so am I. I'll strangle Renee. Dana tried this line on: "I suspected you were sleeping with Renee but...." She shrugged. "You don't have to confess to me when you sleep with someone." Please don't tell me, she thought. This is hell. I'd rather not know. "It's your business," she tried to say sweetly, twinkling her eyes pleasingly, wanting to make Jerri happy, even if it did make her insides feel like a cement mixer was churning there. She added, "I always want you to do whatever makes you happy. I love you."

Jerri looked at her skeptically. "Are you sure?"

"I can cope with it," Dana said.

"I appreciate you trying so hard, Babe. You know, I do care about you more than you know. And I want you to go out with other women too."

Feeling spiteful, Dana said, "Maybe I should." Perhaps she should call Frankie. She remembered saying no to dating her because she had gotten back with Jerri.

Lying in bed alone at eleven, Dana envisioned Jerri and Renee making love, sinking into each other. Their faces laughed with pleasure. It was almost evil. They were setting world records, sexual acrobats, overcharging their circuits. If only they could black out. Choke on their kisses. Cardiac on their climaxes. Dana's imaginings of their sexual merry-go-round reeled around and around in her head. Her pillow was wet. No sound came from her. She was as silent as a minefield.

Her mourning turned into a marathon of misery. She wanted to be held, comforted. Around one a.m. her crying finally subsided. It did not surprise her that she cried for two hours. When Karen left her in Cody to return to Teddy she had cried for five hours. She almost took pride in it, a sign of her love and loyalty to Karen, a devotion like one kneeling hour after hour, praying. On some level she hoped that her suffering would be acknowledged by Karen, pinned with a purple heart.

One a.m. and Rosylyn was not back from the play. She hadn't even called to say she'd be in late. Dana felt a disproportionate amount of anger over this.

At one-fifteen Rosylyn came home. "You awake?"

"Yes."

"Yer too young to have insomnia." She plunked herself on the bed's edge and kicked off her heels. Dana had her back to her so she wouldn't see she had been crying. "Only time I get insomnia's when I sleep alone...you get used to sleeping with a man beside you...then when he's not there you get nervous...I went up to the Starlight Roof after the show for a few drinks...." She clumsily rolled her nylons down. "First time I've taken myself out to a bar alone at night. Thought I'd try it...reach up here and unzip me, Honey. How's yer cramps?"

"All right." Dana hesitated, then pulled the zipper down. She was greatly relieved that Rosylyn had not seen her in front of A.C.T. tonight. Rosylyn looked at Dana with drunken concern, seeing her puffy eyes.

She tugged her dress off, and looked very tired, standing there in her beige slip. She pulled her girdle off, then turned off the light and just plopped down on the bed atop the covers. *She is drunk*, Dana thought. She couldn't even get herself under the covers, and she's sleeping in her slip.

"I hate to think of you having to cry over cramps." Rosylyn rolled close to Dana and placed a comforting arm on her back, and patted. Dana could get drunk just smelling the gin in the air. Rosylyn was an inch from Dana but the covers provided a safety zone, Rosylyn atop them, Dana under them. "Yer good...enough to keep on permanent. Keep up the good work and come Christmas you'll earn...hell of a bonus. Maybe a trip with me to Miami...maybe Palm Springs...." She slumbered off, her arm around Dana, who found she actually felt relieved that Rosylyn lay close to her, an ally, instead of standing up cussing her out for being on Geary Street by A.C.T. Everything was safe.

Dana nestled in under the arm, let it anchor her, knowing what frustration and agitation Jerri would feel seeing this. It was a kind of revenge. And it was an odd kind of comfort.

CHAPTER 11

Jerri kissed Dana's breasts while Dana worried about telling her she had to be back by eleven at Rosylyn's. Jerri kissed her on the lips and Dana tensed up remembering Renee. Dana's eyes caught a snapshot of herself taped to the corner of a Gaugin print. Jerri took that at the zoo when they first met, when they used to see each other every day for the first month straight. Looking at the face in the snapshot, a face with a feeling of excitement and expectation, Dana felt soured.

Her eyes moved to the painting of Jerri she had presented to her earlier tonight. It was leaning up against the dresser. It was done in hues of blue, except for Jerri's body, which lay abandoned in sheets painted to give the illusion that they were waves and wrinkled sheets. Jerri had titled it, *Illusions*, explaining, "The illusion that the sheets are water. I lie in that painted illusion. You can parallel it with how people usually build, paint illusions around those they love or desire. It's a very creative painting. I like it."

It was one of the few paintings Dana had ever finished and genuinely liked. It had actually inspired her so much and boosted her confidence that after finishing it she made a call to City College to inquire about graphic programs there and in the community. One in particular interested her, an adult education program that started in January for free. In just one semester she could have a basic graphic arts certificate that could help her get an entry level job. But she hadn't called the adult education program yet.

"I might enroll in a graphic arts program at an Adult Ed school," Dana told Jerri after hearing Jerri's response to her painting. "I'm lucky I found time to finish your painting with Rosylyn putting on the pressure...." As she talked she realized she was saying the wrong thing. "The pressure on me to paint her."

"Rosylyn said you had to paint her?!"

"No," Dana said timidly. "I told her I wanted to. I've been doing a series of portraits of her."

"Why?"

"Money." Dana felt like a chicken wishbone, Rosylyn pulling her one way, Jerri the other. One would win when Dana broke.

Now Dana glanced away from the painting when Jerri opened her eyes. "You aren't in to this, are you?" Jerri said.

"I will be. Give me time. I just need to warm up."

"Are you spending the night?"

Dana shook her head. "I have to be back by eleven."

"Eleven! The way things are going, it'll take me until eleven to get you turned on."

Dana avalanched kisses on Jerri's lips, wanting to avoid a confrontation. Jerri's lips, the color of heart, parted and brushed against Dana's. Dana kissed her breasts tenderly. She snaked her hand down Jerri's body.

Eyes closed, Jerri smiled serenely, a magic wand waving below. "Will you stay tonight?" she said in a dreamy voice.

"I'd like to," Dana said, feeling she needed an entire night with Jerri to recover from Renee, who was back in L.A.. Her lovemaking took on a certain forcefulness, wanting to reclaim Jerri from Renee.

"I miss you spending the night," Jerri said, cupping her hands around Dana's breasts, and looking up at her. Jerri's skin was a rich sexual tan, her hair alluring black curls. Dana finally began to feel excited. "Will you spend the night?"

"I don't know."

"You'll never spend the night again, will you?"

"Of course I will."

"When?"

Dana became frustrated. She wanted to make love and Jerri was holding it just out of reach, teasing, almost bargaining. "I want a date," Jerri said.

"When I'm off probation from last time I stayed...."

"You'll never be off probation. That's how Rosylyn keeps you in line."

"I'll be off in ten days."

"How about the weekend after next then?"

"Karen's visiting."

"Karen's coming? I didn't know that. Why didn't you tell me? Where's she going to stay?"

"At the penthouse."

"Where's she going to sleep?"

"Well, I guess with me. The next weekend after that I'll spend the night with you. I'll think up a story to tell Rosylyn." She rubbed Jerri's side tenderly.

Jerri was suddenly businesslike as if negotiating a contract. "I guess this is an important event for you, Karen coming to San Francisco. Well, you know, you can do whatever you want with her. Whatever you do is all right with me."

"You think we're going to make love?"

"You just might."

"No. That won't happen," Dana said reassuringly.

"You never know."

"*I know.*"

"Well, let's just say *if* you did want to have sex with her, don't let me inhibit you. I want you to do whatever makes you happy. I mean that. I'm not possessive or jealous."

She's really worried I'm going to sleep with Karen, Dana thought, feeling it was about as likely as her sleeping with Madonna. Before Dana had a chance to repeat reassuringly, "I won't sleep with her," Jerri pounced on her and fervently started making love to her as if she were a valuable mineral about to become rare. She excavated Dana. Dug for gold. Hoarded her. As Dana fantasized it was Karen making love to her—falling prey to Jerri's suggestion..., Jerri struck a vein, sending Dana thrashing into a sexual seizure. As if attempting to stake a claim, Jerri repeated, "You will stay the night, won't you? Think of all the fun we can have."

"I can't. Maybe after Karen comes."

"It's maybe now, huh?" Jerri was quiet, thinking. "I won't be angry about her. But I'll be angry if you don't tell me if something happens." Jerri lit a cigarette abruptly. "I don't like being lied to."

"I've never lied to you or been dishonest." She hadn't told her about Frankie, but nothing had happened.

"You never told me Karen was your ex-lover. You made her out to be a friend."

"She is a friend."

"You're missing the point."

"Dana!" Karen said, smiling profusely, setting her small suitcase on the cement floor of the Greyhound station. She placed her two delicate hands on Dana's upper arms. "You look great. Really great!" Karen kissed her gently on the cheek. She paused to glance joyfully at Dana, then kissed her other cheek. "It's so good to see you!" They hugged tightly. Dana felt electrified with warmth and desire. Karen was so beautiful. Her hair was like poured sunlight, a heavenly lightness to it, falling full around her blue eyes, china white body. She felt thin and delicate and fiery next to Jerri—and so much more loving. Dana would like to fossilize this moment forever. "Teddy's coming back from Lassen by Sunday night to pick me up at the Stockton terminal. I hope he remembers," she said with a nervous laugh. "You know how forgetful he is." Dana did not want to hear about him at all.

They stepped out of the bus terminal onto Seventh Street. A man was laying face down in a dirty doorway. "Is he all right?" Karen said.

"He just drank too much," Dana said.

Karen leaned over his over-sized black suit jacket, frosted with dirt and cigarette ashes, dunked with tiny holes. She shook him gently to see if he was alive. He didn't respond so she shook harder. A gnarled sun burnt face lifted slowly, agonizingly, as if weighing as much as a tombstone. He looked at Karen, trying to focus. Long threads of oily hair rested like noodles around his face. "Are you all right?" Karen said. A yellow-toothed smile soaked across his face. "Well...hellllooo!" Dana glanced about nervously. Karen looked at him and then at Dana, unsure of what to do. Then she quickly opened her big black purse and pulled out a ten dollar bill, causing Dana to protectively glance about again. "Here," she said. "Buy yourself a good hot meal."

"Sweetmeat! Mother Mary," he mumbled smiling. "Can I buy you dollies a drink?"

"Maybe some other time." Karen smiled and took Dana's arm and lead them away. "It's depressing, isn't it?" she said. Dana nodded, looking anxiously about, the thought crossing her mind that some lunatic could open fire, shoot the two lezzies holding arms. This was seedy Seventh Street, not the Castro. Karen was too open and trusting.

If someone ever needed help, Karen responded, often forgetting her own safety. There was that time she got slapped by a big brute for trying to stop him from beating up his girlfriend on a Stockton street corner. Though she admired Karen's Florence Nightingale streak, she wished she would just stick to visiting lonely shut-ins as she did in Cody and Stockton instead of doing crisis care on the streets.

Dana's eyes drifted along Karen's pale neck and down to the soft skin of her upper chest. She was so glad she was here. Karen looked at her and Dana, blushing, quickly averted her eyes to the pavement littered with cigarette butts and gum wrappers.

Karen carefully folded her nylons and placed them in her suitcase sitting on a chair in Dana's bedroom. "I had fun tonight," she said to Dana, who was sitting on the edge of the bed in a light-yellow flannel nightgown. "I'm sorry if you didn't."

She unhooked her bra, her back to Dana. "That one guy, Ken, asked me to call him sometime." She hesitated, then said, "I wish we could have danced together there."

It's all Rosylyn's fault, Dana thought. Her fault that Karen spent her first night here dancing with man after man at the Starlight Roof while Dana and Rosylyn watched from a table. Since her arrival, Karen had been treated like a long lost niece taken under Rosylyn's wing. "We're gonna show you a grand time while you're here," Rosylyn had said within moments of meeting her. "How would you like to go dancing tonight at the Starlight Roof? It's very popular with the tourists."

Karen had hesitated, glancing at Dana uneasily, then politely had said, "We'd love to, Rosylyn," explaining to Dana later that she had been cornered into it.

Dana watched Karen tuck her bra into her suitcase. "You sure are quiet," Karen said. "Tired?" She glanced over her bare shoulder at Dana, still hiding her frontal nudity.

Dana remembered how Karen used to always undress facing her with no self-consciousness until leaving her after their four months together as lovers. Dana was disappointed. Nothing had changed.

"What's the matter? I'm sorry if you didn't enjoy yourself tonight," Karen said. "It must not have been much fun for you there. I just felt obligated to go with Rosylyn since she's kind enough to let me stay here, you know?"

"I know," Dana said, dispirited. She was apprehensive about sleeping in the same bed with Karen after so long. Dana's bare toes twisted on the gold carpet. Karen's back was still toward her. The five beers she had drunk helped her to soak without inhibition in Karen's soft and frail back...into the familiar mole on her right shoulder blade, the blossoming white buttocks. So familiar. She stared at Karen's backside only as she would when drunk. Seeing Karen's naked back soothed her like a tender hand stroking her forehead. Seeing it felt like a kind of attention being paid to her. At least Karen didn't go in the bathroom to change. She eyed the comforting warmth of her body.

Karen pulled a wispy tan negligee over her head. "How about tomorrow night we'll go dancing some place you like? Just me and you?" She stepped into a matching pair of panties, still not turning around. Dana stared at the negligee. She had given that to Karen during their four months together in Cody. She had not seen her wear it since then. The negligee confused Dana. Karen finally turned around and smiled benevolently at Dana, confusing her further. Karen looked at herself in the mirror.

Without thinking, Dana dropped her eyes nonchalantly to her nipples, faintly visible through the negligee. Karen brushed her hair. There was a tenseness between them, an unsureness of what script to play.

Dana stood up, swaying a little from the liquor. She dramatically pulled the covers on the bed back, so sweepingly they looked like the tide retreating. She slid into bed and waited for Karen, half hoping for an ecstatic reunion.

Karen watched her in the mirror. With an amused look, she said, "You looked like you were really having to keep your balance getting into bed. How much did you drink, Sweetie?"

"I'm drunk," Dana said as if not responsible for anything she did tonight.

"I know," Karen said. "I always know when you're drunk."

"How?"

"You get really quiet. And sometimes you say things you wouldn't otherwise. And you always look mad at me."

"I'm not mad at you."

"But you are."

"I'm not. I'm glad you're here." She watched Karen straighten up the sheets on her side of the bed, fluff up her pillow, brush off her feet, and nestle in under the covers.

"I know you're glad to see me. But you can be glad and mad at once." She rolled onto her side, put her hands together under the side of her head, and looked at Dana fondly.

"I'm not mad."

"I can name about ten reasons why you might be mad at me,

some going way back." She looked at Dana sympathetically and guiltily. "You know, I never mean to hurt you. I never want to." Karen looked at the digital light-up clock reading two-thirty, then she turned back toward Dana. "We've hardly been alone one minute since I got here. Let's stay up all night and talk like we used to." She was quiet. "It feels so nice to sleep in the same bed with you again. It's been so long. Too long." She placed her hand gently on Dana's shoulder.

Looking at her, Dana thought about how beautiful she was. She had always thought Karen looked like a young Vanessa Redgrave in *Camelot*. "You look very pretty," she said, wanting to touch her face.

Karen rolled on her back. "You're sweet to say that. Teddy never tells me that." *Teddy again*, sneaking into bed between them. Karen started gesticulating in the air with her hands. "It's been really lousy...since about Easter." She was quiet. "He's always over at the library studying until it closes. I don't understand how someone can study so much and still get C's. I feel like going over there sometime and seeing if he's really there or off with some...." Dana listened as she always had, concerned yet protective of her own feelings. "You know I've never truly been happy with him. I don't want to talk about this," she said suddenly. "Let's talk about something else. How are you and Jerri doing?"

"Jerri?" Dana said. It was odd to hear her name here in bed with Karen; Jerri was from another place and time. "All right, I guess." Dana hadn't thought of her since picking Karen up at the bus station earlier. And then she had been wondering whether Jerri had slept with anyone new since saying they were supposed to do so. "I only see her once a week now. We're always fighting or on the verge of a fight lately."

She felt Karen's hand squeeze her shoulder. "You only see her once a week?"

"She's busy with law school and working and she's got lots of friends and ...." Dana stopped. She did not want to think of her misery over Jerri.

"I've always been jealous of her. I guess she's pretty special to you?"

Dana shrugged defensively, thinking, not like you are. "It's different," she said.

"Different from what?" Karen propped her head up on her elbow, and looked down at Dana.

"Oh, I don't know what I'm saying. I'm drunk."

"Whenever I ask you about her, you never sound happy. She always sounds like she has no time for you. And she slept with her old girlfriend. I'd drop her. You're pretty and sweet and sexy. You don't have to settle for less. I'd walk out on Teddy if I found out he was cheating on me. That would be too much." Karen shrugged. "I don't know where I'd go, though." She looked at Dana.

"You could always stay with me."

Karen squeezed her shoulder again.

They lay quietly beside each other in the dark. Rosylyn's snoring was faintly audible. Dana began to felt uneasy again. She sensed Karen did too. In high school, they would always curl up together in their pajamas and fall asleep. It had always been like that, except for those four months they made love. Then they slept naked and Karen always rested her leg over Dana's hip, saddled to her.

"I sure miss not seeing you all the time and talking to you every day," Karen said. "I've always missed that since you left Stockton." Her hand pressed Dana's side lovingly.

"I miss you," Dana said. "I think about you all the time. I wish I could come back to Stockton with you."

Karen was very quiet, her hand still on Dana's side, but frozen.

"I love you," Dana pressed.

"I love you, too."

"Remember once you said you loved me more than anyone. Is it still...."

"Yes. It's still true."

"Can I hold you to sleep?" Dana said in a drunken voice. "Like we used to in high school?" she added to make it sound innocent.

Karen was *very* quiet. "If it'll make you happy. I want you to be happy. More than you know." Dana shuffled up close and wrapped her arms around her, laid her head on her chest. She felt as if she had come home. For the first time in a long time she was genuinely happy. Her hand stroked Karen's back.

Karen sighed. Dana kissed her neck gently. Their arms wrapped tighter around one another. "I love you so very much," Karen said in an urgent, confessional tone. "Lately I've started wondering if maybe I am gay. I can't get over you."

Then Karen suddenly said, "We'd better not sleep like this. I don't trust myself." Dana shot to the other side of the bed rubber-band-fast. She was innocent. "I don't think we should do that," Karen said uneasily. "It's not the same as high school. It's different now. We're grown. And...." She stopped.

Dana lay dead still.

"It's not that I don't love you. I don't know. It's just.... It's just I'm really scared, you know?"

Dana was quiet. This hurt.

They both lay silently for what seemed like an eternity. Then Karen moved into Dana's arms and they quietly held each other until falling asleep.

CHAPTER 12

"Rosylyn acts like I'm *her* guest just because I'm in her place," Karen said. "It's beginning to make me feel uncomfortable." The day was bright with sunlight, which cast a sheen to the brown and tan, striped satin blouse Karen wore with a skirt. She and Dana walked toward the Powell Street Cable Car stop. Karen took a big pair of tinted sunglasses from her purse.

"I don't want to go out with Rosylyn again tonight," Dana said, brushing a piece of lint off her blouse.

"I don't want to go out with her either. I feel sorry for her, though. She seems so lonely. How long do we have to wait for the cable car? Would I have time to make a quick call?"

Dana nodded.

"Yell if it comes."

Dana stood alone on the sidewalk, not looking at Karen in the phone booth, fearing she was calling Ken, the man she danced with last night. She feared she was calling to tell him they'll be at the Starlight Roof again tonight in an effort to prove her heterosexuality after last night's brush with death. This visit was starting to feel like one big rejection. Dana saw the cable car rolling over the top of the hill. She motioned for Karen to hurry, but saw that she was already rushing out of the phone booth, looking bewildered.

"What's the matter?" Dana said.

"Everything." Karen stared at the approaching cable car. "I've never ridden in a cable car," she said in a controlled even voice.

"They're fun," Dana said feebly, confused by Karen's behavior. "Especially, especially when they go down a steep hill."

"This is going to mess up our whole day," Karen muttered under her breath, and glanced about quickly like a cat caught in traffic. "Where's the bathroom? Do you see one anywhere?" she said urgently.

"That cafe should have one."

Without explanation Karen ran toward the cafe. Dana ran after her like string trailing after a kite that got away. The restaurant was very small and the linoleum tiles were dirty. People sat alone on counter stools eating ham and eggs, scowling in their too-big clothes. Dana avoided looking at anyone, embarrassed to be bee lining for the bathroom. She found Karen staring into the bathroom sink, hands tight on its edges. She glanced at Dana, her eyes full as a fish tank. She smiled unnaturally. "I've probably got you completely wondering about me." Her smile looked painful. "Wondering why I came running in here. My period struck suddenly. The curse. Oh, that's not even funny. That's stupid," she said and suddenly showered her face with tears. "Dana," she said putting her arms up for Dana to comfort her.

Dana clasped Karen to her. "I called...." She stopped. "I called Maurice's." She stopped to dab her eyes with a paper towel. "To see if he was there. To see if he went hunting with Teddy like Teddy said. Maurice. Maur...," she cried. "It's everything I suspected. Teddy was lying. He went with someone else or he didn't go at all. I don't know. I just, I just hung up when I heard Maurice answer. What am I going to do, Dana? I'm not happy being married to him. I don't think I've ever really been."

"You don't know he's having an affair," Dana said, happy that Karen wanted her to comfort her, hold her, rock her.

"I know he is! I can feel it inside myself that *he's having an affair!* It makes me so angry. After all I've sacrificed for him," she said resentfully. Dana brushed Karen's hair off her wet cheek, then kissed her cheek consolingly. The bathroom door swung open. A middle-aged waitress with dyed red hair, red lipstick, and a frilly, little white apron tied around an orange uniform, announced, "Now, we'll have none of that here in this cafe." She glared at Dana holding Karen and pointed at the door.

"None of what?" Karen said.

The waitress, looking frustrated, stammered, "We, we don't want that going on in *our* bathrooms. I'm sorry, but I'm gonna have to ask you to go someplace else." She looked at the green tiled bathroom floor, embarrassed to look at them. "This bathroom's for patrons only." She looked up. "You two ran right in here off the street and didn't order a thing...we just don't allow this sort of thing here. This city may have gone to the gutters but this cafe hasn't!"

Karen had stopped crying. She angrily said to Dana, tossing her purse strap over her shoulder, "Come on. Let's get out of here. It wouldn't be fun having sex here anyway." The waitress looked as if a bee just flew in her mouth.

Out on the sidewalk, Karen said, "I look a mess." Dana saw the waitress staring at them from inside the cafe. "I'm going to file for a divorce just as soon as I ge...get back to Stockton." She talked so fast she practically tripped over her words. "Do you think we could get an apartment..." Dana started to nod before Karen finished her sentence. "...somewhere together? Maybe here? What am I going to do, Dana? What should I do?"

Dana hesitated, then said, "Do what you just told me you were going to do."

"Leave the...!"

"That's what you said. You said you thought you should file for a divorce. And tell him you're moving out."

"You think that's what I should do?" Karen said, her eyes partially visible behind her sunglasses. Upon her lower rims tears were collecting. "I don't feel like breakfast," she said and looked listlessly about. "Do you?"

Dana shook her head and said, "Do you want to forget about breakfast and the cable car and just go straight over to Golden Gate Park now? It's pretty there. You'd feel better there."

"O.K.," Karen said. "He's going to be furious when I tell him I'm leaving. I don't care. I'm not going to sit by while he cheats on me. I bet you he'll try and deny it. Say I'm making it up. I'm just going to go home and confront him. It's crazy being married to him if he doesn't really love me and I don't love him nearly as much as...." She stopped short, looking confused again.

A Cliff House cocktail waitress approached. She looked at Karen; she looked at Dana. She said to Dana, "I'm going to have to see some I.D., Honey." Dana fumbled in her purse for her wallet, embarrassed that only she was asked for I.D. when they were the same age. The waitress examined Dana's license without comment. "O.K., girls, what'll you have?"

"Tom Collins," Karen said, and tapped her long fingernails on the table top.

"Uh, I'll have one, too." Dana looked at Karen fondly, her feet aching from walking all day in the park. She looked at the sunset, ripe with colors, scarring the horizon. It was all so romantic—the sunset, the ocean, Karen here with her.

"It *is* pretty," Karen said as if she only now noticed the view.
"It's beautiful," Dana said, looking at Karen with a soft smile.
They both quietly watched the sunset.

"I feel so rotten," Karen said. "My life is a mess. My marriage is. I've messed you and I up. It's all so confusing."

Dana listened with a calm look, knowing everything would be all right. Karen had mentioned several times now that they would get an apartment together. Dana would do everything she could to make Karen happy. She would make everything better.

"I know it's going to be scary to leave him. I guess....," Karen hesitated unsurely, "it'll be best for me in the long run. Don't you think?" Dana nodded. "You know I've never really been *in love* with him. I love him but...." She was quiet. "He obviously doesn't love me very much or he wouldn't have...." She looked out the window. "A part of me has really been wanting out for a long time. It's almost like I want him to be having an affair so I can escape guilt-free." Dana wondered, what would be a good part of the city for us to get an apartment in? Karen would probably like to be near the park. I'll ask Rosylyn if I can work for her days. If she says no, I don't care. She's not going to stop me from living with Karen. I'm tired of her interfering with my relationships.

"If I'd been smart I would have moved to New Orleans with you like we used to talk about. Remember?" Dana nodded. "I'd have been smart if I had stayed in Cody with you instead of going back to him." Karen smiled appreciatively at Dana. "We'll get an apartment together," she said, trying to sound cheerful, trying to mask her apparent apprehensiveness.

Dana was very happy.

"You know what I want to do tonight? I want to go dancing. Take me to a gay bar," she said, daring to step out. "What are we going to do about Rosylyn? I can't cope with her tonight. I'm too upset. You'd better call her. She's expecting us back."

"What should I tell her?"

Karen shrugged. "Just tell her you and me are going out dancing tonight. Tell her we'll be in later. Don't even mention her coming. She'll get the message."

"Wish me luck."

She dialed Rosylyn's number so quickly she hit an eight instead of a nine, and had to start over, dialing slowly like a child writing 'A...B...C....' She hoped Rosylyn would not be angry. She had always tried hard to please Rosylyn, to be the perfect maid. She had always done what Rosylyn had asked. Just this once it would be nice, and fair, if Rosylyn let her do something she wanted to do. Dana nervously listened to the phone ring, hoping for a longshot, that Rosylyn would be understanding.

A gruff "Hello!" barrelled down the telephone line. Dana considered hanging up and convincing Karen that it would make things easier if they went to the Starlight Roof with Rosylyn. "Hello? Hello?"

"Hello, Rosylyn. This is Dana."

"Where are you?"

"We're at the Cliff House. I'm just calling to say we're going dancing and we'll be in later tonight."

The telephone line was too quiet.

"Ya'll going up to the Starlight Roof?"

"No."

"Where ya'll going?"

"Someplace you don't know."

"How do you know I don't know. What's its name?"

"Calamity Jane's."

"Where's that?"

"On Valencia."

"Oh. In yer old neighborhood. Well," Rosylyn said. "Shall I meet ya'll up there later in the evening? I thought Karen would want to go back to the Starlight.... But I don't mind going elsewhere if you want."

Dana panicked. "I don't think it's a fancy enough bar for you. You wouldn't like it there because it's really crowded and the music is really loud and...."

"Why you taking her there? Sounds as fun as a traffic jam. Why not take her someplace nice like the Starlight?"

It's useless. They will have to go to the Starlight Roof. Dana felt apprehensive and disappointed; if Rosylyn could keep her from going out one night alone with Karen, what would she do when Dana told her she would soon be spending every night alone with Karen?

"Karen liked the Starlight," Rosylyn said. "I could tell. Maybe that young man she liked dancing with so much will be there and she could dance with him again. No harm in a married woman just dancing with another man."

Maybe Ken will be there, Dana thought nervously. Karen could easily slip back into her fear of lesbianism, and maybe then Karen would dance with him all night again. Maybe she would tell him she's moving to San Francisco. Maybe he'd pour on the sweet talk of possibilities. Maybe—no! No Starlight Roof. Karen said we'd go to a women's bar tonight. We're going to get an apartment together. Rosylyn won't like that. I don't care. No one's coming between us. No one, Dana thought nervously, feeling the combined pressures of Rosylyn, Teddy, Ken, Jerri. Rosylyn will probably fire me if I move in with Karen, so what difference does it make what I do now that she's going to fire me anyway? "Shall I meet ya'll at eight at the Starlight?"

"No. We're going to Calamity Jane's." Dana's heartbeat quickened. "It's all young people there. Smoky, too. Loud music like you dislike."

"Don't worry about me, Honey. I'm able to have fun wherever I am if I set my mind to it. If yer thinking I'm too old to be fun, let me tell you, when I was *yer age* I was *always* the life of the party."

"I didn't say you weren't fun.... It's just, uh..., Rosylyn, I appreciate you giving me a good job and nice place to live and all, it's just Karen and I want to go out alone tonight because we so rarely do. I don't mean to sound rude. It's nothing personal.... I'm sorry. It's just I'd like some time alone with Karen." Dana stopped. The line was silent. "Rosylyn, are you there?"

"Of course I'm here. Where else would I be? I'm here getting one splitting headache. Already had one to begin with. I reckon I should stay home and tend to this headache. All that loud music would split my head open for sure. Tell Karen I'm not feeling up to going out. Tell her I'm sorry-. Don't wear yourself out this weekend," Rosylyn said, resentfully. "I've got lots of cleaning and dusting that needs to be done on Monday morning...."

"It's not so bad here," Karen yelled over the loud music at Calamity Jane's and glanced nervously around at all the women dancing, drinking, talking, laughing. "I don't know why I felt so scared about coming to a place like this. It's not bad at all."

"I didn't know you were scared."

"I've never been to this kind of bar, you know. But I really wanted to come here with you. Karen looked at two Asian-American women dancing together in flashy clothes and spike heels, made up like fashion models. Dana's eyes were on Karen.

The other women were of no interest to her whatsoever. She glanced around for a stool for Karen. All the chairs at the tables clustered near the bar were taken. Karen's not going to like standing more after walking all day, Dana worried.

Karen glanced up at the many-colored blinking lights twirling above the dancers, glanced at two sixty-year-old women dancing old-style together, glanced at herself in one of the long mirrors placed around the dance floor, glanced away from an attractive woman eyeing her. Karen started tapping her foot and clicking her fingers to the beat of the music. Dana could not find a chair anywhere. "I'd like a Tom Collins," Karen said loudly over the music to Dana.

"I'd love to buy you one," said a woman standing next to Karen, wearing a page boy, a red-and-white striped shirt and jeans.

Karen blushed. "I'm with her," she said pointing at Dana.

"Too bad for me," the woman said and smiled and walked away.

Karen looked at Dana and laughed.

"I'll get you a drink," Dana said. "Wait here." Karen backed up against the wall as if not wanting to be seen alone.

"Excuse me.... Excuse me...." Dana worked her way to the bar. The bar was very crowded. Dana squeezed up to the bar between a cowgirl type who ignored her and a chubby, eager-looking, young woman who said "Hi." She said "Hi" back. That was all they said. The stocky bartender with short black hair, wearing a white dress shirt with the sleeves rolled up, didn't seem to see Dana. Five minutes passed. Dana worried that someone irresistible might move in on Karen while she was away. She could not see Karen from the bar. Everyone else seemed to be getting their drinks but Dana. The chubby, eager-looking, young woman was gone, replaced by a tall lean man in a tanktop, razor-short hair. She felt slightly jarred seeing a man in this manless place.

He got his drink before Dana did. Ten minutes have passed despite the fact that Dana has given her best pleading looks, her best over-looked and downcast looks to the bartender. She even held a ten dollar bill out like a beggar holding out a cup. Dana began to dislike the unforgivably rude bartender. She disliked the women getting drinks before her. She disliked the smoke that was beginning to hurt her eyes. She wondered, Why am I so afraid to leave Karen alone here?

Finally, a miracle. The bartender pointed at her, the chosen one. "Two Tom Collins," she said quickly, knowing she had a split second to speak or it was curtains.

The drinks secure in her hands, she now had to concentrate on getting them to Karen without someone bumping into her and bouncing the precious liquid down dancing to the floor. She spotted an empty stool. Finally! Karen had wanted to sit down. But how could she hold on to the drinks, hold on to the stool and get Karen over here? Confused, she sat on the edge of the seat, claiming it. She considered leaving the drinks on it like two little watchdogs. Then she looked up and was unnerved to see Jerri looking down at her.

"Jerri," Dana said matter-of-factly, with a slight smile, feeling like she already had been doing a juggling act and now someone had thrown a bowling ball up for her to incorporate into the act. She was afraid to stand up because that would put her in Jerri's arms and if Karen saw that....

In black dress pants, Jerri leaned over and gave Dana a watermelon of a kiss, while Dana glanced around nervously for Karen. Jerri felt like an essential part of the machinery but a part that Dana could not fit in correctly under the circumstances. She noticed a woman standing very close behind Jerri. She was dressed in black, her dark hair was pulled back severely, and she was not smiling. She made Dana nervous.

"I thought Karen was out visiting you this weekend?"

"She's here with me," Dana said guiltily, wondering what she would do when she found out Karen and Dana were moving in together.

"Where?" Jerri looked about the bar. "I'd really like to meet her," she said, smiling like a politician. Dana smiled uneasily.

Karen stepped up behind the woman standing in back of Jerri. Dana was uncomfortable, afraid Karen suspected she had been gone the entire fifteen minutes flirting with this woman.

Unaware of Karen two bodies back, Jerri leaned down and said in Dana's ear, "I'm here with Gloria. She's a new friend from law school."

Dana knew exactly who Gloria was though she had never heard of her before. Dana boycotted looking at Gloria, which also conveniently kept her from having to look at Karen's cool accusing eyes.

"You have my drink?!" Karen canonned out.

"It took me forever to get it. The bartender was practically ignoring me," Dana said with an honest-to-God, Girl-Scout's-promise look, and held the drink out to Karen. Jerri's eyes slid up Dana's arm to the drink, up the arm taking the drink to Karen's perturbed face. Jerri stood up straight and decorated her face with a smile. Dana stood up too, as if they were all giving one another a standing ovation. She felt like a conductor expected to start a symphony. But she had lost her rhythm. "Karen, this is Jerri. Jerri, Karen. Karen, Gloria." Gloria just smirked.

"Hi!" Jerri said with a big beautiful friendly smile, and nodded.

"Hi," Karen said, saluting an obligatory smile back. She glanced at her drink, taking on a sophisticated air, and sipped from it.

A woman with wavy hair and big pink-tinted glasses, a smile as big as her glasses, said, "Would you like to dance?" so loudly to Gloria that Jerri, Karen, and Dana turned as if she was asking all of them to dance. Dana felt relieved watching Gloria disappear onto the dance floor.

"We went to Golden Gate Park and the Cliff House today," Dana said to break the awkward silence.

"I spent the whole day studying," Jerri said and lit a cigarette, blew smoke over her shoulder, and looked very self-assured. "This your first time in San Francisco, Karen?" Karen nodded.

The awkward silences in their conversation seemed louder than the bar's music and bubbly chorus of voices. Dana worried that Karen was jealous and didn't like Jerri. She told me I should break up with her, she thought. Dana looked at Jerri suspiciously, considered Karen's earlier evaluation of Jerri, considered Gloria. How did Jerri find time to go out with so much studying to do? Dana wondered, if Karen wasn't here, would I be the one out with Jerri tonight? Probably not. Feeling hurt, she looked to Karen for sympathy.

Jerri was now waving at a petite woman with a poodle of a permanent as if she was a P.O.W. just come home. "I haven't seen you in so long," Jerri said. "How have you been?!" They hugged like two magnets, causing Dana to feel very awkward and embarrassed. She looked to Karen, who was staring at Jerri hugging the woman. She looked at Dana with an agitated 'you really ought to dump her' look.

Jerri introduced Dana and Karen to the Holy One. "I'm sorry, I'm not sure I caught your name," Karen said. "Moonwoman?"

With a celestial smile the woman said, "Moonwomban."

"Is that an Indian name?" Karen said curiously.

"It's Sapphonite."

"Sapphonite? Where's that? I've never heard of it."

"We're transglobal," she said with a condescending smile.

"Oh."

Jerri interrupted the breakdown in communication. "Moonwomban, you still up in Eugene? Still writing poetry?" They powwowed together, smile to smile. They periodically hugged as if placing wreaths on one another. Dana had no idea who this woman was. She suspected she was a member of the hidden harem. She was humiliated that Karen saw this, feeling like a cobweb in the corner of Jerri's life.

Karen whispered in her ear, "I'd kill you if you hugged and carried on with some woman like that in front of me. Acted like I wasn't even really here. Even Teddy's polite enough not to do it to my face, you know what I mean?"

"It's probably just an old friend of hers," Dana whispered back, trying to save face. "Jerri knows lots of women."

"I bet she does," Karen said. "I don't like how she treats you," she said. "And I don't like her little Saffronite friend. She's a snob." They were quiet. "Who was that Gloria?"

Dana shrugged and looked listlessly at the empty glass in her hand, which she had been holding tightly. She was confused. Jerri knew a lot of women. She'd always talked and hugged them and sort of ignored Dana. That's how it'd always been. Dana always thought that anything bad she ever felt over this was her own fault—her jealousy, her possessiveness, her hang-up. She always had tried to keep her emotions from showing or bothering her, afraid Jerri might leave her if she complained. But now Karen confused her. Karen was egging her on. Karen, who was most always right, was validating her feelings. It's Jerri, not me, Dana thought unsurely. It's Jerri's fault that I feel so bad around her so much, Dana thought, trying the thought on for size.

"Who's Gloria?" Karen repeated suspiciously like a bloodhound catching scent.

"I don't know," Dana said, then egged on by the suspicious look in Karen's eyes, said, "Oh someone she's sleeping with probably." The anger in her voice surprised her.

"How can you put up with all this?" Karen said. "I didn't know it was this bad. She's as bad as Lester and Teddy combined. And here she's practically doing it right in front of you as if that makes it innocent. I've been watching her eyeing all these women since I met her. She even looked at me in that way. I wouldn't let you get away with acting like this if we were sleeping together. No way. I'm never going to be anyone's doormat." 'Doormat' resounded in Dana's head; the insinuated insult hurt. A sexual doormat....

"Well, it's not like I told her *not* to do it. It's what she wanted and...." Dana shrugged.

Karen shook her head and said with a grin, "I didn't know you were a practicing Mormon, a follower of Joseph Smith." Dana could not place the name, although it rung a bell. Seeing the quizzical look on her face, Karen said, "You know, the founder of the Mormon religion and a polygamist. He had a zillion wives." Then she said facitiously, "My God, I just had a psychic flash.... Jerri is the reincarnation of Joseph Smith. That means that Gloria and Moonwoman and you are all fellow step-wives. Oh how glorious, praise the Lord! You always like to give people nicknames—how's Joseph, Jr. sound?" Dana grinned.

Dana felt as if she had been brainwashed by Joseph, Jr. into going along with her having sex with everyone, having to smile and say it was O.K. Joseph, Jr. was still talking to that woman almost tongue to tongue. They even started hugging *again* and Gloria was walking back toward them with a smile and Karen was saying to Dana that *she ought to not take it; She ought to not take it.* The music sounded like a hyena's laugh and Gloria was moving in closer on them. All the hurt Dana had been holding down rose and flooded her. Jerri was hugging Moonwoman *still*. Dana stood up as if by a force beyond her control and grew full with anger, her hands stiff by her side, clenched. Her face was flushed red. She turned to Jerri and placed her hand like a claw on her shoulder and with a gentle meanness pulled back. Jerri and Moonwomban looked at Dana and they looked shocked when they saw the twisted red look on her face like that of a mad animal with furtive eyes.

"What are you doing?" Jerri said, irritated.

"What are *you* doing?!" Dana said loudly. "What are *you* doing?!" Then she looked at the big round incredulous eyes of Moonwomban, of Gloria, of Karen, all watching her. The watching eyes weakened her and made her take her hand off Jerri's shoulder. She looked down. She grew afraid of her feelings, and looked to Karen for direction. Karen looked as spirited as a cheerleader. Jerri looked at Dana, waiting for an explanation. "Do you want to dance?" Dana said in a mad and fearful voice to Karen.

"Sure!" Karen said, animated.

Staring down, all shaky inside, Dana walked out onto the dance floor, not understanding what just happened, but feeling like it was definitely her and Karen versus Jerri and her other women. Her and Karen. Her and Karen. Dana began to pick up the mad rhythm of the music, moving her feet and arms like a warrior in a tribal dance. She did not look back at Jerri. It's over for her and Jerri for sure now. She gained strength from not looking back. She and Karen will get an apartment together. No more Teddy. No more Jerri.

"You did really great!" Karen said, smiling possesively at Dana. "That was perfect topping it off by asking me to dance." Karen's words chased away any doubt in Dana over what she had done. "She deserved every bit of what you did. She had it coming to her."

She had it coming to her; she had it coming to her. The words danced around in Dana's head. She had it coming to her. Dana danced and danced, feeling a strength growing in her from the directive, incessant beat of the music, from the words of Karen, from dancing with Karen for the first time in public, from not going along with Joseph, Jr., from the thought of getting an apartment with Karen soon. Sweat began to form on her neck. "Looks like you scared her away," Karen said with a victorious smile. "She's just gone down stairs. Isn't this wonderful dancing together in public? I love it."

Dana felt victorious. She let the loud music, the dancing, the love of Karen, take her away, forgetting. Jerri was a distant star fading under Karen and her.

She looked over and saw Rosylyn.

Rosylyn stood planted at the top of the stairs, looking about like a plantation owner. She stood out like a giant tomato in drag, dressed in a frilly red dress suit. It humiliated Dana. "Duck," Dana said and pushed down Karen, who laughed as if Dana was trying out a new dance movement. "Rosylyn's here!"

"Rosylyn?" Karen said with disbelief. "Rosylyn?!" Dana nodded. "I can't believe it. I thought you told her not to come."

"I did."

"I feel silly. People are starting to stare at us. I can't dance like this. This is silly. Let's just get up and be adult and go say hi to her.

Ask her to dance," Karen said with a mischievous grin, trying to make light of the situation though she looked very nervous.

"It's not funny," Dana said. "She'll kill me if she sees me. I didn't tell her this was a gay bar. What's she going to think if she sees us dancing together? There goes her liking you." Dana worried that perhaps Karen was mistaken, perhaps Jerri was still here, probably looking at Rosylyn ready to witness her spotting Dana and.... "Please don't stand up. She'll make a scene."

"O.K.," Karen said. A minute later, she said, "My legs are starting to hurt. Let me just stand up real quick for a minute with my back to her. She won't see me. I promise."

"No," Dana pleaded, but Karen had already popped up and back down.

"I think she saw me," Karen said. Dana's legs weakened, overwhelmed with fear. I told you not to stand up, she scolded Karen in her head. She spotted Rosylyn's legs, her hose with the lines up the back, her fat ankles, her red shoes with the gold buckles, walking about the dance floor's edge like two policeman's billy clubs. The feet stopped. They turned this way. They turned that. They stopped again, as still as an unlit box of TNT.

Dana was so nervous she stopped moving. "We ought to stand up and bring this to a head," Karen said. "After all, we are going to live together. We're making fools of ourselves down here. Rosylyn saw me. She knows we're down here." Dana looked at Rosylyn's feet, one of which was tapping impatiently to the beat of the music. The feet began to pick up, shuffle, dance. Dana could not believe it, could not believe Rosylyn would be dancing with another woman. Maybe she was a lesbian after all. The feet were dancing toward them. Dana panicked. Trapped. Cornered. Caught. Dana danced her way up not wanting to be caught down on the floor. Rosylyn was two bodies away, dancing alone like a bear trying to cha cha, staring angrily at Dana, closing in. She looked silly. It humiliated Dana.

"Rosylyn!" Karen said as if surprised and glad to see her.

"Hi," Dana said with a smile that was about to faint.

"I realized," Rosylyn huffed, out of breath, dancing, "I'd never get a word with ya'll unless I danced into this mess. You just can't walk through it or you'll get knocked down. You got to dance yer way in." She stopped to catch her breath. She looked like a big bag of stones bouncing about in an earthquake. And she looked angry.

"Dana didn't tell me what kind of place this was," Rosylyn said. "And I didn't know 'til I got here. But I suspected there was something strange about it from the way she talked about it.... I reckon you didn't know what this place was 'til you got here either, Karen. I tried telling her you'd prefer the Starlight." She cast a disdainful look on all the women. Ignoring Dana as if she was a little child, Rosylyn concentrated on Karen. She yelled, "Why don't we all go over to the Starlight Roof?" She yelled so loudly over the music that everyone could hear. Dana had not been so embarrassed since she was seven and Leroy McCoy pulled up her dress on a day she forgot to wear underwear and everyone saw. Everyone saw. Everyone seemed to be looking at them. Dana wanted to get out of there, even if it meant going to the Starlight Roof. She nodded at Karen to go, and followed Rosylyn off the dance floor and down the stairs; Karen trailed behind them. Rosylyn said under her breath, "Why didn't you tell me what kind of place this was? What are you doing in a place like this? It's a calamity all right. I noticed as soon as I got in the door that something was wrong here. All girls!!"

"That was very rude and inconsiderate of you," Dana said angrily. Something had snapped in her. She had never raised her voice before at Rosylyn, but Rosylyn had gone way too far this time. *She always has to be in control, regardless of what I feel,* Dana thought. *We'll see how much control she has when Karen and I move in together.*

Dana glanced past the coat check into the bottom-floor bar, a quiet bar for talking. She was jarred seeing Jerri staring at her and Rosylyn. "Why're you bringing Karen to a place like this? I know I'm not yer mother and I know it's not my business to say this, but it's not right you bringing her to a place like this, tempting her like this—a nice married girl like her."

It dawned on Dana that Rosylyn had perhaps known all along that she was a lesbian.

CHAPTER 13

"How drunk are you?" Karen said, giggling, pulling off her clothes as if caught in a fishnet. "As drunk as me? Then you're prettyyyy drunk!!! I couldn't help it. I rarely get drunk. But Rosylyn kept buying me all those drinks. And I can't turn down a free drink. She was pretty drunk herself. Hardly could get the key in the front door. I still can't get over her showing up at that bar." She paused, "God, she was like a one-woman posse out to get us!" Karen said, making Dana laugh.

Facing Dana, Karen pulled off her blouse. "Will you unhook my bra?" It felt unreal to Dana that Karen was undressing facing her. The dainty lamp with a frilly yellow shade cast a dim light in her bedroom, causing their shadows to look large and gangsterish on the walls. It all felt subterranean as if Dana was at sea bottom. Everything looked blurry and watery. She felt as if she was floating. She unstrapped Karen's bra. Then she ceremoniously took off her own blouse and unstrapped her bra as if this was an intimate act, this simultaneous unhooking of bras.

Karen spun around with a devilish-angelic grin, her pale breasts staring at Dana. She felt warm inside that Karen undressed facing her again. It seemed unreal still; her drunkenness made it seem more so. But it had all seemed unreal, a dream today—Karen going to divorce Teddy and come live with her, the scene at Calamity's with Jerri, Rosylyn raiding the bar, and now Karen naked before her, a promise of what was to come. It was as if the past never was.

Karen crawled unclad across Dana's bed. Dana beheld the spectacle—the china-like body—all at once familiar and unfamiliar since she hadn't seen it in what seemed like eons. Karen scooted down under the covers while Dana sat watching with anticipation from the bottom of the bed—waiting for a cue as to what she should do. Karen was not wearing a thing but a silly Cheshire Cat grin.

"I haven't been this drunk in ages. God, if Teddy knew what I was doing," Karen crooned. "Dancing at a gay bar with you. Getting drunk and dancing with those two guys at the Starlight Roof. Neither were half as fun to dance with as you, though. God, I'm drunk. Look at me!" Karen laughed giddily. "I forgot to put my p.j.'s on." She laughed as if this was very funny. Dana smiled obligingly, confused. Karen's laughter suddenly slid into silence. Then she said to Dana, "I love you, Sweetie. Come hold me."

Dana crawled under the covers and hesitated before Karen's nakedness. "You've been awfully quiet," Karen said. "Come here," Karen said and clasped Dana. "You're always so sweet. I wish Teddy was half as sweet as you. He's nothing like you. Why can't you be a man? It would make everything so much simpler. Teddy always...." Dana half-heard about Teddy, mesmerized by Karen, warm, close, naked, the familiar lemony smell of her hair, the softness of her body. Dana felt so loved, Karen holding her. Dana loved Karen so, holding her. "You'd never cheat on me, would you?"

"No." Dana held her tighter, felt her breasts all warm and fluidy against hers.

"I love you more than anything," Karen said. "Thanks for everything. You're really precious. You really are." She kissed Dana on the cheek. "I feel better." She rolled sleepily on to her back.

Karen was like a wave perpetually rising, reaching, receding. Dana wanted more than for her to touch just briefly the shore and never remain. "Karen," she said, "I'm so in love with you." She was quiet. "I've always been," she said, her drunkenness encouraging her to talk. She kissed Karen's cheek, feeling it was all right to do so because Karen had kissed hers.

But Karen pulled away. "I'm afraid."

"I'm sorry."

"Don't apologize. I should be the one apologizing to you."

"Why?"

"Oh, let's not talk about all that. It's water under the bridge. Most of it. And the rest is just confusing." She hugged Dana and kissed her cheek, offering an apology, then pulled away. The hug slumbered down into Dana. The kiss felt like a soft pebble touching a pond, sending ripples out.

They were silent for what seemed like centuries.

Then Karen moved quietly and deliberately into Dana's arms. She hesitated there. She said she was afraid and unsure again. She lingered. She kissed Dana's neck. She hesitated again. "I've always been in love with you, too. Much as I've been afraid to admit it to anyone. I'm in love with you, Dana. I want so much to live with you." She kissed Dana's lips. Dana felt as if she was dreaming—Karen touching her—Karen now timidly removing Dana's flannel gown.

Karen started to cry softly, but Dana soothed her with kisses on her eyes, her cheeks, her lips, until the crying stopped, until every last reserve in her was broken down. She could not stop saying how much she loved her. How much she wanted her—the dam broken. She held her so tightly it was as if she was trying to pass through her skin. Her hands moved up and down her body like leaves blowing across earth. She sank into her as if trying to reach her core. She heard, saw, tasted, smelled and felt nothing but her.

She cried out, a ghost escaping from her.

CHAPTER 14

"Rosylyn went out to dinner alone. She's been cool toward me since you left yesterday, since Calamity Jane's," Dana said into the receiver of the phone. "She looked at me in an accusing kind of way. But she didn't say anything. She's making me really uncomfortable here. She's going to flip when I tell her I'm moving out to live with you."

"Dana...." Karen stopped. "Dana, I accused Teddy first thing when I got home of having an affair." Silence. Dana sensed something was not right in Karen's tone. She sounded apologetic. "He denied it. It made me mad. I told him what a great time I had visiting with you, that we went dancing at a gay bar and then dancing at the Starlight Roof." She sounded subdued, sad and guilty.

"Did you tell him?" Dana said anxiously. "Did you tell him you're moving out?"

"Let me finish. I told him to admit he was having an affair. He started crying and saying how guilty he felt. Her name's Gail. A high school cheerleader. Only seventeen. Can you believe that? It's been going on for three months." She almost spoke in a monotone. "But he said he doesn't love her. It's just sex. He kept crying and saying how much he loved me and how after he graduates we'll have a baby. Then out of the clear blue he said, 'You didn't fuck any of those guys, did you?' I said that I didn't. But I felt really guilty about you. He was crying and saying he wouldn't ever see Gail again. He promised he wouldn't. And he practically begged me not to leave him even though I hadn't said I was going to yet.... But I was feeling very guilty about me and you, you know? I thought it'd be best to get everything out in the open. So I said, 'I've got something to tell you you're not going to like one bit.' Actually he took it better than I thought he would. He really didn't act mad. Just hurt. I'm glad I finally told him."

Karen sounded so cold and listless, so unlike herself, that it frightened Dana. Something was not right. "What did you tell him?!" Dana asked, feeling all hot and a little dizzy, suspecting Karen was holding something back, trying to let her down gently.

"That I slept with you Saturday night. And in Cody those four months." She was silent. "He asked me why as if he didn't understand 'cause we're both girls, you know? I didn't know how to explain it. I couldn't tell him I'm in love with you. Especially since he's accused me of never really being in love with him. He asked me if I was a lesbian and he seemed really concerned about it." She laughed nervously. "I told him no, but that it's just 'cause you're a lesbian that it works out that way between us sometimes. Oh, I don't mean it to sound like that, Dana. I don't mean it like that. That's just what I told him. *We know* what it means between us," she said sentimentally, confusing Dana further. "Maybe I am gay. I don't know. Maybe I'm bisexual." Karen took a very deep breath. "It's very hard for me to say this...." She was silent. "I know you won't understand. It's not something I want but it's necessary if there's to be any hope for this at all."

"Hope for what?" Dana was frightened.

"The marriage. Teddy doesn't want me to see you anymore. Or talk to you on the phone. Or write." Karen sounded lifeless. "He said he's not going to see Gail so I shouldn't contact you in any way. He said it's only fair."

Dana's insides jammed up. This can't be true, she thought. Karen wouldn't not see me, not call, not even write. "This is very hard for me to do, but...," she said softly, "we'll just have to break it off for a while until all this blows over. I'm sorry...I never wanted to hurt you again, Honey. I hope you can forgive me. I hope you can understand."

The words started pounding around in Dana's head. No. No. I don't understand. No, don't tell me this. No, don't not see me. No, don't leave me. No. Stop this. "Please don't break up our friendship, Karen. You're my best friend. You said we were going to live together."

The line was silent.

"Dana," Karen said, "you know we've been more than just friends no matter how hard I try to make it otherwise. We're in love," she said in a hushed voice. "It makes it all different. Complicating. Confusing. It's not a normal friendship. It's like there's a part of me that's yours and Teddy never touches that. Do you know what I mean? I haven't given him all of me. It's like I've held part back. And that part was the part I feel for you. I feel like this is our last chance to make the marriage work," Karen said, pleading. "I want it to work. Do you understand? I have to put everything into this marriage and it's not going to work if me and you keep on talking and seeing and loving each other. He wouldn't trust me. I have to put my whole heart into this marriage. Do you understand?"

"We've been together since we were fourteen."

"Think of me."

"I've always thought of you," Dana said desperately. "I want you to think of me this time."

"Dana, don't you understand that I don't want to do this. You act like you think I want to do this. Like I'm rejecting you. I'm not rejecting you. You're precious to me. You know that. Of course I want our love. I love you more than anyone in the world...."

"Then why are you choosing him again? Why are you being so cool and hard?"

Karen's voice loudened. "If I wasn't hard and strong I'd be crying and on the next bus to you, don't you understand? It can't go on like this. I'm *too* torn. It's hell. When I got back home away from you and San Francisco I got sick to my stomach with fear. Look, you know I want children and all that. You never understand that. This is what I have to do!"

"For how long?"

"I don't know how long." Karen sounded exasperated. "As long as it takes."

"A month? A year? Ten years?"

"I don't know, Dana. At least six months. No contact. Just understand. *Please.*"

"No," Dana said. "I don't understand. You've let Teddy finally break us up just like he always...."

"You've always just thought of yourself when it comes to this marriage."

"I've always just thought of you," Dana said, angry at this accusation. "Everything has always been the way you wanted. This is the first time I've really ever asked you for anything."

"I don't want this to be messy," Karen said sadly. "If we keep on talking like this it will only get messier and hurt us all the more." There was a long silence. "There's no easy way to do this. Let's just hang up and be strong.... It tears me apart."

"I'm afraid," Dana said. "I just can't hang up."

Karen said slowly, "Just take the phone from your ear, Sweetheart, and put it back on the hook, and know I love you and always will...." As if singing a lullabye, she repeated, "I want you to do that for me. Take the phone from your ear and put it back on the hook and remember I love you...."

Dana hung up. But her hand was still on the phone, reluctant to let go. Maybe it won't work with Teddy, but maybe it will work and she'll.... Dana took the phone back off the hook. No—don't call back. She doesn't want you to. She put the phone back on the hook. She stared at it, her insides whirlpooling down. She felt as if quicksand was rising around her. She grabbed for the phone. Karen said there's a part of her that's mine and Teddy never touched that. Don't Dana. Put the phone down. She doesn't want you. It's over. I can't believe it. I don't know what I'm going to do. She reached again to call Karen. No! Call Daddy. Daddy, I need to talk to you.

"Well, hello, Angel," Daddy said in his coarse sandpapery voice. "I was just gettin' ready for bed. Why didn't you call collect?"

"I guess I wasn't thinking. I just wanted to talk to you," she said, trying to even out the panicky tone in her voice.

"You all right, Angel?"

He knows something's the matter, Dana worried. "Everything's fine, Daddy." Her insides wrenched up.

"You getting along all right with Mrs. Horstman? She treatin' you fair?"

"Yes."

"You think she'll give you some time off soon to come see your ol' pa? It's been over a year, Angel."

Maybe I should go back to Cody, Dana thought, an anxiety attack gripping her. Karen, Rosylyn, Jerri—I've got no one to turn to really. No one who really loves me and wants me now. Only Daddy. "I miss you, Angel."

"I'm afraid of Lester," she said, not knowing what to say.

"You don't have to be afraid of that punk. If he lays a finger on you I'll get him put away 'til his hair's gray. Your pa'll take care of everything. Just like I always did when you lived here, Angel." An old ache came into Dana's heart. She was the little girl again who reached out for Daddy and found him there sometimes, but just as often not—when he was drunk. "You can't be runnin' from that

103

bastard all your life," Daddy instructed. "I'm gettin' old. Gonna be sixty-eight soon. I'd like to see more of you."

He is getting old, Dana thought. What if he died? The thought was frightening. He was all she had in the way of family, all she had to fall back on. We need each other, she thought. "You don't have to be afraid of Lester. I'll take care of you," Daddy said.

Out in Cody, away from all this screwed up California crap—sky high costs, nonmonogamy, heartbreak, Rosylyn, Jerri, Karen. *Karen.* I could forget them all in Cody. I could start over. I've had it here.

"It's been over a year," Daddy said again, sounding sad.

I want to make Daddy happy, Dana thought. I'll tell him that I have a surprise for him, that I'm going to drive home to Cody tomorrow. I'll start over.

CHAPTER 15

Like a homing pigeon, Dana instinctively moved up Market Street toward Jerri's. The last person she wanted to see in this panicky state was Rosylyn. And she was still angry at her for ambushing her at Calamity Jane's. She needed someone to hold her, a corner to curl up like a fist in before her exodus to Cody tomorrow. She just couldn't make it in California, particularly on her own. Jerri wouldn't deny her one last night. Probably the idea of just one night will appeal to her anyway. Dana felt turned inside out, open, raw, vulnerable. Maybe I should just go to Calamity Jane's, she thought, and get picked up, wiped out. She feared she would lose control of the emotional holocaust in her and start screaming and crying in the middle of Market Street. A street Jerri had once aptly described as 'a walking mental ward.' She would fit right in then. She feared the madness on Market Street tonight. She could come unhinged any second. She could be that obese woman in the red wig muttering, "I ain't no sugar-tit bitch," over and over. Or that man, a walking Woolworth's, wearing a red suit decorated with a button of George Bush, a whistle, a flag pin, a pack of colored felt pens clipped to his coat pocket, a copy of the penal code under his arm, yelling, "Youse all rats! All rats!" at the tourists boarding the Powell Street cable car. Or that downtown lobotomy, fossilized, star gazing at 'Jack-in-the-Box,' a faded blue baseball hat pathetically placed crooked on his head. She walked as fast as her heart beat. Karen will call in a couple of days, she consoled herself. Karen won't go along with Teddy's assassination attempt on them. The thought that Karen would not contact her in any way for six months was debilitating.

There's no way in the world she'd turn herself over to Rosylyn feeling as crazed and vulnerable as she did now. She needed sympathy and Rosylyn would just make it worse. When Rosylyn got home from dining out she would just find Dana gone.

Jerri was not home. Dana sat on her hard gray doorsteps in the dark under a burnt out porch light, waiting. Her insides were like a fist, tight, closed, unable to strike out of her. Her crying was all dammed up in her face. Her thoughts endlessly bombed her. What if Jerri brought someone home? What if she didn't come home? Stop it. You're going to overdose on thoughts and kill yourself. Stop. But the thoughts wouldn't stop.

After an hour, Jerri's white vintage volvo pulled up. Dana hoped she would not be mad. It was just for a night. She'd stay out of the way, sleep behind the toilet if Jerri wanted. The headlights died out.

"Dana?" Jerri said, surprised.

"I'm going to Cody tomorrow. I'm on the outs with Rosylyn."

"Calm down. Come in. Let's talk."

Dana tailed Jerri into her flat, wondering why she was so dressed up—mauve silk shirt, gray slacks, delicate gold loop earrings, hair stylishly blown back, her face a rejuvenated pink. There was an obvious aura of sensuality to her tonight. Once inside, Dana said, "I'm sorry about the other night."

Jerri raised her eyebrows. "Let's have a drink."

Jerri pulled a bottle of red wine out of the cabinet where a half dozen bottles were stored. Dana sat silently at the kitchen table. Neither spoke. The atmosphere was tense. Dana stared at the yellow kitchen wall, at the flyers on the refrigerator—Roxie and Castro theater calendars, a Women's Building calendar, an ad for a political rally against nuclear arms, all plastered on the refrigerator. Jerri poured the drinks. "You never called," she said.

"I didn't think you wanted me to."

Jerri raised her eyebrows and eyed Dana. She set the drinks down on the table and sat down. "I feel very, very ambivalent about you." She stared at Dana. "But I guess you can stay here tonight. If that's what you want." She looked slightly hesitant and distrustful.

"Thank you." Dana glanced away from her scrutinizing eyes. "Excuse me." She went to the bathroom and eyed herself in the mirror. Her hair looked like weeds. Her skin was glassy and colorless. I look like a girl out of a gutter, Dana thought. She opened her purse as if it was a medic's emergency bag and pulled out a comb, blush, and deodorant, knowing she would have to put it all on so artfully that she looked make-upless. She tried to resuscitate her looks, thinking, I'm being really good not to ask her where she was tonight, not to ask who Gloria was. Maybe there's a chance for us.... Her hand shook slightly.

A mildly amused smile rested on Jerri's lips when she saw Dana return as poised, made-up and expressionless as a mannequin trying to sell something. "You look nice," she said politely, then her expression turned stern again. She got up to refill her wine glass, and Dana quickly undid the button above her cleavage, desperately hoping Jerri would want her. Betrayed by Karen, probably fired by Rosylyn now for being gay—rejected twice. She felt that with one more rejection it would be strike three, she'd be out—the dirt on the Ugly Duckling's feet. Not even a dog would want her for its owner.

I'm going to cry, she thought, a lump rising in her throat. She yawned nervously.

"You feel bad now," Jerri said. "But I think it's for the best you leave Rosylyn. Tell me about it."

Dana shrugged. She did not want to tell Jerri the real reason for her crisis, fearing jealousy, wrath, banishment over Karen. "I guess she's mad about finding me at a gay bar...." She just couldn't bring herself to talk to Jerri about Karen. It would ruin any last chance for Jerri and her if a jealous scene exploded. "She's been really cold. Didn't talk. It's awful. I had to leave."

Jerri asked, "You really going to your father's?"

Dana nodded.

"Why?"

Dana concentrated on not crying, trying to maintain control. She shrugged.

"You're running away. I'd rather you stayed here, *temporarily*, until you find another job and apartment. You don't want to live out in the sticks again. Besides, you have to learn to take care of *yourself* and be on your own."

Dana smiled slightly, somewhat relieved.

"But I can't promise I'll be easy to live with even for a short time," Jerri said. "You know...I said it already. I have very ambivalent feelings about you. And now they're at a high pitch, pulling me in two directions. But I'm trying to learn to live with conflicting emotions. And you'll have to, too," she said and Dana nodded.

She was glad that Jerri still wanted her after all. Jerri was going to let her live with her for a while—was going to help her find a job and home just as she had done when she first met her, a disoriented refugee from Stockton, lost and scared. She looked gratefully at Jerri.

Jerri looked so beautiful tonight, hair the color of onyx, body gold-like, a feline grace to her movements, an eloquence. "I'm not mad about the other night—if that's what you're thinking. I was at first, sure." She shrugged offhandedly and lit a cigarette. "I really didn't understand what had gotten into you." She exhaled cigarette smoke over her shoulder, her blowing lips set in an alluring kiss pose. "But my, uh, *friend*, Gloria, and I got to talking and she pointed out how unrealistic it was for me to expect you to never feel jealousy. Like she said to me, 'Only certain gurus in India have succeeded in transcending jealousy.' She's right." Jerri glanced off. "Even I was jealous when Renee split up with me after three years for some little dog groomer she'd fallen for," she said as if still slightly agitated by this. "I don't know," she shrugged. "Maybe Gloria's right. You can't completely eradicate jealousy. You just learn to control it like anger." She was silent, musing. "Maybe it's good you asserted yourself so strongly that night. It's a start. I mean I always have encouraged you to express your feelings more." She laughed to herself at the irony. "I didn't exactly mean like that. But it's a start. I'm not saying I like being the, uh, object of that particular expression. But it's O.K. I'm not mad. So that was Rosylyn at Calamity's, right?"

Dana nodded slightly.

"It's beyond me," Jerri said. "Well, at least you're out of that woman's grip now. You can stay here until you get resettled if it means getting away from her. That's how strongly I feel about this. It should take you a week at most to find a job and a place. I'll set up the living room for you...." She stopped, seeing the stunned look on Dana's face. "It's nothing personal. You know I don't like to be crowded. That's all. It would be too intense."

Dana bit her lower lip, an uprising of tears collecting in her eyes. She concentrated on squelching the rebellion, maintaining control. She would not be a hysterical woman crying for this cold woman's mercy. You can't trust women, she thought. It was too much. It was all too much. She burst. *"Karen's left me!* The words seemed to jump out on their own volition, uncontrollable. She held her hands tightly together in her lap and looked down at them, dropping tears one at a time into them.

Jerri looked confused. "Left you? What do you mean? Were you still lovers?" She came around behind Dana's chair.

"No. She just won't see me or even call or write. Her husband said she couldn't."

"It's all right," Jerri said and put her arms around her from behind. Dana started crying harder. The more Jerri tried to comfort her the more she cried. "Do you want to talk about it?"

"No. I just want to be held."

"Listen, you come in my bed and I'll hold you. O.K.? You didn't let me finish a minute ago...." She stroked Dana's hair. "The living room will be like your room, but that doesn't mean we won't sleep together. Just not every night. I need my space." She kissed Dana's tears away.

Standing in the middle of the bedroom, Dana undressed completely and sat, naked, on the bed's edge, watching Jerri undress, uncover a sanctuary of flesh, toned and tanned. Jerri gave her a quick sexual look, an ambiguous look full of desire and restraint. Then she turned to her antique oak dresser and pulled out two t-shirts, handed one to Dana that said, 'Super Dyke,' and went to the bathroom without a word.

Dana felt as if she'd just been handed a chastity belt. They always had gone to bed naked together. She doesn't want me, Dana thought again, hurt and confused by this barrage of double messages. Jerri was the Queen of Hearts tonight, ready to chop off her already chopped up heart. To top off Karen's rejection, Rosylyn's unspoken renunciation, with a 'Super Dyke' t-shirt, a patronizing pat, and a sisterly hug goodnight. It was like all three—Karen, Rosylyn, Jerri—the Holy Trinity, were in a conspiracy against her to damn her, hammer the nails in deeper. I'm going to Cody to get away from all of them, Dana thought angrily. I can't cope with Jerri wanting me one moment then not the next.

She crawled into bed and lay on the very edge of it. Damn if Jerri was going to get near her with her tear-gas breath, her arsenic-laced saliva, her pocket-knife fingernails. You just can't trust women. Dana held herself tightly.

She heard Jerri flush the toilet, brush her teeth, and answer the ringing phone. She strained her ears to hear. She caught a few words. "I had a lovely time tonight.... Let's.... Soon.... Call me...." Dana was so mad she could burst through her skin. What kind of person would try to torment further someone already devastated by the loss of a love and a livelihood? A sadist. A woman with a razor blade for a heart.

Wearing a fading yellow t-shirt that said 'Maui,' Jerri returned with another glass of wine, and winked sweetly at Dana, despite the tense look on her face. She slid into bed and put her arms around Dana, trying to comfort her. Dana didn't move.

She needed more than ever to make love with Jerri now, the phone call inciting her desire into an urgent need to stake claim, possess her. But it would hurt too much to embrace her longingly and then be rejected. And hurt too much to partake in a platonic hold, lapping up the scraps. She didn't move.

But she needed affection and sensuality, comfort, morphine for the soul, so badly tonight that she finally tossed aside her armor. "I guess I'm just very upset over Karen."

"You sure you don't want to talk about it?"

"It hurts too much."

She massaged her fingers into Jerri's back. Jerri loved massages. She hugged Jerri, still massaging her, her hands moving down to massage her buttocks. She pressed her breasts into Jerri's. Jerri was not responding. But she was not pulling away either, so she crossed the boundary further, running her fingers along her side, and down on to her naked thighs. She would knock that damned ambivalence out of Jerri. She's not stopping me, Dana noted. Make love to me, Dana wished silently to herself, not used to being the initiator. She ran her fingers through Jerri's hair. Eyes closed, Jerri was as quiet and still as a lush immovable island. Dana feared she was falling asleep.

Then suddenly Jerri flung herself onto Dana. She pushed Dana on to her back, pushed her legs open and kissed her lips, saying, "I wish I wasn't so damn attracted to you!" Her tongue dived deep into Dana, who wanted to laugh with relief, ambushed by Desire, rushed by Lust, saved from sinking into an emotional drought. She smiled. She had Jerri. She was so cute the way she often pounced on her like a cat, a sexual jack-in-the-box. Jerri's attack jolted Dana's mind clean like an electric shock.

She let Jerri do whatever she wanted. Jerri made her forget everything, washed her away into a haven of emotional amnesia.

After they made love, Jerri kissed Dana lightly on the lips and teased, "You horrible little seductress. Sexual manipulator."

Dana half grinned, and said, "I'm sorry," the effect of the painkiller, pleasure, still upon her. She did not want the lovemaking to stop. She wanted it to merge into sleep with no thinking time in between, no time for thoughts of Karen to torment her.

"Pardon me, Madam, but I need to use the ladies room," Jerri said with a mock Southern accent.

The instant Jerri left the room the thoughts seized her. Karen will come back to you. Twice before she broke off with you because of Teddy, but she always came back. Did she ever say she wouldn't ever see you or call or write? Stop it, Dana. Don't think about it. The pit blackness started worming its way back into her mind, anxiety started tap-dancing across her nerves.

Jerri returned, looking sexually inundated, and said teasingly, "What's the matter? Did I overcharge your circuits? You in a blackout now?"

"No. It's just.... I don't know.... Karen. I don't want to think about her but I do."

"You will for a while, then you won't. It takes time. You sure you don't want to tell me about it?"

Having just had sex with Jerri, Dana suddenly felt guilty for not telling her she made love with Karen, especially since Jerri asked to be told if Dana ever did. Her thoughts jumbled up—you didn't cheat on her...making love with Karen isn't cheating on someone...she was here first...it's what's most important...it's more as if I was cheating on Karen by sleeping with Jerri, but I feel guilty...I should tell her...besides she practically told me to do it with Karen.

"Jerri?"

"Hummhh?"

"I have something to tell you." Dana was quiet. "Well, I'll just say it.... When Karen was here I kind of, uh, I slept with her. Just once."

Jerri looked dumbfounded. "But you said you weren't lovers earlier tonight."

Dana thought quickly and said, "We aren't. It was just once. Remember you said you slept with Renee once in a while as a friend?" She shrugged. "It just happened."

"I thought it would. But you kept insisting so much it wouldn't. I guess I started believing you. You've caught me by surprise now. I thought you hadn't.... I don't know. Hand me a cigarette. Just tell me about it. Tell me everything and I'll probably feel O.K. about it. I don't know what's come over me." Jerri reached for her marijuana canister.

"What do you want to know?" Dana said nervously. Jerri was so distant suddenly.

"Everything. Just.... Tell me everything." Jerri sounded slightly angry. "Why didn't you tell me earlier? I mean before we had sex. Your timing is...." She shook her head.

"I'm sorry."

"Oh, don't be sorry. I'm just mad at myself. I knew I shouldn't have sex with you tonight. That it would be too intense. Emotionally explosive." She was quiet. "Just tell me about it."

That's mine and Karen's, Dana thought. I can't tell anyone about it. It's ours.

Jerri lit a joint, then rather aggressively whipped her hand to knock out the flame. "Listen, Dana, I don't know if I can take you giving me the silent treatment tonight, you know? I'm having a bad reaction to all this. To the way you're going about all this. You're acting too covert."

"What do you want to know?"

"You know what I want to know. Just tell me. I'll feel better. I won't feel so left out." She shook her head. "This is a cruddy way to feel. Humiliating."

"You're jealous?"

"No," Jerri said and shook her head very quickly, not wanting to have anything to do with that emotion. "I don't know what I am, feel. Just talk!"

"Jerri...." Dana stopped. "I can't tell you what we did in bed."

"Why not?"

"It's, it's too personal."

"O.K. I want you to leave then. I'm not punishing you. I just need to be alone to sort things out. You can sleep on the couch."

"But you practically told me to sleep with her," Dana said, confused by yet another double message.

"You're exaggerating."

"We only did it once."

"Just tell me one thing at least. And tell me the truth. Did you enjoy yourself more with her than me?"

Dana was quiet. Jerri's in a jealous fit, she thought. And she won't even admit it.

"Please answer me. You know how I hate it when you clam up!"

"It was different. I enjoy it a lot with you." But with Karen, Dana thought, it's more joyous and emotionally satisfying, even if she isn't as technically good and imaginative as you. "I love to make love with you, Jerri."

"What's all this? Just level with me. God, this is humiliating. Did you like doing it with her or me better?"

"I can't answer that. It wouldn't be fair to either of you if I said the other."

"Just go," Jerri said. "I know the answer. I just want to be alone," she said in an 'or else' tone.

Dana hesitated, afraid, "I don't want to be alone tonight. I can't be...."

"Why? Because you're upset over Karen leaving you because her husband told her not to see you when he found out you'd fucked. Yes, I can fill in the details you left out. I'm sorry but I don't think I can comfort you tonight. Do you understand? I just don't feel very good about how you waited until just after making love to spring it on me. Your timing was insensitive. Please, go."

"But...."

"I'm sorry, Dana! I can't help you right now!"

"But you slept with Renee and...."

"Go!"

CHAPTER 16

Roused by Jerri making morning coffee, Dana clung to the last vestiges of sleep, a heavenly state with memory was suspended. The waking state quickly invaded, immediately overloading her memory circuits with headlines of her accumulating catastrophes. A feeling of impending doom cloaked her. She looked to Jerri.

"Coffee's on," Jerri said, glancing over at Dana, looking glum, wearing a secondhand Japanese robe, black as her hair. If Jerri rejected her, then she would have to go to Cody, the only city left where someone wanted her—Daddy. Dana sat up on the couch, covering her nudity with a blanket. Jerri set a cup of coffee down for her on the coffee table. "Sleep O.K.?" Jerri said, sitting down in a sea green, Big Daddy armchair. Dana nodded once, not wanting to be any trouble by confessing to only three hours of sleep. "I slept shallow," Jerri said. "But I came to a decision about us."

Jerri gazed at Dana, a death sentence in her eyes. "I'm tired of being a yo-yo over you, wanting you, not wanting you, wanting you. I might as well just say it straight out. I don't think it works with us. It never really has. I don't want to give it another try. We're too dissimilar."

"I won't sleep with anyone else," Dana said, knowing this was a weak last stab at winning her back. The hand holding the blanket up over her dropped to her lap, surrendering a view of her bare breasts, white flags waving as Dana shook her head back and forth to say that she wouldn't sleep with anyone else.

Jerri glanced at her breasts, tossed her uncombed hair back, then looked Dana in the face without saying a word. Finally she said, "It wouldn't be fair if I had sex with other women and you didn't."

"You can sleep with who you want. I don't want to."

Jerri paused, considering this, before saying, "No."

Dana hesitated, then ventured, "Well, maybe we should just sleep with each other."

Jerri looked very surprised hearing this. She set her coffee down firmly on the coffee table like a judge's mallet. "I don't want to be monogamous with you, Dana. And I don't think I want to have to deal with you having sex with other women either. I know I always said it would be all right if you did. But that was just speculation. I misjudged myself, perhaps. I was overly optimistic. I'm sorry. Overall it's been more pain than pleasure for us. It just doesn't work."

"What would make it work? What do you want to be different?"

"I don't know. Nothing. I guess I'm just not into the relationship enough to want to put up with all the problems."

"I told you I wouldn't sleep with anyone again...."

"You're missing the point!" Jerri's jaw clamped closed.

Dana broke the silence. "Just tell me what you want. Is there some way you want me to change? Do you want me to talk more about my feelings? Read more books?"

Jerri took a deep breath. "I don't want you to change," she said. "You're fine as you are. You're one of the sweetest women I've known."

Dana blossomed inside.

"But," Jerri said, "I guess to be totally honest, I just don't love you enough to want to be monogamous with you either."

Dana looked at the coffee in the mug in her hands, dark and still. She felt like throwing it in her face. She did not look up. She did not move. She wanted to disappear away to where there was none of this.

Jerri sat down by Dana and took her hand in hers. She patted her back. Dana felt like recoiling. "Dana, I'm sorry. I never meant to hurt you. You know I do care about you. I care about what happens to you." The last line messed Dana's mind up more. Too many double messages. She looked to Jerri needing genuine compassion. A slight smile roosted on Jerri's closed lips. Dana had seen that smile on her before. It had always frightened her. It was as if Jerri was enjoying this. It was beyond Dana's comprehension, that smile. Her palms turned cold and clammy. "I think we shouldn't see each other at all for awhile to finalize the break. At least two months." Why was she always so cold and mathematical, Dana wondered resentfully. "Then we can get together and talk. Maybe we could be friends. Possibly. We'll see." Dana heard an echo of Karen saying that they couldn't see one another again for at least six months. No one wanted to see her. She didn't deserve this. She had always been nice to all of them trying tried to give them whatever they wanted. She had been patient, long-suffering, unselfish, devoted, giving and loving. Why was this happening now? "You can stay here a week, like I said, until you find a place and another job. But, well, I'll be gone to school a lot, so...you can sleep on the couch. O.K.? Set up camp in the living room."

"No!" Dana said angrily. She was definitely going to leave for Cody today. She glared at Jerri.

"Tell me what you're feeling," Jerri said.

Dana was as silent as a ticking time bomb.

"Come on, Dana."

Dana's fingers fidgeted around the handle of her coffee cup.

"Tell me, are you going back to Cody?"

Dana nodded, knowing it would irritate Jerri. Jerri shook her head very slightly, trying to curb her disapproval. She took a sip from her coffee and said, "Who knows, maybe it would be for the best." She nonchalantly looked at her fingernails.

She just wants me to go to Cody now, Dana thought angrily, so I'll be out of her way. How did I ever fall in with such a cold selfish person? She's worse than Lester. She's a sadist. The way she smiles when I hurt. I don't care if I ever see her again.

"What are you going to do now?" Jerri said like a social worker.

"Leave! You don't want me here. Obviously. You never really did. You only wanted me for one thing."

"You really want to be ugly about this, don't you, Dana? And you wonder why I say it doesn't work with us!" Jerri turned her head away sharply. She was silent. "Let's not be like this. This is really immature. Let's be civil about this. Tell me, what are your plans now?"

Dana said slowly, coolly, "To go to Cody to get far away from you."

Jerri looked dumbfounded. Dana had never been mean before.

Dana flashed back on all the times Karen made her leave, upon the bitter things she would not say fearing Karen would cut her off forever. She was always playing the sweet angel, Daddy's little girl, wanting to win favor, even when being rejected. This was different though. There was no hope for Jerri and her now. Jerri had made that all too clear. This was a cremation. It was final, no hope for an afterlife. This was the perfect arena to air all of her bitterness. Jerri didn't spare me anything. She hurt me all she could, Dana thought resentfully. I'm not going to leave smiling and understanding this time, all my anger and resentment locked inside. "Jerri," Dana said in a mock-sweet voice as if about to eulogize the relationship, "I don't want to be your lover anymore either." She looked at the coffee table and said, "I never *really* wanted to be with you. I mean, not like I did with Karen. I'm *in love* with her. I wanted her but I got you and you were pretty and smart so I tried to make it work with you. And I did love you. I liked sleeping with you. But yes to your question last night, I did enjoy it more with Karen."

"I know all this," Jerri said. "But you need to know some things too since we're being so honest. Since we got back together I've been seeing Gloria on and off. It started out casually but now it's heating up. That's part of why I want out."

Dana picked up her purse and clothes with a yank, wrapped the blanket around herself, quickly dressed in the bathroom, and left without going back into the living room where Jerri was still silently sitting.

She stepped out into the sunlight, and felt as if she was dissolving into it—falling apart into it.

Standing before Rosylyn's door, Dana was afraid to use her own key to open it. All she wanted was to pack her car with as much as it would hold and arrange for the rest of her belongings to be sent to Cody. Feeling desperate, like she was hitting rock bottom, she prayed that Rosylyn would not be angry with her. She bit her nails, staring at the gold hallway carpet, feeling like a lost child, knowing she was fired for sure now for not coming home last night. She knocked lightly on the door. No answer. Rosylyn must have gone out for breakfast.

Sliding her key in the lock, Dana stepped in and walked quickly to her bedroom. Packing her belongings, she hoped to be gone before Rosylyn returned. All of this was Karen's fault, she thought bitterly, grabbing a handful of scarves and socks. Karen's messed me up again. And it's my fault for letting her mess me up again, for being so stuck on her. I wish I knew how to get over her. Loving her is too painful.

She was surprised to see Rosylyn suddenly standing in her bedroom doorway. "Where have you been?" Rosylyn looked mad as a grizzly. Her nightcap was sliding off the side of her head and her eyes looked sleep infested. Even her nightgown looked lopsided. She was having a difficult time making her words work and was alarmingly silent after asking where Dana had been. This was a miracle. Rosylyn was speechless. Dana could make a quick escape while Rosylyn was stuck in a state of vocal incapacitation.

Pack quickly, get out of here, tell her to mail the rest of your things, Dana thought, really hoping the silence was an unexpected act of divine intervention.

She repeated her earlier prayer at the door since it seemed to be working: God, don't let Rosylyn be angry when I tell her I'm going.

"What are you doing? And where were you last night?" Rosylyn said.

Dana said slowly, "I'm going home to Cody. And it's my business where I was last night."

Rosylyn didn't reply.

In silence, Dana packed quickly.

Rosylyn finally layed into her. "Yer quitting on me without even giving notice? You think you can just leave without warning? Who do you think you are to treat me like this? I expect two weeks notice at least. I'm not sure you understand who you're meddling with, young lady. I will not be tampered with. I will not let you go without an apology and an explanation and a word with my lawyer to see if you have broken any verbal contractual obligations to me. Now let's sit down and have a serious discussion about this. I haven't had breakfast. Come in the kitchen."

Totally confused now, and intimidated by the attorney threat, Dana slid back into her pattern of doing what Rosylyn told her to do. This pattern had a hold over her as strong as Karen's.

I don't know how to break away from Rosylyn, Dana thought, feeling trapped, miserable, unable to see a way out, feeling like a child who had only been packing her pillow to run away. She felt helpless, following Rosylyn into the kitchen.

As if it was a potent negotiating weapon, Rosylyn said, "Here, have a piece of cold chicken. Do you want some orange juice?"

Too nervous to eat, Dana said, "No, thank you," confused by the change in Rosylyn's attitude. "I'm not hungry."

Rosylyn flung her hand at a few flies darting about. "We need to get some fly killer strips." She bit into the chicken leg. "Now what's this talk about going home? You have the opportunity here to become a famous painter, to be someone. I can help you as a patron. Many an artist would die for the opportunity to have a patron."

Rosylyn paused.

Dana could not believe that Rosylyn was talking about being her patron instead of firing her. And she wondered if she really wanted her as a patron. At one time it sounded promising. But now she was wary of any promise from anyone.

"I need a maid. And yer a fine little maid. You're dependable ninety percent of the time. And I'll let you slide on the other ten because you're so young." Rosylyn concentrated on biting the chicken meat clean down to the bone, staring out the big glass panes to the distant shorelines of Emeryville and Berkeley across San Francisco Bay.

Time seemed suspended. Dana was silent. On one level she was relieved that Rosylyn was not firing her. She really didn't want to go live with Daddy in Cody; it had been a panic reaction. Dana felt a sudden relief. Rosylyn would take care of everything. She was offering a ready-made life to fall into—security, boundaries, home. She offered order to her life, now directionless and frightening due to the break ups.

"We'll try two more weeks of probation," Rosylyn said in a soft voice. "And if everything works out we'll increase your salary by three hundred dollars."

Dana was dumbfounded over the promise of a huge raise. She did not understand why Rosylyn would want to keep her on at three hundred dollars more after all that had happened.

"Do you want to stay or not?" Rosylyn said.

Dana glanced quickly down at her hands intertwined nervously on her lap. Forget Karen. And that two-faced Jerri. You've got to make your own way and not run home scared to Daddy. You can save money here. Three hundred dollars is an incredible raise. Forget Karen.

"Sometimes I wonder what's on yer mind." Rosylyn took another chicken leg from the refrigerator.

I don't want another lover for a long time, Dana thought, trying on this new thought for size, aching to be free of the emotional tyranny. I'm so tired of it not going anywhere but into pain and loneliness. I need to be free of this. I need out of this. I don't think I could live through another lover and getting emotionally beat up again. I'd rather be lonely. I'd rather be alone without a lover than get hurt again. Being single can't be any worse than going through all of this pain with lovers and so many breakups. God, I want out of this. Help me to get out. I'll work for Rosylyn. I need the money. And maybe I'll sign up for the graphics program that starts in January. And then I'll look for a job as a graphic artist. I'll get the hell out of this penthouse purgatory.... Hold your breath just a little longer.

"Do you want to stay on or not?" Rosylyn repeated.

"I'll stay for a while longer," Dana said. She hesitated before continuing, afraid of how Rosylyn might respond to what she was about to say. She mustered up her courage, her anger at Karen and Jerri's rejection fuelling her words. "But on the condition you respect my privacy and quit asking what I'm doing with my time off!"

Rosylyn looked as if she was about to reprimand her, but stopped, a very calculating look in her eyes. She tried to sear Dana with her intense gaze.

If she could, she probably would brand me with an R, Dana thought and stifled a grin.

Rosylyn saw the slight smile. Again she stopped herself from retaliating with words. She looked unnerved.

A long silence ensued.

Then Rosylyn suddenly said in a serious, souvereignly tone, "Don't forget it's Saturday. I expect my usual hot dog to be served to me at one."

The comment struck Dana as comical. Nothing like a hot dog to placate Colonel Roz. Dana completely repressed any sign of laughter inside, knowing it would be suicide to laugh at Rosylyn and her hot dogs. Hot dogs were her empire, and everything was right in the world when a royal servant humbly served her the prized delicacy, a symbolic salute to her status. "Of course, at one," Dana said, knowing this was the easiest way out of this confrontation, to let the Hot Dog Queen think she reigned forevermore.

CHAPTER 17

"There's few people I trust. I trust Simon Johnson, my lawyer down in Nashville. He's my right arm. And I reckon I trust you somewhat," said Rosylyn, climbing into bed with Dana. "Now if you asked me do I trust Mr. Horstman, I'd say I once did ninety-nine percent and that was my mistake."

Dana did not feel uneasy sleeping with Rosylyn anymore. It was comforting, she thought, comforting in some weird kind of way. Her being here talking keeps my mind off Karen, Jerri, the pain, the fear, the loneliness.

Before sleeping, Dana was most prone to depression over losing Karen. It had been a month since Karen broke off with her. Rosylyn always anesthetized her and talked her to sleep, that dream state that was her only real peace.

The familiar smell of Rosylyn's gin breath once again filled the room.

Dana was moved with pity for Rosylyn, an alcoholic victim of gin, victim of Mr. Horstman and that unknown thing he did to her. And never able to have babies.

"I trusted Mr. Horstman for twenty-eight yearsssss too many," Rosylyn slurred. "But I couldn't be blamed—he always treated me like a queen. You should a seen him on our anniversaries. He'd always fly us someplace great. New Orleans. Hawaii. Houston. I don't like foreign countries. We were gonna go to Palm Springs for our thirtieth this year but...." She stopped. "On our twenty-fifth he surprised me with a new Cadillac." Silence. "You hear something on the patio?"

"No." Without thinking, Dana lightly touched Rosylyn's forearm to reassure her everything was all right. Then realizing where her hand was, she quickly withdrew it, embarrassed.

"When I was a young girl—I was a good looking young girl," Rosylyn suddenly announced, and added, as if defending herself against Dana's touch, "had half a dozen boyfriends before picking

Roger Horstman. He was just a poor ol' farm boy when I met him from a little ol' town called New Johnsonville." She sounded sentimental and bitter. "Was living on a farm with his Mama and Papa and seven brothers and sisters. And working the register at Crawdaddy's Liquors. I'd go by there everyday to get ale for my daddy. And I'd always be turning poor Roger down for dates because he was just a poor ol' country boy, owned nothing.

"But we had money. My family did. Owned a vacuum cleaner business. It's not that I didn't like Roger, it's that I was afraid my mama'd disown me if I dated him. She wanted me to marry money.

"Well, what happened was Daddy died suddenly and we, Mama and me, were left with a whole vacuum company we didn't know nothing about running. So Mama sold it and gave me a percentage. It was just enough so I could do what I'd always dreamed of doing...studying acting and singing in New York City." Dana could not believe what she was hearing. "I'd always had this natural aptitude for drama. But Mama put her foot down. You see she thought acting was like being a harlot. She was very old fashioned. But I knew the real reason was she didn't want me to leave her behind a widow alone. But I was intent on going...." The phone on the night stand rang, startling, Dana. She picked up the receiver.

A male voice blasted, "Dana?!"

"Yes."

"You come near my wife ever again and I swear you'll live to regret it. You put your damn bulldyke eyes on her again and I'll, I'll...."

Dana hung up on Teddy, disturbed.

"Who was that?"

"Wrong number."

"At this hour?" Rosylyn was silent a moment. "Maybe that burglar's back, calling to see if we're here."

Maybe we should check the broom closet, Dana thought and stopped herself from saying aloud, laughing to herself, no, no one was trying to break in. "It was a wrong number," Dana said patiently. "Did you go to New York City and study acting and singing?"

"Yes, I did. I took the train to New York City without even telling her. About six months after Daddy's heart attack." Dana felt mentally assaulted by Teddy's viciousness. She contemplated calling Karen about it.

"I'd never gotten out of there if she'd known I was going. I sent her a telegram from New York. Before I knew it Mama was on the phone threatening to kill herself. Scared the living daylights out of me. I was on the next train home. That put an end to my stage career.

"I decided as long as I was trapped in Nashville I was gonna do what I pleased. Next time Roger Horstman asked me on a date, I went. Mama raised a fuss—but she didn't threaten to kill herself," Rosylyn said with a chuckle. "Awful way to get someone to do what you want." Dana wondered if Rosylyn would ever resort to manipulating her like that when she eventually departed.

What would Rosylyn do if Dana left her for another job? She had decided for sure to go to the Adult Ed graphics program in January, and had informed Rosylyn, who kept telling her it was a bad idea.

"Roger was a handsome young man with jet black hair. A real sturdy build. And smart. Seemed like a boy that was going somewhere. Said he was going to go to college and study business. Mama laughed when I told her that. She said he'd never get off his Daddy's farm.

"Mama refused to come to the wedding. I think I hear someone on the patio again. It's a good thing we team up together to protect one another at night."

"It's just windy tonight," Dana said, amused by her paranoia. Rosylyn had such vanity she seemed to think all the burglars in the world naturally gravitated to her sky-high estate nightly. She probably thought her penthouse was the central target of all organized crime in the country. Though amused, Dana patted Rosylyn's arm again, and felt genuine warmth and concern. Rosylyn was so lonely.

Rosylyn let out a sigh. "Well, she eventually came 'round to accepting us. Probably because he took me to live on his daddy's farm only two miles from Mama's. She wanted me close by. And she figured Roger would inherit the farm someday. But after two years Roger moved me down to Knoxville to the University there. But there was nothing she could say about it because I was married. It was different running away as a single girl versus being a married woman with responsibilities to her husband. Mama didn't write for the first three months. Then she just up and moved to Knoxville.

"After Roger graduated we moved back to Nashville, Mama following of course. He convinced Mama and me to invest our money into his hot dog business. That was the start of his success in hot dogs." She was quiet for a long time. "And I guess that was about the same time he did what he did and kept doing for almost thirty years until...." She stopped. "Well, he's sitting down in Nashville all alone because of it. Doesn't know where I am. I just told him I was separating from him." Dana felt a little embarrassed over Rosylyn divulging such personal information.

"Simon Johnson said Roger's furious over me going and not saying where. But I'm not coming home 'til I get his word that...." She stopped again, then suddenly chuckled. "He'd never think to look for me here. In the kook capital. It's all right here for a short spell, but not for permanent living. Nashville's better living. Listen, Honey, when I go back next month how'd you like to come along and be our maid? We got a mansion on hundreds of acres." Highly uncomfortable, Dana didn't respond. And Rosylyn did not push the issue. "I got another offer then, Honey. How'd you like to go to Palm Springs, on me, for Christmas?"

"All right." Dana had been dreading Christmas. But better Christmas in Palm Springs than in the penthouse. She could use a change of scenery.

"We'll call it a bonus."

CHAPTER 18

Dana watched teenage girls swish by on the sidewalk wearing sunglasses and not much else, heads held high, heels hitting the pavement pompously, a look of determination in their eyes. Sitting in a sidewalk cafe with Rosylyn, she watched the Mercedes, BMWs, Jaguars, Volvos and Cadillacs, engines growling, owners looking impatient with the traffic.

Traffic jams, flashy cars, strutting debutantes, a sad row of palm trees, hoards of expensive shops.... What was the big deal about Palm Springs, Dana had wondered since arriving.

A waiter, feigning a French accent, stepped up and said, "A turkey sandwich for the pretty mademoiselle. And for her lovely Mama a beef sandwich."

Rosylyn suspiciously eyed the brown bread imprisoning her precious roast beef. She cast a skeptical eye on a fluffy pile of alfalfa sprouts touching a razor-thin slice of orange. "There must be a mistake," she said. "I didn't order brown bread."

"I'm sorry, ma'am, everything is served on whole wheat bread."

"I'd like some white bread."

"I'm sorry, ma'am, we don't serve white bread."

"Don't serve white bread? I've never heard of such a thing. What kind of restaurant is this?" She cast a quick suspicious glance around the premises.

"I'm sorry, ma'am," the waiter repeated, looking helpless before her wrath. "Would you like to order something else? We have many fine salads on the menu. Crab Louis. Spinach. Caesar."

"I want a beef sandwich on white bread. And if you can't supply that I'll go elsewhere."

"I'm sorry, ma'am..."

Before Dana knew it they were hailing a taxi and her delicious looking sandwich was being whisked away by the hands of a perturbed waiter. "Over priced health food dive posing as a decent restaurant," Rosylyn muttered to herself, surveying the traffic.

"Their idea of food out here is brown bread and alfalfa sprouts and avocados. Palm Spring's just one big tourist trap California-style. There's no relaxing to be had here," Rosylyn grumbled. "We'll get a pizza or some chicken delivered to our room."

Dana had been greatly disappointed when she learned Rosylyn had booked them for seven nights at the Holiday Inn. She was further disappointed upon realizing Rosylyn was content that they should spend most of their time in their room, lying on the bed watching the HBO station, with occasional visits to the pool or the cocktail lounge. Dana had envisioned staying in an extravagant hotel with a hot tub and palm tree on every private patio, tropical flowers everywhere, strolling musicians and masseuses. But Rosylyn had said that she always stayed at Holiday Inns because they were dependable and you got what you paid for.

Riding in the taxi, Dana was very solemn. Some vacation. Painful thoughts of Karen come to mind. Dana questioned whether she would ever be happy again.

She walked slowly down the Holiday Inn hallway to their room, hungry and depressed. She noticed a plump short woman, black hair piled on her head like a twirling tornado, stop and take a double take at them as they passed. The woman wore bright red thongs, and a red, yellow and blue-striped towel was draped over her arm. A smile of recognition exploded on her radish-colored face, and her hairdo nearly toppled off her head as she exclaimed, "Rosylyn!"

Rosylyn stopped dead in her tracks and fixed her eyes on the creature in the aqua-marine bathing suit. She looked ambushed. A number of seconds lapsed before she said politely, "Thelma, fancy running into *you* of all people here in Palm Springs."

"Small world, as they say. What are you doing here?"

"Vacationing."

"Six months and no one's heard a word from you down home. We'd never stopped to think you'd be hiding out at the Holiday Inn in Palm Springs all this time. I'll give you credit for a clever choice, old girl."

Rosylyn held her head high, towering a whole foot over pumpkin-shaped Thelma. "Let's just keep it as our little secret, old friend to old friend." Rosylyn winked in a hostile manner and bulldozed forth a smile. She uneasily watched Thelma glance once too often at Dana, trying to solicit an introduction to the curiousity-rousing, pretty, young thing standing so attentively by her side.

Rosylyn made no introductions.

Thelma stuck out her hand. "I'm Thelma Carrothers, an old Nashville buddy of Rosylyn's." She pumped Dana's hand up and down, smothered her with smiles, looking as if she wanted to befriend Dana to better pry into Rosylyn's present life. "And what is yer name, Honey?"

"Dana."

"Dana who?"

"Dana Wilkins."

"Well, this certainly is a lovely young lady yer with," Thelma said and turned her eyes and smirking lips back to Rosylyn's peeved face. Turning back to Dana, she said, "Yes, Rosylyn and me have been friends for centuries." Rosylyn's lips noticeably soured. "I'd never have guessed she was in Palm Springs. And I'd never a thought I'd run into her here. This is a minor miracle. You know, Honey, Roger doesn't have the faintest notion yer here."

Rosylyn shot her a 'keep your mouth shut' gaze.

"Roz, Honey, for the life of me I don't know why yer acting like this." She put her hand on her hip. "We're all surprised by yer behavior. Running off like that, not telling a soul where you were going. Why some people even think you're dead."

"I reckon it'd put an end to my misery," Rosylyn said abruptly, shifting her weight from foot to foot impatiently.

"That's no way to talk, Rosylyn, Honey. There's people back home that genuinely care about you. We worry over you."

"Funny thing you would be worrying about me with all the problems you got, Thelma. Yer time'd be better spent worrying over yerself."

"You...!" Thelma stopped herself. She regained her composure and said mock-sweet, "I'm just trying to help."

"I know, Thelma. Trying to pry into my business as usual so you can run back to Nashville and compete with the local paper for spreading gossip. Best help you can give me is to forget you saw me here. Because it's really none of yer damn business, Thelma."

Thelma's bouncy cheeriness turned into pure pounce. "Honey, it wouldn't make a difference to Roger if I told him you were here or not. He told me and Rita flat out just two weeks ago that he didn't want to know where you are." She looked like a black-headed ratty-eyed gnome now. "He's not the type to come crawling looking for you, begging on his knees for forgiveness like you'd like. He's a man of dignity. And yer just a small hurt woman turned meaner than the whole situation warrants. Roger'd rather not know where you are," she repeated for effect.

Dana envisioned Rosylyn picking up the little mole by the neck. It was not right that she should publicly snipe at Rosylyn in a Holiday Inn, particularly during the holiday season. There was a wiry, tiny, gray-haired lady pretending to wait for the elevator, occasionally sneaking disturbed and curious glances at the two bitches balling each other out in a civilized hotel. This Thelma was causing a public spectacle of Rosylyn's personal life. Dana felt angry and protective.

Thelma had the nerve to repeat a third time, "Roger doesn't want to know yer here, Honey."

"What do you know about what Roger wants, Thelma? I'm gone six months and you've suddenly moved in as an authority on Roger Horstman. You're just a casual business connection of the lowest kind to him, Thelma." She shook her head.

"I'm only repeating what he said to me and Rita. He said he'd rather not know where you are. He said 'cause you didn't want him to know he's not gonna bother finding out. He's pretty damned angry about all of this," Thelma said hotly, as if angry about something herself. "You don't know what kind of man yer tampering with."

"That's like you, Thelma. One party with my husband and you think you know more about him than I do after three decades. Kindly keep your malicious gossip to yerself." Their gazes locked threateningly.

"Well, I hope yer getting professional counselling for yerself."

"I'd advise the same for you and Rita," Rosylyn retorted.

Dana did not understand why this woman was so hostile toward Rosylyn. She crossed her arms nervously. No one treated Rosylyn like this and got away with it. Dana would never dream of talking to her like that. She marveled at how well Rosylyn was retaining her composure. "Thelma, this is the last straw. You have finally pushed me too far. When I return to Nashville you needn't ever count on me for anything. In fact, just forget you saw me here, forget you ever knew me to begin with because that's exactly what I plan to do concerning you!"

Thelma's body tightened up and she leaned forward like a big fist put forth. "When you come back to Nashville? I don't reckon you'll want to come back when you find out what yer dear husband, whom you know so well, has been up to."

Rosylyn looked a little unnerved. "What is that supposed to mean?"

"It means yer playing yer cards all wrong, Honey."

"What are you exactly trying to say?" Rosylyn looked ready to sock Thelma's tiny teeth out.

"Simply that you may think yer the one dealing this game, but yer not."

"And I suppose you are. One would think so hearing you talk."

"Rosylyn, you want to know what Roger's been up to?"

"Looks like yer determined to tell me." Beneath Rosylyn's hostile eyes loomed a distant, vulnerable, wondering look.

"Well, that boy's been over there every weekend since you left. Every weekend. Well, he's not really a boy. He's a young man, twenty-eight years old. A charming and smart young man. Good looking from what I heard. You really ought to relent, Rosylyn."

"Relent," Rosylyn muttered, looking slightly defeated but not wanting to show it. "So now I'm being made out to be the bad guy?"

"Forgive and forget," Thelma said with an acid tone and victorious smile. "Let bygones be bygones."

"I'll take you up on that advice, Honey. Thank you," Rosylyn said, much to Dana's surprise. "As far as I'm concerned yer a bygone who'd better *be gone,* Thelma. You'd better clear out of town."

Thelma's mouth dropped open. "You don't own this town."

Dana felt as if she was in the Wild West. If they had guns, they'd be pacing off.

"Well, yer inspiration enough for me to buy up this town just so I can run you out of it."

"Yer just a hurt and bitter woman, Rosylyn Horstman. I can see how eager you are to take pot shots at whoever strolls yer way. I won't take this personally."

"Take it personally, Thelma. Get out of Palm Springs."

"Who is this young girl?" Thelma suddenly inquired. Rosylyn was quiet, forcing her to squirm with curiosity. "Where did you meet this girl?" She demanded accusingly, "Is she staying here with you? Who is she?"

A devilish look skirted across Rosylyn's face. Thelma turned to

Dana. "You don't know the kind of woman you're with."

"She's a nice woman," Dana said, eager to shut this malicious woman up and show her loyalty.

"You're obviously as young and naive as you look. Rosylyn, you should be ashamed of yerself."

"I'm only ashamed of myself for ever having stooped so low as to be a friend with yer kind...."

"Oh ho, is that it! My kind?! Well, Honey, I've always seen right through yer game. You act so high and mighty and holy, well, I've always known what you are. You acted so shocked twelve years ago when I attempted to be honest with you about what was going on between us."

Rosylyn laughed. "You mean to be telling me twelve years later that you've thought to this day that I was interested in..., well, yer stupider than I ever realized, Thelma Carrothers."

"Interested you were, Rosylyn Ann Horstman. That's why you've despised me all these years. You've despised yerself for feeling as you did. You never owned up to it, Roz. I did. And you hated me for it."

Thelma then glanced from Rosylyn to Dana back to Rosylyn. "Or perhaps you finally have owned up to it, Dear."

Thelma was slapped. A clean, quick, efficient slap across the lips. She instinctively lifted her elbow to defend against further blows. When she saw one slap was the extent of the damage to be inflicted, she turned to Dana and said loudly, backing down the hall, "I'm warning you, Honey, you don't know what type of woman yer with. She's a...." Rosylyn stepped threateningly toward her, silencing her with eyes aimed at assassinating. Thelma quickly ducked behind her motel room door and slammed it shut. A chain lock slid into place.

Rosylyn took Dana's elbow and aggressively shuffled her into their room, cussing, "Damn busybody. Verbal sniper. It's no holiday in this inn with Thelma Carrothers down the hall. I'm sorry you had to listen to her filth. She's got the filthiest mouth in the South. I want to set you straight, Honey." As Dana sat on the edge of the bed, Rosylyn stared at her intently. "You're to forget everything you heard out there. Now, let me set you straight. Twelve years ago Thelma and I were very close friends. Thelma thought she would take advantage of that. Well, I was, and am, a married woman, and not about to do any such thing as she propositioned. I was shocked by her behavior. I committed an indiscretion she's never forgiven me for. I told Mr. Horstman and a couple other people that Thelma was queer and on the make for me. Of course that got back to Thelma and everyone else in Nashville. It ruined her career as a beauty salon operator. She's never forgiven me for that. She's despised me since.

"I'm just telling you this because I want you to understand what happened out there in that hall. She's a vicious and malicious woman out to hurt me for hurting her once. She never got over it and never will. I've always managed to respond politely to her jabs all these years, but today she went too far and forced me to get rough with her to shut her up. Don't think I have a habit of slapping people. That's the first woman I've ever had to slap, Dana. It's best you just forget everything you heard today. I don't expect you to understand this."

Rosylyn turned her back toward Dana and looked at her angry face in the mirror. She muttered to herself, "Damned if she thinks she's gonna go back to Nashville and spread filthy rumors about me. Roger'll hear from me first." She turned around to Dana. "I don't like Palm Springs. Especially with Thelma Carrothers in it. I don't even like the Holiday Inn anymore. Nothing's worse than a stupid gossip slandering someone respectable down into the dirt they lie in. I've always had enough pride not to stoop to her level. Dana, you'd better book us on the next flight to San Francisco before I bust her door down and...!"

On the plane home, Rosylyn sat silently entrenched in the seat, staring straight ahead so intently she could burn a hole in the plane with her hot gaze. "I'm going to call Mr. Horstman and tell him I want a reconciliation. This separation's gone on long enough. You can be our maid in Nashville. You can even be an artist for our business, painting hot dogs on ads and such."

A hot dog artist. Dana cringed at the thought. I'm not going to Nashville. The graphics program starts in two weeks. I've got a thousand dollars saved and all my debts paid off. I can make it without Rosylyn if I have to.

CHAPTER 19

"You'll never guess who's here in Cody and who's gone?"

"Who, Daddy?"

"Lester married a girl and moved to Louisiana to work in her daddy's auto parts store. And your best buddy's here. Separated from her husband again. She told me she didn't think she'd go back to him this time around." The line was silent. "With Karen in town, you'd have your best buddy here. Come on home, Angel."

Dana was so stunned that she did not reply for a while. "How long has she been there, Daddy?" Perhaps she *had* finally left Teddy.

"Said she'd flown in on Christmas Eve."

"So she's been there three days."

After talking to Daddy for ten more minutes, Dana quickly dialed Karen's mother's house. Karen was free again.

Karen answered the phone. "Dana? How did you know I was here? Oh, you must have talked to your dad. I ran into him. I'm so glad you called. I was going to call you as soon as I got up the nerve. I left Teddy."

"What happened?" Dana said, trying to smother the happiness in her voice.

"I caught him seeing Gail again. He's such a goddamned liar." Karen stopped to catch her breath. "He told me it wasn't as easy as he thought to give her up. I actually had the nerve to tell him I felt the same way about you."

That must have been when Teddy called and threatened me, Dana thought. He must have been afraid Karen would try to contact me.

"You know what he had the nerve to say to me? That he hasn't sowed his oats yet because we got married so young. He expected me just to accept that as justification and to just forgive him. He's been calling here everyday begging me to come back. But I won't. I've had it. He can have Gail." She paused, then said, "I've missed you so much. I thought of coming directly to San Francisco but...." She paused again. "Rosylyn's there. And I've been confused. It's all happening so fast, you know? So I'm here. I really was going to call you but you beat me to it. I really want to be with you."

There was only one thing Dana needed to know. "Are you going to divorce him?" Her lips pressed firmly together, hoping.

"Probably, but I don't know."

The words resounded through Dana's mind, *I don't know, I don't know.* She felt she'd been hearing that forever from Karen, voiced or not; it was like her own personal national anthem. Just to see how Karen would respond, Dana said slowly, "Rosylyn's going back to Nashville to her husband. And Jerri and I split up for good."

"Really!" Karen said, sounding pleased. "Why not move back to Cody then? Your dad really misses you, Dana. And you know his health has never been that good, high blood pressure and all. And Lester's gone. We could get an apartment. Or I could come out there. But I really would rather live in Cody or somewhere else in the country than in a big city. Why don't you come here?"

"I don't know," Dana said, feeling slightly apprehensive.

"Well, why not?"

Dana asked herself that same question. Why did she hesitate? In the past she had never hesitated to come when Karen called. Why not go? All of her past pain answered. Karen leaving to marry Teddy. Karen moving to Stockton. Karen telling her at the Cody Rodeo she had been writing him throughout their four month separation, even though she had been Dana's lover during it. Telling Dana to leave Stockton. Backing out on coming to San Francisco to live with Dana. Calling to say she wouldn't contact Dana for at least six months. Karen could not be blindly trusted anymore. She was capable of hurting Dana too much. As much as she desired to go, Dana hesitated for the first time.

"What's keeping you in San Francisco?" Karen said.

Dana was full of ambivalence, confused. "What's for me in San Francisco?" She thought about this, then said, "My art career. I've signed up for a program where you can get a graphic arts certificate in one semester, a basic-level certificate."

They were both quiet. Finally, Dana dared to ask, "Well, what's in Cody for me?"

"I'm here."

"For how long?"

"Dana, why are you pushing me to make a decision I'm not ready to make? Can't you tell how upset I am? I need you. What more can I say? I'll probably divorce him. There's a ninety percent chance I will. If that weren't true do you think I'd ask you to come to Cody? You aren't willing to take any risks.... Look, I'm confused. It's scary to consider becoming a lesbian. But I keep thinking that I really wish you were here. I want you here. I do miss you, Dana. I'm in love with you. But it's your decision."

"And what if you go back to Teddy?"

Karen exploded. "I'm too emotional right now to be thinking of the future to decide what's best for you or me. I don't know any of that. I've been praying that I'll do the right thing. But all I know is I'm in pain now and I wish you were here and if you make me say that one more time I'm going to wish I never asked you to come."

Dana was overwhelmed. Her every desire was to say yes, but she had been hurt too many times. A new, slightly more powerful self resisted the temptation.

"I'm sorry if I've sounded pushy and selfish but...," Karen said and then was quiet. She took a deep breath. "I just need time with you to know for sure. You know I've always thought I'd be happier with you." She was quiet. "But it's always scared me. I want to be with you on this separation to find out. So that's why I don't know if I'm divorcing him. It depends a lot on me and you. After six months with you I think I'll know."

This was unbearable. Dana was simultaneously repelled and attracted. How could she possibly suggest Dana be on best performance for six months matched against Teddy? Damn, why did it always have to come down to her or Teddy? Why couldn't she just be loved for herself? Dana wanted out of this game. She had always been on the losing end. She was full of anger and pain. Had she no say in this game? Karen was summoning her again and it frightened her how much she wanted to come to her. Dana was quiet, paralyzed between desire and recoil, anticipation and anxiousness, pain and pleasure, deadlocked by conflicting emotions. She had gone over a month without a lover and it had been hard.

"Maybe you need time to think it over," Karen said. "I don't blame you for being reluctant. I know I've hurt you many times. But will you think it over?"

"Yes, I will."

"I love you," Karen said and gently hung up on Dana, causing her to crave her intensely. Hung up on. Cut off from her love. Karen always knew how best to produce an effect in Dana, who longed for her to fill this hollow loveless loneliness. Karen. You are torturing me. Please stop.

While cleaning the lunch plates off the kitchen table, Dana listened to Rosylyn on the phone. Rosylyn was fully made-up as if making a debut, wearing the green suit jacket with a matching pleated skirt that Dana gave her for Christmas. Rosylyn had given her diamond earrings. "Roger? It's Rosylyn.... Well, aren't you gonna say a thing? It's been six months!"

Dana pretended not to listen. She sensed this call to Roger was a turning point, like hers to Karen. "Well, you'd think you'd be glad to hear me.... Of course I know you're mad I disappeared, but I'm mad about why I had to go! Sometimes a separation is the best medicine for a situation like this."

Dana pushed her bangs out of her eyes and started sponging down the counters. "I'm in San Francisco.... Why here? Why not here?...I know there's lots of those here," Rosylyn said and glanced at Dana. "I don't have a thing to do with them so it doesn't matter if they're here or not.... I've been here the entire time except for two days in Palm Springs. You won't believe who I had the rotten luck to run into there.... Thelma. She had the gall to make accusations about me and my maid similar to the trash she made up twelve years back about her and me." Rosylyn laughed as if Roger was laughing along with her at crazy Thelma and her asinine accusations. "What do you mean why was my maid with me? You know I never travel alone.... Of course we shared a room...I know I never took Georgia Anne anywhere. She had a husband. And I had a husband to travel with. What are you driving at, Roger Horstman?!" Rosylyn was silent. "I know yer angry over this separation but that's no excuse for making low blows."

Worried, Dana glanced at Rosylyn every other second. The more difficult Mr.Horstman made it for Rosylyn, the more difficult it would be for Dana, particularly if she decided to leave for Cody to be with Karen.

"Well, I'm glad to hear you do, Honey. I was beginning to think you didn't want me to come home.... No, I don't want Georgia Anne back. She let me down. I've got a good maid here who you'll like," Rosylyn said and rubbed her nose.

Damn, Dana thought, she's really planning on me coming to Nashville. She stopped sponging the sink, mesmerized by Rosylyn's words. "I'm not giving Georgia Anne the job back. I've already promised this girl the job. And that's a term of me returning. She comes with me.... Attached to her so quickly? She's been my right arm out here, Roger." A devious smile skipped across Rosylyn's lips as she calculatingly added, "She's been like a daughter to me...."

Rosylyn listened for a few minutes then yelled, "Me having her *as a maid* is not at all the same as you having the boy."

The sponge still in her hand, Dana stared at Rosylyn, spellbound. She never realized how deeply attached Rosylyn was to her. She was not a convenience, she was a necessity. No wonder Rosylyn never fired her for staying away those nights and for the Calamity Jane episode. She was a necessity. Rosylyn talked as if she possessed Dana. This woman in the green suit and dyed red hair had a definite plan for Dana's life. This woman talked as if she controlled Dana's fate. "The girl comes with me!" Rosylyn yelled again.

Dana was stunned by the strength of Rosylyn's feelings for her. She was just a kid in a Pontiac, thirsty on a hot day. How did she end up as a commodity to be haggled over like a slave for sale? It was beyond Dana's comprehension. And how did she end up as a competitor in a tug-a-war over Karen? She tried to make sense of how her life came to this moment, but she could not.

Karen and Rosylyn were both trying to stake claim to her. Both talked confidently as if Dana would do what they wanted in the end as if she was some powerless pawn. Highly uneasy, she crossed her arms tightly and nervously tapped her foot, listening to Rosylyn carve out an imagined future. "We can let Dana have the big yellow room upstairs. She's almost completed a series of twelve nice portraits of me you'll like. We need to give her a room to paint in. She'd be a business asset. She can paint one hell of a hot dog. She can paint them for our business."

Dana cringed again at the thought of becoming a hot dog artist.

"Let's get one thing straight before I return—about the boy."

Listening to Roger, Rosylyn's mouth dropped open as wide as a canon's. "No, Roger! I mean what I said before I left. It's me or him."

Sprinkling Comet in the sink, Dana listened closely for clues as to who the boy was. It sounded incriminating. Rosylyn married to a homosexual? Not to mention a lesbian for a maid. And an old friend who was a lesbian. Rosylyn was practically in the center of a homosexual harem. Perhaps she really was gay herself. Dana's lips rose in an amused smile. That would explain the strange possessiveness and strong feelings. But Dana once again dismissed the idea as being too far-fetched.

"I will not come until I have yer word of honor that you will not indulge in seeing the boy anymore. That boy's not ever gonna be there for you like I am, Roger."

After a long silence, hand on her hip and elbow bent like a crowbar, Rosylyn barked, "Yer just thinking of yerself!" A light sweat accumulated around her neck. "What about me? All these years I thought we were childless.... You made yer bed. Now lie in it. That boy is illegitimate! Born in adultery! Raised in deception!"

Dana feared Rosylyn would have a heart attack. "It doesn't make any difference if you only slept with his mother five times and never after you got her pregnant. Yer missing the point. You sneaked to see him for twenty-eight years behind my back and you gave money for him to be raised on." Rosylyn suddenly became very quiet. Something seemed to be draining from her face as she listened, the very life in it.

In a weary weighted-down voice, she said, "If that's how it is, Roger, that's how it is. We'll have to stay separated until we can reach a compromise." The phone fell into the receiver and Rosylyn agonizingly gazed at it. She turned to Dana, triggering her into arduously scrubbing the sink for the nineteenth time. No eavesdropping maid was she, but a dedicated maid minding her business of sinks and cleansers.

Eyes watery, gazing at Dana, Rosylyn said, "I was only married to him two years and he cheated on me and got this girl pregnant. Then for twenty-eight years he sneaked to see the boy and sent him money. He didn't have nothing to do with the boy's mother after getting her pregnant, but that didn't make him innocent. I never knew about any of this until just before coming to San Francisco. Here I thought we were childless and unable to have children all these years and he had himself a son." She tried to stop from crying, turning away from Dana briefly to regain her composure.

Dana placed a comforting hand on Rosylyn's shoulder for a moment, genuinely feeling sorry for her.

"I'll be damned," Rosylyn muttered, her fist clinching then relaxing. "If he'd a told me then I might have forgiven him and we could have raised the boy together. I would have loved to have a son. A daughter even more. Half his is better than none at all. That's half of why I'm so mad. He was only thinking of himself and how to protect his own hide. I had a right to that boy, too. For twenty-eight years I never knew I had a son of sorts. But twenty-eight years later is too late to find out. You know how I found out?" Dana shook her head with a look of compassion. "Roger was in Detroit on business and I decided to surprise him with new file cabinets at his office. Well I was cleaning out the old ones that had been in there for decades and I came across a file labelled 'Personal Accounts.' Naturally being curious I looked inside. It was full of Father's Day cards, some old and yellowed, and 'Dear Dad' letters, many asking for money. I'd no more live with him seeing that boy now than I would if he had a mistress."

Rosylyn reached up and pushed Dana's bangs out of her angelic innocent eyes. Her hand then drifted down onto Dana's shoulder and paused there. "I reckon we'll just have to stay here." She smiled sweetly at Dana. Then she turned, muttering to herself, "Playing a waiting game on me, well I can out-wait the son-of-a...." She turned back to Dana as if lost.

Dana did not know what to say. Full of compassion, she realized how much she herself had come genuinely to care for Rosylyn. She loved Rosylyn. Rosylyn had always been there for her when no one else was. She was the one person who had consistently wanted her around. She was a savior of sorts. Didn't Rosylyn hire her when she really needed help? She shuddered thinking of Rosylyn's wrath if she learned Dana might go to Cody. Her wrath would be double potent, escalated to extremities by Mr. Horstman. But Dana felt a compulsion to decide now about Karen and Cody.

Dana considered going to Karen. It frightened her, the possibility of being rejected again. Six months down the road and Karen might go back with Teddy. Then where would Dana be?

At least if she stayed here with Rosylyn she could support herself through adult Ed. night school, and in just five months she'd have a graphics certificate. Karen might be a dead-end. Karen, Rosylyn, Karen, Rosylyn. Dana was deadlocked.

Rosylyn continued gazing at Dana like a hypnotist trying to consume her. "I'm glad yer here as a maid, and especially a maid that's more than a maid." Dana's cheeks reddened as Rosylyn smiled at her in a sweet solicitous way. "I'm beginning to trust you more than my own husband."

You have to decide now, Dana thought, panicky. Tell her now whether you're staying or not.

Rosylyn was unusually affectionate in her expression and with her hands, one of which was now gently rubbing circles on Dana's back as if sensing Dana must be persuaded. "You know yer a darn good painter. Those portraits look just like me. I know I've been quiet about my plans as yer patron. But I intend to buy them from you for two-thousand-four-hundred dollars, that's two hundred a painting. Then I'm going to get you in a gallery. I'm going to launch you as an artist in our business."

Rosylyn was a career with a future, and what did Karen promise for the future? Nothing. A gamble. The cards have always been stacked against her in the past. Why be fool enough to think it will be different this time?

Karen's hurt me too much, Dana thought bitterly. No matter how much I love her, I won't just let her suck me up to spit me out again. With Rosylyn as my patron there is opportunity as an artist. And security. And caring. No, I won't go to Cody. I won't go until.... Her mind reeled trying to figure out what she would need in order to decide to go to Karen. Until what? Until.... That's it...until I see divorce papers.

"You'd think you'd be thrilled to hear what I just said," Rosylyn lamented. "You look like someone's got you up against a cliff with a gun." She slightly shook her head.

"No, no," Dana said quickly, shaking her head, ready to consent. She smiled. "I think it's a wonderful offer."

Rosylyn's face became rosy as a plump plum hanging high, then suddenly dropped into a business-like expression. On cue, Dana quickly eclipsed her own smile. Rosylyn was right. They must get down to this serious business of being separated. Months of hard work were ahead, of having to persevere and wait, and of studying graphics and painting.

The thought crossed Dana's mind that Rosylyn and she were gambling, holding onto a bad hand hoping to bluff and win the pot, the one each loves on her own terms. And if they both lost they would wind up in a penthouse with each other and plenty of fried chicken as a consolation prize.

She felt a peculiar camaraderie with Rosylyn, a fellow refugee. They shared a purpose, this separating off, denying themselves their loved ones, wanting the hurting to stop, wanting their own terms. Rosylyn was right. This was how it must be accomplished. A separation.

Until the divorce papers are in her hands.

She will write Karen and spell out her terms.

CHAPTER 20

In the belly of Dana's bed Rosylyn was soundlessly harbored. Dana sat in midnight light on the edge, hoping, once again, that Karen would divorce Teddy. It had been three months since she spoke to her. The one saving grace during this time had been her painting and attendance at the graphic arts program at the Mission District Adult Education Center, which had been bolstering her self-confidence.

Dana had not had a lover for four months now, wanting to prove to herself she could make it on her own without one. It had not been easy, particularly at first. After the first six weeks of being single, she had suffered from a feeling of such despair one night that she had feared she might be going over the edge from depression, loneliness and self-doubts.

She had reacted to the attack of despair by going to Calamity Jane's, hoping to find a quick fix. A heavy-set butch in leather and little handcuff earrings had radared right in on her. Without even asking her to dance, she firmly took Dana's hand and led her onto the dance floor and into a slow dance. By the end of the song, they were french kissing as they danced, something Dana had never done in a bar, much less with a stranger. She had been more or less just going along for the ride. Then the woman, while gazing at Dana with sleazy eyes, had softly suggested, "Let's get out of here and go somewhere private." Instead, Dana had quickly returned to Rosylyn's.

The experience had only served to add a new dimension to her loneliness. She didn't return to the bar again after that, deciding to stay sexually uninvolved until she felt less desperate or until Karen....

She had to admit, however, that it had actually been getting easier as the months passed.

Sitting on the edge of her bed now, she quietly took off the new blue slippers Rosylyn bought her the day before. She felt tired from painting all evening to have finally finished the twelfth and last portrait in the series, *A Day in the Life of Rosylyn Horstman*. She saw them in her mind's eye. The portraits were rendered so realistically that they struck Dana as quasi-comical when lined up side by side. What would my life look like in a series like that?

Sliding into bed next to Rosylyn, possible paintings for *A Day in the Life of Dana Wilkins* flashed through her mind. A painting of her painting the painting of Rosylyn and her glorious fried chicken. Her serving Rosylyn the Saturday hot dog, her "Roz dog." Her painting that live model at class this week, a nude who actually brought in a motorcycle to pose on. Dana and Rosylyn in bed, Rosylyn in a nightcap, watching a Dallas rerun. The envisioned paintings took on such a grotesqueness that Dana found herself actually laughing at herself in them. She imagined herself in a painting where she stood stiffly in her maid's uniform holding a broom next to Rosylyn, a take off on the classic portrait of the farmer with a pitchfork and his wife, American Gothic. The thought of that one further tickled both her funny bone and creativity, and she began exaggerating her own expressions for effect. Eagerness in her eyes at Calamity Jane's, so carefully dressed and made up, hoping, hoping for "The One." Wide-eyed, french kissing on the dance floor with that leathered-up butch. Little dragon flames coming out of her eyes, tied up, naked, with banana tit splits, Jerri lighting up a cigarette as they fought. Extremely serious looking, dancing practically down on her knees with Karen seeing Rosylyn's ankles and shoes come closer and closer at Calamity's. Sobbing loudly as a bridesmaid during Karen's wedding ceremony while clutching that little white basket, much to the horror of the wedding guests and minister. On her hands and knees with a big magnifying glass scrubbing Rosylyn's kitchen floor.

Dana had never quite looked at her life in this way, and enjoyed doing so. She fantasized about how she could make a fortune doing *A Day in the Life of...*portraits of people.

She considered how gratifying it was to finish the series of Rosylyn after having spent her life only half completing paintings, always sidetracked by the ups and downs of lovers.

Today had been a good day. One of her favorite instructors, Ted Jenkins, had told her that she was one of the most talented students to pass through the program. "Stick to it, and you could make it big," he had said.

Dana saw her art as a possible way out of this unsatisfying life where you never seem to get what you really want. She had experienced a feeling of power in doing her artwork lately. Her hope regarding Karen, coupled with her artistic dreams, continued to keep her going.

Tucking her pillow under her head just right, she hoped Rosylyn would come through on her promise to buy the portrait series for two-thousand-four-hundred dollars. Rosylyn had been disgruntled that Dana had devoted far more time to her graphics classes and homework than to the portraits. Hopefully she was not so disgruntled that she expected a discount.

Dana remembered how angry Rosylyn had been when she told her that the graphics program entailed five nights a week, from seven to ten p.m., for five months. She recalled how on the first night of class, Rosylyn had pulled out tickets to *The Little Foxes* at A.C.T. and had said, "Look what surprise I have for us tonight." Dana had replied, "You know I'm starting graphics school tonight."

Rosylyn had tried to convince her that nothing happens during a first class. "When Mr. Horstman was at the university, he missed first classes a number of times without any trouble. In fact, we once went to a play on the first night of one of his classes."

Dana had raised her voice and said, "You're not going to stop me from going to graphics school." Rosylyn had gone to the play alone. It had felt good to stand up to her.

As Dana lay still in bed now, she felt Rosylyn squeeze her wrist, one of many displays of affection steadily on the increase since her showdown with her husband months back. Dana was startled that Rosylyn was awake this late. Her drinking had started earlier and earlier since that telephone confrontation with Mr. Horstman over "the boy," an event that had since left her face stained with a sour determination like that of a badly bruised boxer staying afoot round after round.

Why was she awake, Dana wondered, worried. She suspected that only a whale of a worry could cut through her drunken state to keep her up this late and keep her deadly quiet for a full five minutes before revealing she was awake. An onslaught of talk would soon follow, vocal chords running rampant in her bed once again. Nothing was Dana's alone anymore, not even the privacy of her own bed, not even her slippers.

Sometimes she felt like a moon revolving around Rosylyn's life.

She felt like a martyr to Rosylyn, even in sleep, an around-the-clock maid, as reliable as the mail, always delivering. Rosylyn needed a sleeping companion and Dana was always there through thunderous snoring, worry storms, rain or shine the maid came through. God will surely bless her with Karen after making sacrifices such as these.

Rosylyn slurred, "Did you finish the final portrait of me?"

"Yes," Dana said, eager to be paid.

"Good girl. We'll get Mr. Horstman to buy them when he and I get back together. He's very generous. You can get twice more from him than I offered. I've been thinking all night that this separation's gotten old. I'm tired of this town. I'm tired of living penned up in a penthouse. I've been thinking I should just book a flight to Nashville next week and settle this once and for all. Hand him the divorce papers to sign if he don't see eye to eye with me by now. I'm willing to compromise. He can see the damned boy two times a year," she said grudgingly. "Call and book me a flight first thing tomorrow."

"How long will you be gone?" Dana said like a forgotten hostage, unnerved by her patron's pronouncements.

"I can't say how long I'll be gone. Could be a month or more. You'll stay here and watch the place, with pay. Don't worry, I'll be back for you."

Dana's immediate response was to deliberate over Karen: Rosylyn's going to make her husband decide, could I force the issue with Karen as well? Make her pick now. Karen, I want to know. I'm tired of this loveless limbo. She released an anxious sigh as she heard Rosylyn slip off into sleep, snoring softly.

The telephone cord stretched across the kitchen counter to the stove where Dana was frying two eggs for Rosylyn. The receiver was jammed between her ear and shoulder as she whisked orange juice and reached for salt and pepper, and made airline reservations for Rosylyn. Then she quickly dialed Karen's number, dreading this moment. To call Karen meant to jeopardize a dream that had kept her going these last three months, the dream that Karen will be hers again. Dialing Karen was Russian Roulette. Listening to the phone ring, Dana looked like a large piece of blown glass, fragile, translucent pink, icy hard eyes, uncomfortable in her own angular cool body. Her every desire was to melt. *Karen*, she said to herself as if praying.

As the phone rang, a distant memory rose in Dana's mind—Karen and her at age fourteen, Christmas day with Karen at her door with a small wrapped box, sun and snow glowing behind her. In the box was a shiny silver buckle, embossed with wild horses, inlaid with turquoise. Beautiful.

A creamy and cool "Hello" slid slowly and seductively through the cross-country line.

Dana hesitated.

"Hello?" Karen cooed like a purring panther.

"You sound happy," Dana said, seeing Karen's happy face in her mind's eye. Another memory suddenly flashed—her face soaked with happiness, kissing Dana, saying 'I love you, I love you,' her red hair falling all over Dana, the cold Cody winter outside. Dana asking, 'Would you marry me?' And Karen replying, 'You mean if you were a guy? If you had been a guy I would have married you instead of Teddy.'

"It's you...," Karen said, sounding ambushed. "I didn't expect a call from you after that letter...." She was silent, then suddenly said with glee, "Dana! This is a, a big surprise. How have you been?"

"All right. I've been in the graphic arts program and in June I'll graduate, hopefully. The teachers say it can help you land an entry-level job in the graphics field."

"Good for you!" Karen said.

Dana paused then said, "Rosylyn's going to Nashville on Tuesday to talk with her husband about coming home."

Another memory came to mind—Karen in Stockton crocheting a long sleeping cap for Teddy. It was red-and-white striped. Karen saying, 'Don't worry, Dana. Yours is next. It's going to be all white with a big white tassel on the end so I can find you in the dark.' Very confusing as they were not sleeping together then. Dana wondered what brought those sleeping caps to mind. She had an ominous feeling as if someone on their deathbed suddenly flooded with flashing memories of their life, the final review.

"Are you going to be her maid in Nashville?"

"No. But I haven't told her yet. I'm not going to rock the boat until she's moving back for sure. I've already rocked it enough by going to school."

"I've been helping Mom get a lot of work done out here," said Karen. "We wallpapered her bedroom with a pink-and-white striped pattern with real soft, pretty, pink flowers." Dana remembered when they were fifteen, she and Karen had wallpapered Dana's room with a Cheshire Cat print that Karen liked. "And I helped her make a bunch of apple dolls for this bazaar. We've become real close again." Karen stopped momentarily. "We've talked like we've never talked before. But I don't want to run up your phone bill with all this, so...." She was quiet. "I'm glad you called." She sounded as sincere as a parrot.

Dana wished she never called. It was too strained. Her long limbo with Rosylyn looked half-decent next to these moments of casualness on Karen's part. She did not understand Karen's behavior. She felt as if she was being saluted by a sorority sister. She coiled up inside tighter and tighter. She remembered how warm and loving Karen had been when they made love that last time. She felt suddenly greedy for these warm memories as if they too were slipping from her into a cool distance. The tension finally broke in her. "Why are you acting like, like so cool?" A morgue like silence ensued. Then Dana asked, "Are you going back to him? Is that it?"

In an apologetic wisp of a voice, Karen said, "Yes. I'm sorry. I was afraid to tell you. I don't know I'm...." Silence. "I'm sorry." Silence. "Dana, it's been really lonely out here and you wouldn't come to Cody and give us a try and...."

"Bullshit, Karen!" Dana said, shocking herself. She had never sworn at Karen before. "It's not my fault."

"Don't yell at me."

Something finally broke in Dana. She was so angry she could blow a planet out of orbit. "I'm so sick of you pretending to be straight," she said in a voice racked with anger and anguish. "I'm so sick of all of it."

"Dana, get control of yourself," Karen scolded, having never heard Dana retaliate so forcefully before.

Control, Dana thought, control. Take control of yourself. Take control away from this cold controlling bitch. Control yourself instead. Dana's brain felt as if it was filled with a hot swirling liquid. She felt a scream surging upwards inside, stampeding to her vocal chords, which stopped any scream from escaping.

I am so thankful I decided not to join her in Cody, hard and lonely as it has been, Dana thought. She remembered Jerri once telling her that important decisions must always be made objectively like an attorney acting on your best behalf. She sensed a new power from having acted on her own best behalf.

Dana told Karen good-bye.

Later at supper, Rosylyn eyed her. "You've been dragging about all day. You coming down with something?"

Dana shook her head. She swallowed a nasty spoonful of peas, fearing they would jam up on the lump in her throat that had developed after her call to Karen this morning. Whenever she was afraid, the lump came, but it had never stuck all day before. Dana feared it could only come unlodged by a magnificent scream, such as the silent one hammered up inside her still. She feared that scream careening for release.

What would Rosylyn do if the scream suddenly and uncontrollably wailed out like a siren across the sanctimonious supper table, causing peas to pop off plates, squash to slam up into the ceiling, and sirloin steak to sail into the chandelier?

Rosylyn did something she had never done before—she set her fork at the side of her plate. She looked Dana directly in the eye. "What's troubling you, Honey?"

A tear escaped, slid down Dana's blushing cheek. Damn traitorous tear. She wiped the evidence away and did not look at the intense gaze. Rosylyn was as silent as a searchlight. Her silence was suffocating to Dana. It seemed to say: gasp for air, give in, confess, surrender your soul.

It was tempting. The ultimate in security—someone else as landlady of her life.

"Are you afraid of staying on here alone for a spell?" Rosylyn probed. Her eyes had an unusual gentleness and understanding. "Is that what's worrying you?"

CHAPTER 21

Rosylyn was gone.

Sitting cross-legged on her bed, Dana felt as if her life had been stripped of everything but art. She felt like a maiden abandoned in a tower. This penthouse was high-class solitary confinement.

She stared at the strange face in the cold mirror on the wall—Dana Wilkins. Colorless complexion, sad eyes, lost in fear again. The loneliness wouldn't leave her alone.

Rosylyn had been gone just two days and Dana was a Siberian stage set. She was startled by the intensity of her fear of being alone. She thought she was getting over that. Hadn't she gone four months without a lover and proved she could be alone? Why the sudden panic attacks since Rosylyn left? The chilling realization came upon her that Rosylyn's presence, coupled with her hopes—now dashed—about Karen, somehow masked the massive fear barrelling down upon her now. It frightened her to consider she might be dependent on Rosylyn. It was confusing. How could she be dependent on Rosylyn of all people? This couldn't be true.

Totally alone, there was no buffer left between her and her insecurities and self-doubts. They rose up and haunted her. She felt that no one loved her, not even Rosylyn—she'd gone back to Mr. Horstman just as Karen always went back to Teddy.

Dana terrorized herself with how her future would be a loverless doom, a hibernation of the heart, all feeling slowly wrinkling up inside. Lifetime career—Karen's widow. What a horrible thought. Or even worse—what if she was so entrapped that she was fated to spend her life as Rosylyn's maid and hot dog artist in Nashville? What a terrifying thought.

But she felt presently powerless to stop lousy fates from happening. She rubbed her cold bare feet. She missed being touched. I've gone long enough without a lover, she thought. I need a lover. Not one I'm in love with. A safe one.

Dana took the scrap of paper with Frankie's number, hidden

away like one last Valium, out of her jewelry box.

All one hundred freckles on Frankie's face smiled upon seeing Dana again, and they did not stop smiling until the cold wind bit her and Dana as they sped north across the Golden Gate Bridge on her gargantuan motorcycle. They were heading toward the Russian River for the weekend, an idea of Frankie's. Wearing a big, white, motorcycle helmet, Dana held onto Frankie's back like a koala bear.

The sky choked with clouds and San Francisco Bay's wicked waves whipped about wildly. A sensation of speed sailed through Dana as if there was an open hole in her chest. All she was conscious of now was being shot clear through with speed while holding onto this almost stranger for dear life, Karen and Rosylyn thousands of miles away. It seemed unreal. She felt like an astronaut with a big helmet flying into unknown voids.

There were two good things to this frightening ride—she didn't have to converse and she could forget her troubles. The fear of death consumed her full attention. Possibly her last minutes on earth would be pitifully spent, riding on a metal machine up an asphalt strip while pressed against an acquaintance's ass.

Two hours later, they glided up to the Village Inn in Monte Rio, sitting serenely on a redwood forest embankment above the Russian River. The air was crisp and clean. Frankie gently removed Dana's helmet and said, "You're a good rider."

"You're a good driver," Dana said, dreading a weekend of stilted comments and awkward silences.

Dana was still anxious even though the bike ride was over. Why be fearful? It was so pretty here, she told herself. There should be no reason for fear here. A warm fire crackled in the Inn's lobby, which was filled with soft sofas and armchairs, and flanked by large windows peering onto a deck overlooking the deep green river. It was a magical atmosphere. What better place to hide away in on a gray and chilly day? Why was she so afraid?

"I like to come here in the Spring," Frankie said. "It's pretty here, huh?"

"Yes, it is."

Silence again. A pair of ventriloquists could greatly help them out.

A woman with long brown hair and dangling earrings showed them to their room on the second story.

One double bed stared up at Dana. She had only had sex with two other women ever, and she had been highly infatuated with both. The emotional camouflage was missing here. Dana doubted she could handle casual sex with a woman. Frankie was vastly more attractive, though, than that steamroller butch at Calamity's who wanted to flatten her out "somewhere private."

Neither Frankie nor Dana had closed the door yet, standing tensely by it. "I reserved this room because I thought you would like it," said Frankie.

Dana looked at Frankie then quickly averted her eyes to the river. "The river's pretty," she said nervously, glancing out the window of the room. Frankie closed the door and Dana instantly understood claustrophobia.

Frankie smiled too warmly at her. She is cute but she's about as sexy as a giraffe, Dana thought, feeling confused and conflicted. I *had* wanted a safe lover. Perhaps this is *too* safe. When Frankie took a step toward her, Dana nonchalantly walked to the other side of the bed and busied herself with her overnight bag. Frankie removed her brown leather jacket, then started pulling off her burgundy sweater, revealing two, mammoth, pinkish breasts. Flustered, Dana thought, she doesn't waste any time.

Sitting on the bed's edge and pulling off her boots, Frankie smiled and asked, "So this is your first time on the river?"

Dana nodded. First time on the river. First time over her head sexually. She felt as if she was about to become a casualty of casual sex. Did Frankie really expect it immediately?

"I'd like a drink," Dana said. A dozen drinks. *That's the only way I'm going to be able to go through with this.*

"There's a bar and restaurant downstairs," Frankie said, putting on a blue shirt and white pants, then sliding on a fancy pair of tennis shoes. "The waitress is great. Her name's Marla." Her eyes twinkled at Dana like the two, little, diamond earrings she wore. Then she got a serious look. "To be honest with you, I don't drink. I just got out of a rehab program last month. I'm an alcoholic. A recovering alcoholic. I've been on the wagon for two months. I'm in A.A."

Her words stirred Dana's heart a little. She seemed more intriguing. "Good for you," Dana said. She quickly added, "I rarely drink," not wanting Frankie to think she was an alcoholic because she had asked for a drink. "I won't drink this weekend either if that would make it easier for you." She wondered, why am I surrounded by alcoholics lately? Rosylyn, now Frankie, and Jerri always loved her liquor and drugs. It's odd that they're all drawn to me considering I rarely drink or do drugs. Dana teased herself, maybe you should switch from painting to acting in liquor commercials; you could make a mint with your talent for attracting drinkers.

The only light in the pink room was from the moon. "I really had a nice day," Frankie said, wearing striped pajamas.

"So did I." It *had* been a nice day. Frankie had treated her like a queen and seemed to dote on her. She prepared a picnic lunch from Bartlett's, the local store, and served it on the Village Inn's deck. Then she asked Marla, the waitress, to bring coffee and desserts. Marla was very charming and attractive. Then they went for a walk in Armstrong Redwoods, a majestic and beautiful park. She asked Dana all about herself. Where was she from? How did she like the graphics program? What kind of painting did she do? What movies did she like? For the first time ever Dana had done all the talking. Then Frankie treated her to a delicious dinner at Fife's resort, a gay-operated business like almost every place on the river.

Dana hoped the wonderful day would not be spoiled by bad sex. "I'm not tired at all," Frankie said suggestively. "I'm full of energy. Would you like a back massage?" She reached over and started rubbing Dana's neck with a gentle strength. It felt good.

Then Frankie straddled her butt and rubbed her back. "Relax...." Dana felt as if she was sinking into warm water, drifting off.... If the pores in her skin could sigh, they would release a heavenly chorus of sweet release. Ummmm.... It made her forget everything. Magical masseuse. She had not felt this good since.... No. Do not think about Karen or Jerri.

"Roll onto your back," Frankie commanded in an experienced manner.

Dana obeyed. She was as limp and pliable as a marionette now, not wanting Frankie to take her pleasuring hands from her. Frankie massaged her endlessly. She was a Santa of sensations. It felt so good, warm, and secure. I wonder how she is sexually, Dana found herself wondering, much to her own surprise. You can do whatever you want.

As if on instinctual cue, Frankie moved her lips onto Dana's neck. Then on to hers. Their lips tangoed erotically.

Dana laughed to herself, remembering her earlier fear upon seeing this large bed leering at her. Frankie had seemed so sexless. Holding her tightly now, Dana craved more. More. This woman was a sexual wizard. Her insides flipped inside out with pleasure. This was sorcery.

Sex for breakfast. Sex for lunch. Sex for dinner. They had been on a three-day marathon, only breaking once for Frankie to attend her weekly Alcoholic's Anonymous meeting on Sunday night when they returned to San Francisco from the river. Dana felt like a bottle of champagne come uncorked and fizzing. Sex with Frankie was an addictive sweet. Frankie's only desire seemed to be to please her.

"I think I'm falling in love with you," Frankie said in a vulnerable and needy way, her pendulous breasts resting against Dana's. They were in Rosylyn's bed, which Dana preferred because it was a double king and exciting. Real taboo. "It scares me a little." She looked at Dana for reassurance. "This is the first relationship I've had sober."

Dana did not know what to say. The sex was fabulous but she was unsure what she felt apart from it. She felt a fondness but.... It just wasn't the same as.... Forget Karen, Dana scolded herself. Frankie is good for you. You feel more powerful with her. No one has ever been so nice to you, so why not love her? Give her a chance.

"Can I ask you something personal?" Frankie said. "Am I your only lover?"

Dana leapt at the opportunity to provide a measure of reassurance. "The one and only! Did you think I had another lover?"

Frankie blushed. "It's not my place to say, it's not my business."

"Say it," Dana said, sliding her fingers across Frankie's ribs, threatening to tickle her.

"I thought Rosylyn might be your lover. Or you her kept woman. When I met you I thought that." Frankie laughed trying to make light of it.

"You're kidding? That's crazy!" Dana's cheeks turned red.

"Not really. You're a beautiful young woman living in a penthouse with a lonely, middle-aged, rich woman who you're always fretting over; so, well, I just thought it was a possibility. She seems to have a real hold over you."

Dana was unnerved that this stupid suggestion was so upsetting. "I am not her kept woman!"

She repeated it silently to herself, *I am not Rosylyn's kept woman.*

CHAPTER 22

"Why don't you like to talk about old lovers?" Frankie said. Dana quickly began kissing her lips, pushing her down on the living room carpet, her lips a cork trying to plug Frankie's voice. I don't want to think about Karen, she thought, running her hand up the back of Frankie's shirt, knowing how easily Frankie could be distracted.

As they made love, Dana found herself fantasizing about Karen. She banished the image. Sometimes Karen felt like an incurable disease, just when she was starting to get over her.

Afterward Frankie told her, "You're the best lover I've ever had." Dana enjoyed hearing that. It was not the first time she'd been told that. Karen had said it too.

They lay still together, enjoying the afterglow. "Sex is so much better sober," Frankie said. "I'm so grateful to A.A. It's turned my life around. Would you like to come with me to the next group?"

Dana was hesitant. "You better do that alone. I don't think I'd fit in an A.A. group." She wondered if Frankie thought she was an alcoholic.

"A.A.'s twelve steps to recovery have helped people with all kinds of problems. You don't have to be an alcoholic to go."

"I've never been very comfortable in groups," Dana said. "I don't even like parties that much. But if you really want me to go with you, I'll go."

Frankie thought intensely then announced, "If you don't want to go to A.A., maybe we could try some other twelve-step groups together. I plan to keep with A.A., but I have been curious about trying some other groups, like ACA or SLAA."

"What does all that stand for?" Dana asked.

"SLAA is Sex and Love Addicts Anonymous. It's for people who are addicted to sex, romance and relationships or any combination of those three. It's for loveraholics. People who are afraid to be without a lover or feel really empty without one. I have a problem with that. And I obsess over women I fall in love with."

Dana was quiet. "It's normal to obsess over someone you're in love with."

"It's not healthy."

Dana wondered if she might be a sex and love addict, as ridiculous as that sounded, but she did not tell Frankie this. Instead she dodged the issue and asked, "And what's ACA?"

"Adult Children of Alcoholics. That's for anyone raised by an alcoholic parent, or in a dysfunctional family."

Strike two. Dana felt that she was that too. Daddy was an alcoholic and so was Grandma Wilkins, who half raised her. She began to feel very uncomfortable with this topic.

"There's a group for everything," Frankie said. "It's exciting. You were in Cody and Stockton so you probably don't know all this. All the groups are based on the twelve steps of Alcoholic's Anonymous. There's Overeater's Anonymous, Cocaine Anonymous, Debtors Anonymous, Incest Survivors Anonymous, Gamblers Anonymous, Smokers Anonymous, Narcotics Anonymous. Let's see. What else?" She paused. "Workaholics Anonymous and Prostitutes Anonymous and Families Anonymous. Emotions Anonymous.... Oh yeah, and Domestic Violence Anonymous and lots of others."

This was unbelievable. Surely Frankie was making this up. Dana decided to play along. "And there's T.V. Addicts Anonymous and Suntanners Anonymous. And Shoppers Anonymous."

They both laughed. Then Frankie said gravely, "It's a serious matter. Every one of the groups I named do exist in San Francisco or the greater Bay Area."

Dana thought it was weird that Frankie had memorized so many of them as a school kid would the Gettysburg Address. Was she addicted to these twelve-step programs? Perhaps she should tell Frankie about Group Addicts Anonymous? Dana was quiet, deciding Frankie would not find that funny. Frankie Astaire and the twelve steps, it was fitting.

"And I've saved two for last that I think you might like." Frankie said this in a dramatic fashion as if she was about to click her fingers and have a waitress appear to announce the two house specials while leaving a menu of twelve-step groups to pick from. "Artist's Anonymous. That's for artists addicted to not doing their work, who spend most of their life doing everything but their art work."

Strike three. That's me, Dana thought. I haven't done my painting all week since meeting Frankie. "I can't believe there's an artist's group like that." She thought about how much she wanted to do her painting, but how often the forces of life swept her away from it, lovers, money problems, worry. But she had been doing it more now, at least during those months she had been without a lover. She considered that painting and the graphics program were to her what A.A. was to Frankie. Art work was her own private group, a redemptive force.

"The groups I think you might be most interested in are Al-Anon or Codependents Anonymous. They're really the same. They're for people who are with alcoholics and find themselves taking care of them. Or just people who are caretakers in general. People who lose themselves in others and have no or little boundaries. I think you show some codependent behavior, particularly with Rosylyn."

Dana was still. She felt Frankie was crossing her boundaries. This was not fair to be judged and psychoanalyzed like this. Frankie barely knew her. She had felt adored and idolized by Frankie until this moment. It was disillusioning.

Frankie propped herself up on her elbow and looked down at Dana. "Which'll it be, Honey? Do any of them grab your interest? We could shop around until we find one that we both want to go to."

Dana did not want to admit that she could possibly fit in so many. She considered that she might be more messed up than she realized, but she didn't want to be in a group. If Frankie wanted her to go, she'd go. But only once—to help Frankie stay on the wagon.

"You pick," Dana said, disheartened by the whole subject.

CHAPTER 23

Three weeks later, Dana was sitting at a table at Calamity Jane's after attending her fourth twelve-step group with Frankie. It had been an Al-Anon group. The week before it had been Frankie's A.A. group, and before that, Artists Anonymous. Next week they were going to Sex and Love Addicts Anonymous. Frankie had orchestrated it all as if she was lining up season tickets, hot dates. To Dana, it seemed more like confession and communion than a date. What happened to having fun? Perhaps she should turn this relationship over to a "Fun Power." The only fun they had was in bed. Outside it, Frankie continually acted like her psychoanalyst, was somewhat suffocating and tended to talk too much, particularly about A.A.-related subjects. Dana once had a friend, Lisa, in Cody who was in A.A. and was really helped by it, but she never preached about it as Frankie did non-stop with that judgmental edge. If Frankie said one more time, "You're in denial," Dana was going to bop her one.

Dana had wanted to go dancing tonight to do something fun after all the intensity of groups, graphics classes, painting daily and lectures from Dr. Frankie and Colonel Roz.

Sitting in the bar, Frankie asked Dana, "So, what group have you liked best so far?"

"Artists Anonymous. The ACA group was moving, too. So was the Al-Anon group tonight. Hey, look at that woman sitting in the corner," Dana said, nodding in the direction of a tall Swedish-looking woman sitting alone, reeking of sexuality. Her lips were painted pink and her hair shined as brightly as a halo. "Do you think she's a transvestite?"

"Why do you say that?"

Dana watched a smile slowly rise on the woman's full lips. She stood up, revealing a perfect figure held in tight designer jeans and an equally tight purple top. "Jerri, Honey, over here," the woman said in a creamy voice and waved. Dana wanted to die seeing who just invaded the bar. Her cheeks turned as pink as the blonde's lips. Jerri bee lined into the woman's gargantuan bust, hugging her and stinging her with kiss after kiss. A jealous heat rose in Dana. That woman was stunning, strikingly attractive.

"Her lover's not so bad," Frankie said, studying her. "Hey, isn't she the woman you were with when I first met you here?"

"You've asked me about ex-lovers," Dana said, "well, there's one." She watched Jerri walk suavely and confidently to the bar and order drinks while keeping her eyes flirtatiously strapped to the big blonde like some prey that could get away. The blonde played at averting her eyes every ten seconds from Jerri's watchful claim. Why does this make me so jealous, Dana wondered, irritated at herself.

Jerri glanced at Dana nonchalantly then back at the blonde.

It was unnerving. Frankie was stone silent, surveying Dana's every facial twitch. Looking sullen, her freckled cheeks seemed to fatten.

Frankie abruptly asked, "How long have you two been split up?"

"Four months."

Frankie dove her hands into her pocket for cigarettes with a certain forcefulness. She put a cigarette in her mouth. She struck a match. "Is she an alcoholic?"

Dana watched Jerri present a drink to the blonde, who nodded a thank you and tapped her finger on the rim of the glass before taking a sip.

"I never really thought about it," Dana said, irritated by the question. Frankie was like a bloodhound always trying to sniff out alcoholics and codependents, constantly talking on the topic. "Why don't you take a blood sample to find out?" she said, resenting Frankie's holier-than-thou attitude.

Frankie took a long drag off her cigarette. "She's a good candidate for A.A.," she said, eyeing Jerri. "I can always tell, I've got an uncanny instinct for it."

Dana thought, with a tambourine, A.A. armband and "Save-your-soul" sandwich board, Frankie's evangelical calling could be complete. She grinned over *that* picture.

Jerri glanced around the bar again, then at Dana, who felt like a bar stool the way Jerri looked at her so indifferently.

She talks so intimately with that woman, leaning across the table. She's probably talking about sex, Dana thought, knowing Jerri. The blonde let out a huge laugh and Jerri kicked her chair back slightly with a charmed smile.

Frankie jumped up. "I'm going—"

"What?" Dana said before Frankie completed her sentence.

"I'm going to the bathroom." She cut across the bar like a storm trooper, slamming right past Jerri's table, almost knocking into her.

I'm glad I never told her much about ex-lovers, especially Karen, Dana thought, if she gets this jealous just seeing an ex in the same room with me. Frankie's worse with jealousy than I am. This is suffocating.

Jerri turned and looked intently at Dana. She leaned to the blonde, whispered, then walked over to Dana, who shrunk with every approaching step. If Frankie found her talking to Jerri....

"How are you?"

Dana was quiet.

"I didn't ask you out. I just asked how you were."

Dana blushed. Jerri sat down. The blonde watched them. Dana was as self-conscious as if she was on a TV game show.

"Do you want me to leave?"

Dana didn't answer. Jerri looked gorgeous.

"That woman's the one you met here that night we got back together, huh?"

"It's not your business," Dana said, noting that Jerri was indeed drunk. Perhaps Frankie was right. I don't like you, she thought defensively, trying to protect herself from Jerri's sexual web. I don't love you anymore, I don't feel anything for you, I don't want you around, she said to herself as if trying to ward off evil temptation with voodoo chants. Why had she suddenly become so vulnerable?

"That's true. It's none of my business." Jerri gazed at Dana, looking very sensuous. "It's good to see you, Dana. You look really good."

Dana glanced at the blonde, who looked as if she would like to torch Dana. Jerri was so insensitive. That poor woman. I'm glad I'm not her, Dana thought, remembering how much it hurt being Jerri's lover. "What happened to Gloria?" she asked.

"I broke up with her a while back.... How are things for you?" Jerri's face looked sincere and caring, qualities Dana had rarely seen on that cool and confident face, perpetually tainted with carelessness.

"I'm doing better. I'm almost done with the graphics program I enrolled in. I'm painting a lot. I'm out of debt and have some savings. I just bought a stereo for my studio. Everything's changing for the better." She didn't mention that she had been twelve-step dating with Frankie, wanting to avoid Jerri's ridicule.

"Good." Jerri was quiet, looking at her. "I'd like you to call me sometime."

"Why?"

Jerri looked at her with devilish delight. "Remember the fun we had?"

"I should go right over to her and tell her...."

"Sharon's her name."

"Who is she?" Dana said, irritated.

"I live with her. We met three weeks ago and she moved into my...." Jerri stopped, seeing the shocked look on Dana's face. But Jerri wasn't the type to live with a lover. The hurt resurged in Dana. She felt as if Jerri wanted to brand the rejection in deeper, scar her forever. Why was Jerri playing with her like this? "I may live with her but I'm still free to do what I want. That's how we both want it."

Joseph, Jr., Dana remembered, and grinned. "I'm in a relationship with Frankie now," she said, still grinning. "She's in love with me. Please go back to your table before she comes back."

"Do you love her, Dana?"

Dana didn't answer. She's not really right for me, she thought, but she's better than being single and lonely. She looked at Jerri and thought, and better than being in your harem.

Jerri winked. "Call me."

Frankie came out of the bathroom, trying to look unaffected by Jerri's presence.

"Call me, Babe," Jerri whispered, eyeing Frankie with amusement. Frankie stalked over like John Wayne. Jerri stood up. Frankie sat down and put her arm around Dana, who did not look at Jerri, staring at the tabletop instead. God damn it. How can she just so casually step up and wreak havoc with my emotions? Jerri just stood there, waiting to be introduced.

Frantically, Dana whispered to Frankie, "I can't get her to leave."

In an aggressive low voice, Frankie said to Jerri, "What do you want?"

Jerri threw her hands up like a criminal surrendering. "Don't shoot. Someone might get hurt."

"Leave us alone," Frankie said, looking like a bull. "You're drunk."

Oh no, Dana worried, she's going to pull out her tambourine, armband and sandwich board. She was relieved that Frankie kept quiet.

Jerri took a step back and looked at Dana, looked deep into her trying to tap her sexual core, make it bleed. A longing rose in Dana and met Jerri's unforgivably seductive last shot.

"Jerri," the blonde bawled out. "Get your bloody ass over here before those women knock your head off. If they don't, I will!"

Jerri sat down with the blonde and they resumed talking intimately as if nothing happened.

"Let's go home," Frankie said. "I'm getting where I can't stand bars." She stood up and took Dana's hand, leading her out. "I can't tolerate the drinking and sexual games anymore. Bars are a force field of denial."

Dana glanced at Jerri as if a force beyond her control had taken hold. Jerri smiled. It was true. Jerri wanted her now that Dana had another lover.... *Call me, Babe.*

Dana put the key in the penthouse door, feeling that Frankie was very unattractive tonight. "I can't wait to get into bed," Dana said, feeling very tired. Why couldn't Frankie be more exciting?

"Should I take that as a compliment?" Frankie teased.

"Silly," Dana said, lightly pinching her cheek.

A voice boomed from the kitchen, "Is that you, Dana?" Dana was stunned. Why hadn't she called first before returning from Nashville? "Yes, it's me." Nervously, she whispered to Frankie, "You better run before Rosylyn sees you."

Frankie looked bewildered. Her words collided on her lips like a five car pile-up. "What's...don't.... What's she.... Shit!"

"Shhhh," Dana said, her finger at her lips.

Frankie reluctantly stepped away. "I'll call you later," Dana whispered, quietly closing the door.

"Is someone with you?" Rosylyn yelled from the kitchen.

"No, I'm alone."

"Where you been?"

Dana stepped into view. "At a meeting," Dana said, not wanting to set Rosylyn off by saying Calamity Jane's. A fifth of gin, half-empty, stared up at Dana, who was shocked to see Rosylyn's condition. She looked as if she swallowed a liquor store and a bartender or two. God, what happened in Nashville?

"What kind of meeting and with who?" Witches burned in Rosylyn's eyes.

"An Al-Anon meeting with a friend. When did your flight get in?"

Rosylyn nursed her drink, silent as fire. "What the hell are you doing in a group like that?"

Dana shrugged and reached in her purse. "Here's a pamphlet on it with a list of twelve-step groups on a variety of subjects." It was a feeble attempt to help Rosylyn with her alcoholism and smoking.

Rosylyn completely ignored the pamphlet. Her glare could split a city in two. She's trying to suffocate me with guilt, Dana thought. I wouldn't be surprised if she had a private eye watching me, reporting, 'Yes, they fucked every day everywhere, on the rug, on the couch, in both beds.' I'm not your kept woman, Dana found herself thinking. I haven't done anything wrong.

"Help me to bed," Rosylyn suddenly said.

Silently, Dana helped her undress and into bed.

"Yer coming to bed now, aren't you?" Rosylyn said. "It's near midnight."

"Let me change and I'll be right in." After a month of freedom and twelve-step groups, Dana found she was uncomfortable with Rosylyn, repelled by her drinking.

She changed quickly into her pajamas and silently slipped into the kitchen to call Frankie. "It's me," she whispered. "Sorry about all this."

Frankie was silent. Finally, she said, "Is everything all right?"

"I'm not sure. Rosylyn is really upset about something but won't talk about it. I'm hoping she'll tell me when we go to bed...." Dana stopped, realizing she said the absolute wrong thing.

"To bed? The same bed?!"

How am I going to explain this, Dana thought. "Yes, the same bed. She doesn't like sleeping alone. She's been afraid ever since you hid in the broom closet and she thought you were a burglar. She thinks the burglar will return—"

Frankie interrupted with, "That's a new one on me."

"Frankie!"

The line was silent.

How could Frankie hassle her at a time like this? What would it take to convince her that Rosylyn and she were not lovers? She felt impatient. "Listen, just five more weeks and I'll have my graphics certificate and get a new job and be out of here. Please be patient, Honey. I'll call you in the morning. Rosylyn's waiting. I don't want her to get suspicious."

"Well, you've got me suspicious."

"Frankie! Please. Don't start. You know it's not true."

They exchanged cool goodnights.

It had been so easy having a lover again with Rosylyn away. Now it seemed impossible.

"You are now first lady of the penthousssse," Rosylyn slurred and squeezed Dana's hand in bed. She left her hand encased around Dana's. "You've got a job with me for life if you want." She patted Dana's hand. Then she moved her arm around Dana's arm and clutched tightly as if hanging on for life. "Yer like a daughter to me," she said in a desperate and needy way. "I'd do anything for you like you was my own....."

God, what had happened to Rosylyn?

Dana was bewildered. A feeling of power ran wild in her. The tables had turned. Rosylyn would do anything for her. She was strangely full of the sense of security and well-being power imparts. She knew Frankie would label this "sick." But a part of her also did recoil from the intensely needy clutch.

Rosylyn started talking laboriously. "I reckon the bastard wants the boy more than me." She was silent. "We went a month without him seeing the boy, except once, on a trial basis, then he said he wanted a divorce. He's got the papers drawn up. He says he wants a divorce." Rosylyn tried not to cry.

Dana stroked her arm sympathetically. "It'll all be fine."

"And there's nothing I can do to stop him."

Dana felt the grip grow tighter around her arm. She felt sympathetic and repelled.

"He wants to divorce me after thirty years."

"Don't think about it now," Dana said, not knowing what to say.

"I've got enough money so we could live anywhere you want." Rosylyn's voice rode with fright. "New York, Miami, Hawaii, Phoenix or even Cody if you'd like that. You can select your dream location to live. We'll call it a fringe benefit." There was a long silence.

Dana gently patted her arm, feeling sorry for her, wanting to comfort her, knowing how painful it was to be rejected by someone you love and depend on.

As Rosylyn lapsed into sleep, she anchored her arm solidly around Dana.

Dana did not sleep for a long time, nervous. Being Rosylyn's maid was one thing, but being Mr. Horstman's replacement was another.

CHAPTER 24

"Please understand," Dana told Frankie on the phone. "Do you think I enjoy Rosylyn being this upset? Drinking so much? Do you think I like having my freedom limited?" Between Frankie and Rosylyn, Dana was beginning to feel very hemmed in. Yet they both also made her feel needed and powerful.

"One wonders," Frankie said. "You're acting totally codependent with her, reinforcing her alcoholism. You say you're not a kept woman but a codependent is a kind of kept woman, especially with someone like Rosylyn. You're so naive. I also think you have a real problem with relationship addiction. Call it codependent, kept woman, relationship addict—it's all alike. I'm glad we're going to Sex and Love Addicts Anonymous on Monday. Remember, it's at five-thirty for an hour."

Dana felt like a target practice. What happened to their easy going and fun relationship? It was disenchanting. The honeymoon was definitely over. They used to have trouble talking together. Now Frankie talked all too well. A royal know-it-all. Dana resented being analyzed and lectured to so much. She felt that Frankie used the twelve steps to step all over her.

Dana turned the potatoes down from boiling to simmering. Frankie's kept woman accusations were making her angrier and angrier. "Let's not fight," Dana said.

That sullen silence.

"When will we see each other again?" Dana sensed an ultimatum was close behind. "I want to see you tonight."

Dana was silent.

"If you can't get out I'll come there after she's asleep."

"No."

"You've totally slipped into dysfunctional behavior," Frankie said. "This is as serious as me starting to drink again. What is this thing you have with her?"

Feeling pressured, Dana gave in. "O.K. Come at midnight. She'll be out cold by then. I'll meet you in the hall, but only for a little while. And promise to be good."

At eleven-fourty-five Dana lay in bed next to Rosylyn, who was snoring loudly. She felt bulldozed about by Rosylyn and Frankie. They seemed like two sides to the same coin, the only difference being their age and that Frankie had stopped drinking. Both would swallow her whole if she let them. Rosylyn's arm, in her sleep, swung around Dana like a stifling strait jacket.

Depressed, she dutifully slid out of bed and tiptoed to meet Frankie, feeling lonely and empty. Her lack of real feeling for Frankie only made her feel more empty and lonely.

Frankie stood in the hallway in her leather jacket, collar up, smiling. Again Dana had the uncomfortable thought that she was looking at a version of Rosylyn twenty-five years younger. The same red hair. The creamy skin. The neediness. The problems around alcohol. The chain-smoking. The manipulativeness. The lecturing behavior. They even pouted alike.

"Can I come in?" Frankie said and kissed Dana.

Dana took her hand and led her to her studio. This was crazy. How had Frankie ever pressured her into this? Frankie sealed her lips against hers and wrapped her arms about her like an orangutan. "I miss you." She kissed Dana's neck, felt her breasts. "I love you so much." She started unbuttoning Dana's nightgown.

"You promised to be good."

"I will be good," Frankie said mischievously. "Very good. The best."

Dana did not know how to stop her because it felt so good.

"Oh, Frankie," she said, her voice sliding into a sigh. "We can't do this here." But she wanted to. She wanted to sail away into a sexual wonderland away from those sickly emotions that had been plaguing her.

"Do you think I'd do this if it wasn't safe?" Frankie said melodically like a country western singer, slowly pulling off her shirt, kissing Dana. "Trust me. She's asleep. I can hear her snoring. Everything is safe, Honey. I love you." Whenever she said that her eyes got a soft wet glaze. Dana averted her eyes. If she could feel so sexually aroused by Frankie, why couldn't she love her?

They half-haphazardly collapsed onto the studio floor. If there's one thing Frankie was talented at, it was definitely sex. She was passionate, giving, intensely sensuous.

A mischievous grin galloped across Dana's lips upon realizing she was being watched by Rosylyn's eyes in the portrait of her eating fried chicken, which was still resting on her easel. The eyes were looking right at Dana, who felt like a porno star sprawled on the studio rug. I have a life of my own, Dana thought defiantly, challenging the watching eyes, and simultaneously feeling aroused by their disapproving voyeurism. God, sex was deliriously good in this forbidden atmosphere.

Feeling full, blossomed out, she knew they had better stop before their luck turned. She forced herself to be more sensible. "Frankie, Honey, you better get dressed. Better go. I'm getting nervous. I don't hear her snoring."

A pout spilled full onto Frankie's forlorn face. Dana put her pajamas back on and started dressing Frankie, who grew more sullen.

"Don't be mad," Dana said.

Frankie was stubbornly silent.

"We'll see each other soon."

Frankie was unresponsive. Dana started to feel angry. What was it about redheads, Frankie, Rosylyn, even Karen, they were all so stubborn and selfish. What did she want? For Dana to make love with her until dawn? They stood still, checkmated. Ten minutes passed. Much longer and they'd turn into bookends.

It dawned on Dana that Frankie was forcing her to pick—Rosylyn or her? She felt immobilized. "Rosylyn's going to wake up," Dana warned.

"Go back to bed with her," Frankie said like a black bowling ball blasting a strike.

Dana heard a rap, rap on the door. "Are you in there, Dana? Are you painting this late?" The door flew open, revealing a sleep swollen face that snapped wide awake seeing Frankie.

Thank God, we're dressed, Dana thought.

Looking stunned, Rosylyn's face under a pink nightcap, reddened like a burner. Dana glanced at Frankie resentfully. You wanted Rosylyn to catch us.

Rosylyn stared at Dana demanding an explanation.

"Rosylyn...," Dana said, faltering, falling back on formality. "This is a friend, Frankie. I was showing her my paintings. Frankie, this is Rosylyn."

"Mrs. Horstman," Rosylyn corrected abruptly with an angry and arrogant tone.

The antiquated southern formality at this particular moment struck Dana as funny, and she stifled a grin.

Dana's worst fear had come true.... Colonel Roz meets Frankie "A.A." Astaire.

Hands holstered on her hips, Rosylyn glared at Frankie, who glared right back. They looked like mother and daughter. "Forgive my manners but it's two a.m. and I'm half asleep so say it I will.... I don't much care for yer looks."

Frankie gave her standard reply these days, "You're drunk." Then she added, "You should try A.A. You're an alcoholic. Admit it. That's the first step to recovery, Roz." She quickly turned to Dana and demanded, "Are you coming with me? You've got to rescue yourself from this pit of dysfunction. Only you can save yourself, Dana. Only you." Then Frankie suddenly grabbed Dana's arm and started to pull her out of the room. Just as quickly, Rosylyn grabbed her other arm and reeled her back in. Frankie pulled her the other way, Rosylyn the opposite, and a painting for *A Day in the Life of Dana Wilkins* flashed into Dana's mind, causing her to laugh. A painting of Rosylyn and Frankie playing tug-a-war with her poor arms while the eyes in the sacred fried chicken portrait witnessed all. It struck her as absurd and she could not help but laugh. Then she thought of how the painting would have looked had Rosylyn entered the room thirty minutes earlier, and laughed even harder: Rosylyn in her nightgown and nightcap was pulling on Dana's leg one way while Frankie, under Dana, in position sixty-nine, tried to tug her back in place under the ridiculous chicken painting.

Dana's laughter caused Frankie and Rosylyn to both drop her arms and stare at her as if she had gone mad. Dana tried to stifle her laughter but had a hard time. Their stares turn to glares—Rosylyn's quasi-confused and Frankie's mean. Dana had never seen such a mean glare before as Frankie's. It unnerved her that Frankie could be so hateful. It's true, this is what Frankie wants, to force me to choose. The thought angered Dana. Frankie wanted Rosylyn to find them having sex under her prized portrait and then fire Dana.

"You'd better go, Frankie," Dana said angrily.

A smile briefly appeared on Rosylyn's lips.

Dana trailed a fast-walking Frankie to the door. Frankie spun around. "I almost started believing that crap that you're just her maid. You're so cheap, you can be bought. You're sick. You're dysfunctional! She's dysfunctional! She's sick! You're both sick! You're not going to suck me into this pit of dysfunction. No matter how much you deny it, *you're a kept woman*. Why don't you just admit it? And admit that you're sick?" She glared at Dana who was somewhat dazed by Frankie's behavior. "I don't want to be a part of any of this. I've got to get out of here.... Better run to bed now," Frankie said nastily.

Dana cemented her lips closed. Her eyes flickered about wildly. Damn it, if that mouth said another mean thing...!

Frankie walked out the door.

Dana was dazed. That was someone who was supposed to really love her. She felt like crying, but she must face the impossible task of Rosylyn. Chin up, girl.

Rosylyn was in the kitchen mixing a drink. "Don't think that was a surprise," she said. "Nothing surprises me any more, and I've known since the day I met you what you are." She shook her head. "That girl looked like a hard-core queer. And by the hate in her eyes looking at me, I'd say she wasn't new to you. Is this what you've been doing while I was away?" She shook her head. "I don't blame you entirely. This city's to blame. So queer here it's fashionable. So fashionable you can become that way here before you know what hit you. I don't feel that comfortable here myself." She was silent a moment. "I reckon I'm partly to blame for leaving you here alone and lonely and wide open for whatever hard-core decided to target in on you."

Rosylyn was quiet for a long time, nursing her drink. "We'd be better off somewhere clean like Salt Lake City. Book us a flight to Salt Lake for this Friday. We'll see if we like it there." Rosylyn left the room.

Standing alone in the kitchen, Dana turned off the light and stood still in the darkness, feeling trapped. I do not want to be Mr. Horstman's replacement. I am not your daughter. I do not want to be in any way like a kept woman. She realized that the security and money Rosylyn had provided her were not nearly as important as being free and doing what she truly wanted to do, even if that was scary. Perhaps it was better to be insecure and poor instead of financially secure, stifled and trapped. I've got to get a place of my own and be totally on my own. But I feel powerless over Rosylyn, and Karen and Jerri still. And whatever drove me to Frankie. God, help me.

CHAPTER 25

"Did you make our reservations to Salt Lake City?"
"No. I plan to stay in San Francisco."
"And become a hard-core queer?"
Dana's face turned crimson.
"Honey, I care about you very much. I'd hate to let you go to a life like that. It's a life of loneliness, unnatural acts, liquor, back alley bars and girl after girl. That's what a lesbian's life is. Thelma's living proof. Now at one time—and I'm only telling you this because I hope it helps you—I almost acted on an unnatural impulse." The name Thelma blinked on in Dana's head. So it was true after all about Rosylyn. "And I'm only telling you this because I want you to know most everyone goes through this and you have to say no to it like I did, like the rest of us did, so you can lead a normal and decent life. You just have to say no for your own self-respect. All's it takes is saying no."
"No."
"That a girl."
"No! No, I won't go to Salt Lake City with you."
If Rosylyn squeezed the sides of her breakfast tray any harder her knuckles would pop off. "This is yer last chance, Honey," she said with a tough voice. "We're leaving this filthy city."
"Why are you so afraid of gay people?" Dana asked loudly, surprising herself with the question. "They never hurt anybody."
"I thought you wanted more for yer life than to just be a queer."
"I do."
"Well, there's hope."
"I want more from life than to just be a queer. I want to make a living as an artist and I want another queer to share my life with."
"Now don't be disgusting, Dana. You think yer daddy would be proud of you saying yer looking to spend yer life with another female?"
"Well, what are you asking me to do?"

"What's that supposed to mean?"

"Aren't you a female and aren't you asking me to spend my life with you in Salt Lake City or wherever and sleep in the same bed with you every night like we've been doing?"

The tray lifted up off Rosylyn's lap and hung suspended. The words broke on her lips, "You thankless—how dare you!!! Don't you ever try to drag me down in your dirt." She smacked the tray back down so hard an egg flopped into her lap, the orange marmalade fell over, and Dana ran out the door chased by a screaming voice. "Get the hell out of here! You thankless queer!" Dana grabbed her purse, and heard Rosylyn yell, "You filthy queer!" again as if trying to purge herself of the word, of the accusation. Peaches yapped and yapped. She's nuts, Dana thought, resisting the urge to say good-bye with one grand slam of the large door.

Outside Rosylyn's apartment complex, Dana felt she could pop apart with anger. Rosylyn had no right to talk to her like that, but she did feel relieved to be free of her.

Until she realized she was still wearing her virgin white maid's uniform with the frilly Shirley Temple collar. How humiliating to be seen in public in this. But it's either go back and surrender to Rosylyn in order to get her clothes or walk straight ahead and don't look back, or to either side at possible smirking lips. Her anger fueled her forward.

What the hell are you going to do now? She asked herself.

Fear answered—call Frankie.

You can't call Frankie. Not after last night.

But you're free for her to have you now.

But I don't really want her.

I do now.

You're just scared. She remembered a woman at the A.A. meeting saying, "Besides being an alcoholic, I'm also a relationship addict. I don't care who I'm with as long as I'm with someone, even if they're totally wrong for me, even if they're abusive, even if they don't love me, even if I don't love them."

Look, you've got to make it on your own, Dana told herself, without anyone, without Frankie, without Rosylyn, without Karen. Stop being afraid of yourself.

Her nerves were running wild and she asked herself, where are you going to sleep? Where are you going to work?

I could go to the Holiday Inn or Hilton and apply as a maid. The thought amused her, imagining herself applying in a maid's uniform on a Sunday morning, then also asking for a room for the night at the same time. And who would she have for a reference but Rosylyn. She'd probably buy the hotel if she found out I worked there as a maid. "I can't live without my maid," Dana said aloud to herself in a melodramatic Southern drawl.

She decided to check into a motel until she figured out what to do with herself and how to rescue her belongings from Rosylyn's. Her nerves were livelier than a cheerleader's. She got her Pontiac out of the garage, drove to the Castro area, and checked into a motel on Upper Market Street, close to Jerri's. It made her feel somewhat secure knowing an ex-lover was just a couple of blocks away, even if she did plan to be alone. This minor indulgence wouldn't hurt.

There was a Gideon Bible in the dresser drawer, a seascape on the wall, an autumn print bedspread, a sanitized glass and a bucket for ice. It was all reassuringly familiar as a home should be. She took a shower. She turned on the TV, trying to distract herself from the growing dread inside. The soap operas didn't console her.

She sat on the double bed, watching an old rerun of *Cheers*. Absently, she gazed around the room. The TV didn't hold her attention. Her thoughts were too frightening to think. What a lonely room. The later it got the lonelier she got. And the darker it became the more fearful she felt. A ripe night for panic attacks and nightmares.

After two more hours of anxiety, she was so distraught that she decided it was okay to call Jerri.

"Dana? I was wondering when you'd call," Jerri said in a cocky voice. "What's up?"

"I'm at the motel around the corner from you—in room seven."

"Lucky seven. I'll be there in half an hour, Babe."

Two hours later and still no Jerri. Dana was humiliated to be lying in bed naked waiting for her. But what other choice did she have? It's either naked or in her maid's uniform. She scolded herself for being such a fool. She wanted to cry but was afraid to when she was so completely vulnerable and alone, victim to Jerri and this seemingly endless night and unsympathetic motel room. The glass in the mirror glared, the overhead light cast surreal shadows, creating a grayness over all the colors in the room, the hospital green, latrine yellow, muddy browns. The room felt like a holding cell.

Finally—a knock on the door. "You look cute," Jerri said, walking straight in, smiling at Dana standing wrapped in a sheet. Jerri looked tired. "I'm sorry I'm so late. Sharon and I got into it over the phone." She looked around the room. "What are you doing here? Is this all for me?" She smiled suggestively.

"I left Rosylyn."

"It's about time, Babe." She nodded her head approvingly, catching her eyes on the trace of cleavage visible above the sheet. "Where's your girlfriend?"

Dana shrugged. "It's over. It ended last night. I wasn't really ever into it. It was nice at first but then she started getting too possessive, and analyzing and dissecting me to pieces all the time. She was really mean at the end. I never really loved her."

"That's how it always goes," Jerri said. "We don't want the ones who want us, only the ones who don't." The words made Dana uneasy. She recalled someone at the Al-Anon group saying she had spent her whole life pursuing women who didn't really want her and rejecting the ones who did. "Love's a funny game," Jerri said. "I'm not even sure what love really is. Do you know what I mean?"

Dana didn't reply, thinking, Karen.... Love.

"Do you have a robe I can put on?" Jerri asked, undoing her jeans and pulling off her top. She was never one to waste time.

"I walked out on Rosylyn just with my purse and maid's uniform. You can wear it," Dana said with a giggle.

"No, thank you. Reminds me of a trashy lesbian novel I just read called, *Maid for Her*. She sat down on a tan vinyl chair, looking sophisticated, sexy, and comfortable in her nudity, which Dana could not help but covertly glance at. Jerri exuded sexuality. Her smile was deliciously sweet. A night in bed with Jerri could make her forget everything.

"Where are you planning to go from here?" Jerri asked, reaching into her purse and pulling out a joint.

"I don't know."

"You can't live here forever."

"I'll work it out. I'm getting my graphics certificate in five weeks." She considered how that was a big motivational force in her life now. "I've got enough money saved to last two months. And I can sell my car if necessary. I'll try to get a graphics job."

"You've really changed since I first met you," Jerri said. "You're more gutsy. I like that. You used to be so passive. It used to drive me...."

They were both quiet.

Then Jerri said, "Sharon moved out on me last week. Just like that. She couldn't take me hitting the law books so much. What was I supposed to do? I'm studying for finals. She wanted all my attention. She got angry when she called and found I was going to see you tonight. She wants everything her way." Jerri took a long meditative drag off her joint. Jerri's addictions were becoming more and more apparent to Dana. "Let's keep it light tonight. Fun. No heavy stuff."

Dana felt as if Jerri was just here to use her to strike back at Sharon for moving out. Well, I'll use her first, Dana thought self-protectively. Cool casual sex is all Jerri ever wanted from me anyway. Jerri must be what they mean by a sex addict, Dana thought. I know I have a little bit of that too, but at least I *try* to love the women I sleep with.

Dana felt vulnerable making love. Like a reflex reaction, she started wanting Jerri back, much to her chagrin. Why couldn't she just have casual sex without getting hooked on the person or the sex?

"Don't be so serious," Jerri whispered. "Just enjoy." She made it sound as if they were playing touch football.

Afterward, Jerri fell asleep and Dana lay awake. She felt like a planet taken out of the gravity pull of the sun, let go spinning in space. She held on to Jerri, but Jerri was not really there for her. Empty inside, Dana stayed awake long into the night, wondering if she was hitting rock bottom. She felt an inexplicable and confusing pull toward Rosylyn and resisted this lurking undertow.

After three hours of sleep, Dana woke to no Jerri, no note, no nothing. I've had it, she thought. I'm never calling her again. I've said that before, though. Maybe I am a sex and love addict. That sounds awful. But look at last night. I did feel powerless over my neediness. A part of me knew it was the wrong thing to do. Jerri's all wrong for me, yet I keep going back to her. I need something.

She contemplated what the best revenge would be: to have Mormon literature or Sex and Love Addicts Anonymous literature mailed anonymously to Jerri. Better yet, how about putting her on both mailing lists under the name of Joseph "Jerri" Smith.

She got out of bed, put on her maid's uniform, and felt at a loss as to what move to make next. She thought, I'll stay at this motel for now.

Dana paid for a second night, and drove to Rosylyn's to get her clothes and as many belongings as possible. It's scary to leave Rosylyn's and have no job, no home, no lover, no one.

Everything was quiet inside at Rosylyn's, too still. The curtains were drawn. The kitchen was empty. She stepped into the hallway leading toward the bedrooms. A large figure stepped from the side, startling Dana. "What are you doing sneaking in here?" It was only ten a.m. and Rosylyn was drunk already. Her hand clawed into Dana's shoulder and shook it lightly. The bottom rims of her eyes were red, and her lower lip pouted out, glistening with liquor.

"I wasn't sneaking in. You didn't answer the phone. You didn't answer the door."

"Where were you last night?"

"At a motel."

"With who?"

"That's none of your business."

"You're hopeless." Rosylyn retreated to the kitchen and poured herself another drink as if trying to drown herself. She seemed to be taunting Dana drinking two drinks at once, daring her to stop her, save her. She looked near suicidal.

Dana did not know what to do. She felt powerless over the situation like a lifeguard who couldn't swim.

"I should fire you," Rosylyn slurred, sitting down at the kitchen table, miserable. "But I need a maid so I can't let you go." She was quiet. "I need you here."

"Rosylyn, I'm sorry, but I want a place of my own. I'm moving out."

In a desperate voice, Rosylyn said, "If it's more money you want...."

Dana suddenly started feeling like a ship in a bottle, ready to sail, but caught. To desert Rosylyn now would push her into the grave. Dana did not want to do that to her.

"Please don't go now," Rosylyn said, a lost look in her eyes.

"I'm sorry but I can't take care of you," Dana said. "I do care about you. But you have to care for yourself more. I can barely take care of myself now, let alone someone else. I'm going to stay in a motel until I find a place."

Rosylyn threw her a curve ball. "Will you work here days? An eight-hour shift? The same pay as live-in plus three hundred dollars instead of room and board."

Rosylyn was a master at hooking her back in. Dana was quiet, considering the offer. "I'll do that until I find a new job," Dana said, knowing she needed the money. She would have to endure this situation just a little longer until school was over and she got a graphics job. She said, "I'll stay at the motel until I find a place." She couldn't believe she'd let herself stay with Rosylyn.

CHAPTER 26

Dana propped the graduation certificate from her graphic arts program up on the night stand in her new sublet. The best thing to happen this month was graduating from the program. She felt on top of the world. She pulled out a typewriter to start her resume. The last class had been on the art of resume writing and hunting for graphics jobs in San Francisco.

In one more week Dana would move into her own studio apartment in the Upper Mission district near Mission Dolores. For the last month, while looking for the right place to call home, she had sublet a Noe Valley studio apartment. Most of her belongings were still at Rosylyn's awaiting the move to a permanent residence. Dana had sold her Pontiac to create a bigger savings account, a buffer zone which she thought she needed in order to make the transition into a new home and job more securely.

Jerri had called earlier in the month. Dana had found the strength, despite her attraction, to say, "I don't want to see you. I don't want to sleep with you ever again. It's not healthy for me." When she hung up the phone, she knew the break was for real this time, final.

As she typed in Dana Wilkins, the phone rang. A gray cloud enclosed her as she listened to Bud Mason, Daddy's long-time best friend. After talking to him, she called and made an airline reservation for the next flight to Cody.

"I'm sorry, we did all we could." The doctor's eyes were compassionate in a businesslike way, hidden behind thick black glasses. Bud Mason put his arm around her shoulder tightly.

Her insides locked up. She didn't even get to see Daddy one last time. The heart attack killed him an hour before she arrived in Cody.

"Is there someone staying with you tonight?" the doctor said pensively.

Dana shook her head. She just wanted to be alone. This was unreal. Daddy couldn't be dead. *Daddy is dead.* The words were like a sledgehammer slamming into her heart.

In a state of shock, she was driven home by Bud Mason. In front of Daddy's house she sat still, silent. "You sure you don't want me to come in, Dana?" Bud Mason said compassionately. Dana broke down and sobbed and they hugged each other tightly. His eyes filled with tears. "You know he was like a brother to me." They held each other and mourned for a long time.

From the porch, she stoically waved good-bye to him. Grief overwhelmed her as she stepped into Daddy's house, her childhood home, rented from Bud Mason to this day. Daddy always gambled away any potential down payment for a house.

She sat down on the old, green, living room couch and cried. Daddy was not here. Out of habit a part of her expected him to be. She found herself saying, "God, please, please...." But there was nothing to pray for. He was dead. She felt angry at God and at Daddy for leaving suddenly, angry at herself for not visiting him.

Looking around the house, she felt a great emptiness. This was not at all the homecoming she had always imagined. Daddy's brown reclining chair—empty. His cigarettes were beside it as if any moment he would step in and light one. She sat in the chair. No Daddy. Her mind felt like one big whirling grief monster, a tidal wave of blackness, wetness, despair, insecurity.

Now I have no one. No family left. She caught her reflection in the mirror above the mantle, which was cluttered with old cigarette cartons and ale cans. She was a little girl crying for her daddy. Damn those ale cans, cheating her out of so many moments with him when she was growing up. Daddy died and left just as suddenly as mother did.

Feeling lost and frightened, she called Karen to tell her Daddy died. No one was home. So she dialed Rosylyn to tell her.

"I'll be right there," Rosylyn said compassionately. "I'll be on the next flight. Don't you worry. Rosylyn will be there to take care of everything. The funeral. The estate."

"No," Dana said quickly. "Bud Mason, an old family friend, is helping with all that. He's the executor."

I should have never called her, Dana thought, listening to Rosylyn persist in trying to talk Dana into letting her come to Cody. Dana resisted, telling Rosylyn in a louder and louder voice that she could take care of this on her own.

Hanging up, she felt washed up on an unknown shore. No Daddy. No Karen. Only herself, alone in Cody now. She had wanted to prove she could make it on her own—but not to this extreme. The silence here was suffocating and frightening.

She remembered a painting of Daddy, unfinished, lying in her closet. Pulling it out, she thought, I will finish this. She would paint Daddy in all alive and always have him here.

Unable to sleep, she painted him in as if trying to resuscitate him. She painted long into the night. Painting was once again a kind of healing for her. She could feel him here with her. Warm, loving, unseen.

When the sun started rising, she crawled into Daddy's bed and sunk her head into his pillow and fell asleep, his completed painting watching over her nearby.

The next afternoon, from the living room window, Dana was shocked to see Rosylyn's feet swing out of a taxi. What was she doing here in Cody? Was this a grief hallucination, Dana wondered. No, it was definitely Rosylyn. The cab driver set two walrus-sized suitcases on the pavement. Rosylyn was dressed in a cowgirl-style pleated skirt, a white blouse with a bolero, two glistening gold bracelets, and softball-size diamond earrings. She wore an ocean of blush on her cheeks. I'm surprised she isn't wearing a cowboy hat, Dana thought, resenting her lively demeanor. Was Rosylyn hard of hearing now on top of everything else? I said funeral not wedding.

Pausing before the dirty white picket fence, Rosylyn looked at the light green house with white shutters, eyeing it like a real estate appraiser. She's probably contemplating buying the house, Dana thought angrily. Why such big suitcases? Was she planning on moving in? She did want out of San Francisco. Dana felt nervous. She leapt up and yanked the door open. "Rosylyn, what are you doing here?" she asked angrily.

The taxi driver set her suitcases down on the porch. Rosylyn eyed her poor maid dressed in jeans and a brown blouse, hair half-combed, eyes red from crying, a tired look on her face.

"Everything will be all right, Honey. Rosylyn's here," she said and wrapped her arms around Dana, reeking of airplane cocktails and lilac perfume. If she hugged Dana any tighter, she'd bend her bones. They have only hugged once before and Rosylyn seemed to be making up for lost time under the guise of consolation. Dana blushed as the taxi driver looked at them. Rosylyn dipped into her purse to pay him.

Stepping inside, Rosylyn was silent as she sized up the old sofa, the Frederick Remington cowboy prints, the bookcase full of magazines, such as *Field and Stream, National Geographic, Popular Mechanics,* the crumpled ale cans everywhere, and Daddy's reclining armchair, taped together where the vinyl split apart. She looked at Dana with even more pity. "You just rest and I'll tend to tidying things up for the funeral and whoever might stop by to pay their respects."

Rosylyn picked up Daddy's ashtray, some twenty butts dead in it, and dumped it in a tin wastebasket. Dana watched her, growing angrier. She had wanted to leave everything just as Daddy had left it, wanting to retain his presence as long as possible. Weakened by grief and fear, she barely had energy to resist Rosylyn's siege of the house. Was this really happening? Daddy's dead and Rosylyn's here now?

"Where should I put my suitcases?" Rosylyn asked.

"Rosylyn, I didn't invite you to come here," Dana said as she thought, I slipped, calling her in a panic. It's funny, but I do feel less anxious with her here. I hate this dependency. I really don't want her here. Totally feeling at a loss as to what to do, she thought, God, if you're there, please grant Rosylyn a happy life somewhere else apart from me.

"I'm just here to help," Rosylyn said.

Exasperated, confused, Dana said, "Look, the funeral's tomorrow. Since you're all the way out here, you can stay until after the funeral. But you have to go the day after tomorrow."

She carried Rosylyn's suitcases to her old bedroom as Rosylyn said, "Looks like yer Daddy was expecting you to come home someday,"

Dana felt a pang in her chest. Daddy had left her room just the way it had been when Dana left—Cheshire cat wallpaper, the shelf lined with stuffed animals, an old stereo with her Anne Murray, Patsy Cline, Willy Nelson and Emmylou Harris records.

Rosylyn stepped to the white dresser and picked up an old photo of a pretty young woman with blonde hair standing before an old Chrysler. "Was this yer Mama?" Dana nodded. Somehow everything hurt now.

After a silence, Rosylyn said, "This room's like a museum of you. That bed's awfully small. Don't you have a double in this house?"

Daddy would rise from his coffin at the sight of Rosylyn in his bed, particularly Rosylyn trying to get Dana in his bed with her. "I'm sleeping in my Daddy's room, *alone.*"

Rosylyn walked into Daddy's room and eyed the dingy olive-colored walls, tattered patchwork quilt, rack with two rifles, a pile of dirty clothes in the corner, a carton of Winston's on the night stand, a half-full bottle of Whiskey. She eyed the Senior class photo of Dana and another of Dana as a small girl in a white dress and Sunday hat. Coughing, Rosylyn whipped open the curtains and snapped the shade up, opened the window. "I'll start in cleaning this room first thing tomorrow for you, Honey, after the funeral. You'll feel better in a clean house."

Dana was mortified. Daddy's room would stay as he left it. It was not Rosylyn's to touch. "No, I want it left exactly as it is!" Dana said loudly. "And I'm booking a flight for you to leave in two days."

That night Dana watched Rosylyn washing the dishes after serving Dana a dinner of pork chops and potato salad.

Dana thought, this is a real role reversal. Does she think if she becomes my maid I might let her live with me? Dana imagined the sweet revenge of making Rosylyn mop already sparkling clean floors daily, disinfect clean toilets, vacuum clean carpets, just as she always made Dana do.

Dana looked out the living room window into the darkness, missing Daddy. The phone rang. "Dana, I just heard the news from Mom. She just called. I am so sorry, Sweetheart. Are you all right?" Karen said.

Dana would have liked to cry, but not in front of Rosylyn, who was too interested in every opportunity to comfort her, particularly physically. "It's very painful." She felt choked up. "I'm still shocked.... Rosylyn showed up here this morning uninvited." Her eyes watered up.

"When's the funeral? I want to be there, if that's all right with you."

"Tomorrow at two." Dana sensed Rosylyn eavesdropping, the dishes suspiciously quiet.

"I'll be there," Karen said.

The line was silent.

Dana finally said "I'm glad."

"I loved him," Karen said. "And I love you."

Dana felt raw and vulnerable, the pain of Daddy having split her open, left her weakened. Karen slid deep in her. She felt her warmth. The past never was. There was only their love for each other in this moment of consolation. Dana was needy for that love, a familiar love, family. She hesitated, then said, "I love you, too. I'll see you tomorrow."

More tears collected in Dana's eyes. She tried to stop them from spilling over but was unsuccessful at controlling them. Rosylyn saw the tears. Dana then felt Rosylyn's hand on her shoulder, then her fingers running through her hair. "It'll be all right," Rosylyn said. "In time you'll get over this and yer Daddy will be a happy memory. It'll be all right, Sweetheart." Rosylyn continued stroking her hair. Then she kissed Dana's forehead. She kissed Dana's eyelids, kissing away the tears. Dana panicked, fearing her lips would be next. She turned her head. Rosylyn stroked her hair again. "You just cry, Honey. I'm here to take care of you."

Dana stood up and walked to the bedroom, wanting her freedom from Rosylyn more than ever now, disliking and pitying her at the same time, caring for her and then resenting her. Dana wondered, is Rosylyn here to help me or is she just here to help herself?

CHAPTER 27

After the funeral Dana was lying in bed alone. She could not sleep. Daddy's room was dark as a tomb. She was remembering sitting in the church today praying that Karen would show up as the minister said, "Frank Wilkins was always there to lend a helping hand to whoever needed it. He will be missed in Cody, and especially by his daughter Donna." The mispronunciation had been jarring and embarrassing. She had thought, resentfully, why was I so foolish to open up and trust Karen even for a moment?

"You've had a long, hard day," Rosylyn had said when they got home. "I don't think you should sleep alone after a funeral." Rosylyn was there for me more than you, Karen, Dana thought bitterly.

The darkness was disturbing tonight. She flashed back to Daddy in his casket, Daddy but not Daddy, dressed up like for a banquet, lips and cheeks unnaturally pink, hair combed back in a style he never wore before. She had bent down into the coffin to kiss him good-bye, and stood up suddenly when that sickly hard cheek iced her lips.

This room is too deathly dark, she thought. It was as quiet as a graveyard. The light-up clock read midnight. Was that a knock on the door, Dana wondered? No, it was her imagination. But a minute later she heard a rap, rap again. She slid out of bed and walked to the front door, where she heard a muffled voice say, "Dana." She didn't recognize the voice. God, some pervert got her name out of the obituary column. "Dana," the voice said more loudly.

She recognized it and opened the door. Without speaking, Karen hugged her tightly. Dana was hesitant but then hugged her back. "We'll miss him," Karen whispered softly. "I'm sorry I missed the funeral. I just got in. It's a long story. I've got Mom's car. Let's go for a ride. Rosylyn asleep?" Dana nodded. "I didn't call because I didn't want to wake her. Let's just go."

"But I'm in my pajamas," Dana said, wiping the tears from her eyes.

A smile alighted Karen's lips as she said, "Do you remember when we were in junior high and we snuck out in our P.J.'s and T.P.'d Mrs. Pippin's trees?"

"And she knew we did it," Dana said. "Remember she said her neighbor asked who did it, and she told her 'Students, that's how they show their love for me.' And the neighbor said, 'Well, I'm glad they don't love me.'" Their smiles beamed in the moonlight. "I'm glad you're here, Karen."

Karen reached over and stroked Dana's head tenderly, then embraced her for a long time again. "I'm so sorry about your dad," she said in a quiet voice.

Karen headed the Oldsmobile out of town. They glided up a stark highway that emptied into the mountains. The high beams wiped out the blackness ahead. It was desolate outside. "I came as soon as I arrived in Cody." The tempo of Karen's words was hurried, the tone bittersweet, a combination Dana often heard on her lips. "I'm not going to lay all kinds of Teddy crap on you because I know you're not up to it. I'll make it short. He's so damned possessive he threw a fit because I was coming to see you even if for your dad's funeral. We were fighting all the way to the airport and he made me miss the plane, so I had to catch a later one." She drove so fast Dana expected the car to lift off any moment.

"I won't forgive him for making me miss the funeral." Dana was silent a moment. Karen clamped her lips closed and stared straight ahead angrily. "I'm beginning to feel no love for him for weeks at a time. It was a mistake to go back with him again. I'm going to leave him for good this time, I've decided."

"Slow down," Dana said, noticing the speedometer teeter on eighty.

After a silence, Karen said, "How are you doing, Sweetheart? I've been worried about you." She reached over and gently stroked Dana's arm.

"I'm really sad. But I'll survive."

Karen was quiet, then said, "Time will heal it."

It sure is taking its time, Dana thought skeptically, healing me of you. Though she didn't feel devastated anymore, she still loved Karen more deeply than anyone in the world. A part of her always missed her, even if the feeling was more bittersweet than obsessive now. "When are you going back to Stockton?"

"In four days. I have to get back for a wedding for my friend,

Kathy. I'm a bridesmaid...but after that I'm leaving him. When are you going back to San Francisco?"

"I don't know. Daddy's death is making me re-evaluate my whole life, try to figure out what I really want. I don't want to die and never have lived the life I want to live.... Bud Mason told me today I could rent the house if I wanted. It's got me to thinking. I never really have felt at home in San Francisco. It's so expensive. I don't think I'm a city girl. And I *really* want to get free of Rosylyn. I'm afraid she won't leave tomorrow for her flight.... Where are we going?"

"To the dam."

As they drove to the dam, Dana told Karen about graduating from the graphics program and moving out of Rosylyn's while still working for her during the day.

Dana wondered why Karen brought her to Buffalo Bill Dam. It was eerie there. The moon glinted harshly through the purplish black sky. Standing on the edge of the dam, their voices were swept away by the wind into the torrents of water barrelling down onto suicidal boulders far below. The stars sparkled. It was a catastrophically romantic atmosphere. The water was violent. Feeling silly in her pajamas, and chilled, Dana turned to get back in the safe, still capsule of the car. Karen grabbed her wrist. She said something but Dana could not hear her, so she moved in closer. Karen folded her up into her arms, sheltering her. They did not speak, sealed together in silence for a long time.

The moment felt absolute. Beyond compassion.

They got back in the car and drove slowly and silently back to Cody, Dana's head on her shoulder, hand on her arm. The crisis of Daddy caused her to set aside caution. She needed love now, and Karen was here for her.

It was as if they made love up on that dam in its passionate atmosphere.

Rosylyn served Dana breakfast in bed and turned on the TV in Daddy's room to *Good Morning, America*. Looking at the TV, Rosylyn said, "I reckon we better get started after breakfast on getting yer Daddy's things all boxed up."

"What?" Dana said.

Rosylyn stared at her. "You don't want his belongings reminding you of him. It's time to box them up. We'll have them shipped back to San Francisco if you like or we can have an estate sale."

"I don't want them boxed up yet," Dana said firmly. Rosylyn would not box Daddy away. "Besides you have a flight to catch today."

Rosylyn said rapidly, "You have a job to get back to, too. Now didn't you say Bud Mason was the executor of the estate? There's not much to settle here what with him renting this place and leasing the gas station."

Dana thought about how Daddy was always just scraping by. He perpetually had been in debt from gambling. It's true, his estate consisted only of his belongings and truck.

"Well, I'll call this Bud Mason and get him to get the ball rolling so we can get things settled and get home. Peaches' probably missing us to death in that kennel." Rosylyn added, "We'll help Mr. Mason get a new renter in here." She looked like a prosecutor trying to sway a jury.

A renter in Daddy's house? No. No strangers living in this house as if Daddy never was. Him all boxed away, reduced to a few boxes somewhere while strangers laughed and lay about in his house not caring two hoots about who he was.

"You just don't understand anything," Dana said. "I'm not coming back until I decide to. And you're not in charge here. You've got a flight to catch today and you better not miss it."

In a mocksweet voice, Rosylyn said, "I understand, Honey. You've lost yer Daddy. You're sick with grief. Confused and upset by it all, which is only normal. You should be upset."

She slid her arm consolingly around Dana's shoulders. "But yer Daddy's gone, Honey, and you have to face up to that. Hard as that is to do. Hanging onto his house and things won't bring him back, Honey. Trust me to do the thinking until you feel better."

Trust her to do the thinking? Never. "Rosylyn, I can take care of everything just fine. And I just might not be coming back to San Francisco at all!"

"You don't have to be my maid if that's what yer thinking."

Dana relaxed a little until she heard, "I've got an offer you won't refuse if you got any sense at all and I think you do. If you don't want to go back to San Francisco, we'll stay here. I've been aching to move away anyway. I'll buy a big ranch house and be yer patron and promote you as an artist here. I'll get a maid for us. Would you like that? You won't even have to work. We'll try to make something of you out here."

"Yeah," Dana said bitterly. "You'll make a kept woman of me."

Rosylyn looked as if she would like to slap those words clean off those ungrateful lips.

CHAPTER 28

"Here, Sweetie. Mom baked you meat loaf and an apple pie. There's gravy in the tupperware." Karen set the food in Daddy's refrigerator, and brushed lint off her blue cotton skirt. Her eyes ran along Dana's sad lips and pale cheeks. She playfully knocked Dana's bangs out of her eyes, then ran her fingers gently through her hair. "Where's Rosylyn?"

"I don't know. We got in a huge fight this morning and she split. I can't get her to go. We fought last night too."

"You may have to call the police to get her to leave," Karen said.

"No," Dana said, "That's not the best method...."

"You're right, it might take the National Guard."

Dana laughed, then said, "I'd feel ridiculous calling the police to report a house guest who won't leave."

Karen said, "I'd like to report a house guest who won't leave." Then she switched to a nasal tone, imitating a switch board operator at a police station. "I'd like to report one too at my home. How long has your's been there? I hear that the number one crime in Cody now is the house guest problem. In fact, it's a national epidemic. I'm sorry, ma'am, but way out here in Cody our resources are so limited that we don't even have a House Guest Removal Squad yet like the big cities do."

They laughed together.

Karen popped a grape in her lips, which were lightly colored with lipstick. She plucked another grape and put it in Dana's receptive mouth. "I packed a big picnic for us—salami sandwiches, pickles, diet coke, homemade chocolate chip cookies. Let's drive up to Yellowstone for the day. Just me and you." She smiled sweetly.

"What happened to the tofu sandwiches and carob cookies?" Dana teased.

"It's too hard to stick to natural foods. I lost my will power." Karen shrugged. "Besides I figure I'll die either way eventually so why not have fun and eat what I want?" The sun poured through the kitchen window and illuminated her strawberry blonde hair. "I left the engine running," she said with a mischievous smile. "I was going to kidnap you from Rosylyn."

Dana smiled. Karen was always so impulsive, always surprising her, never predictable. She grabbed her purse and put on her sunglasses and told her, "I'm ready."

On the highway, Dana said, "Do you realize the older you get the faster you drive?"

"Don't sass me, little lady," Karen said in a mock Texas accent. "Why don't ya come on over here and set yerself down right beside me? Give them cowboys somethin' to holler about?" Dana was reluctant. "Come on, little cowgirl. I don't bite." Karen grinned.

"Don't tease me."

"I'm not picking on you," Karen said, surprised. "I was just trying to cheer you up."

"I'll feel better when Rosylyn goes.... I really think I might stay in Cody." Dana was quiet. "I kind of feel responsible for Rosylyn. I know I shouldn't. I'm all she has. She's very lonely. An alcoholic. Her husband is divorcing her and she's really distraught over that. I hope she doesn't get suicidal. I feel guilty thinking of leaving her. I've been planning to for some time now."

Karen didn't reply for a while. Then she said, "She's really in love with you, isn't she?"

"No," Dana said. "She's just really attached to me for some reason. I'm like the daughter she never had. I don't know if she's gay. It's hard to imagine. But she does act like she *has* to have me in her life."

"Well, I've been straight, too, Dana, but.... Well, you know you're special, Dana."

"What do you mean?"

"She could be married and in love with you—like I've always been.... I know she's in love with you."

"She thinks lesbianism is disgusting and immoral."

"She's just scared.... I know, I've struggled with it myself. It's so confusing. But I'm almost positive now that I'm gay. I'm admitting it to myself." Dana was relieved to hear Karen finally admitting it. But Karen quickly changed the focus back to Rosylyn. "But if she's in love with you like I suspect, you should get away from her." She nodded decisively. "Don't feel guilty about leaving her. It's not like you're leaving her. You're just quitting a job. God, it's not like you're her lover. You have to do what's best for you. Just like she's watching out for her own interest. Do you think she's thinking about what's best for you at all?" Karen paused, then said, "Really she's just a garden-variety terrorist whose seized your place. You've been taken hostage."

Dana laughed at the idea, then was quiet.

"You know what I really feel guilty about?" Dana said. I feel bad because I was hoping for an easy out with her, one I couldn't be blamed for, and then Daddy died and...."

"Oh no you don't! Stop right there. You didn't bring on your dad's death. Don't give it another thought."

Tears gathered in Dana's eyes. The combination of Karen here beside her, Daddy being gone forever, and the sadness she felt for Rosylyn, easily brought up tears. Karen reached out and took Dana's hand, and pulled her toward her. "Sit by me. It'll make me happy. It'll make you happier."

Dana scooted over. Karen dropped Dana's hand on her thigh. Dana wondered, is she just being so affectionate because Daddy died and Rosylyn's giving me a hard time?

"Wouldn't it be great if we just kept on driving for as long as we wanted? Down the Rockies all the way to Mexico. Good-bye Teddy. Good-bye Rosylyn," she said lightheartedly. "No more hassles."

"No more headaches."

"No more heartaches."

"For Christ's sake, slow down."

What a wonderful picnic that was, Dana thought, sitting in Daddy's armchair later that night. And what a good dinner Karen's Mom made. Damn, where's Rosylyn? It was midnight and she still had not returned after disappearing this morning. Feeling manipulated, she grabbed her purse and the keys to the pick-up.

She's probably passed out drunk in town somewhere, Dana worried bitterly.

In the pick-up, she searched the sidewalks intensely. This was not the first time she had done that. She recalled nights when Daddy didn't come home until she retrieved him from the bar. She drove up the side streets. No Rosylyn anywhere. Suicide? And Dana to blame. Stop those crazy thoughts, she scolded herself. She pulled up to the bar Daddy used to go to. No Rosylyn. Another bar.

No Rosylyn. Another and another.

Dana stepped into the murky atmosphere of the fifth bar. A bartender in a checkered vest and red bow tie was wiping a glass dry. A voice told him, "My husband was no good. Sometimes you get so mad you'd like to hire a professional killer. Pour me another." The bartender glanced uneasily at Dana as she approached Rosylyn. Rosylyn looked over and stopped talking. Her lower lip hung out, glowing wet. She tried to focus on Dana, holding on to her glass and to the bar top as if they were life rafts. "What are you doing here," she muttered, looking hurt and angry. The bartender wiped off the counter by her glass.

As motionless as a coat on a hanger, Dana gazed at Rosylyn, a haunting memory of Daddy, drunk, invading her mind. She glanced at the bartender, embarrassed that someone was witnessing this. "Do you want a ride back to the house?" she asked.

Rosylyn looked at the bartender with a bulldog expression.

"This girl's...let me tell you...I flew all the way from San Francisco to help her bury her father and now she's trying to kick me out of the house."

"Oh, are you Frank Wilkins girl by any chance?" he said, his bald head shining under a sole overhead light. Dana nodded. "I'm sorry about your father. I didn't know him all that well but he did come in here once in a while."

"I've given her money for a long time to help her," Rosylyn muttered. "Gave her a home and...."

"Nice guy your father was," the bartender baritoned out, "the little I did know him." He glanced uncomfortably at Rosylyn.

"Thank you," Dana said.

Rosylyn glowered. "She's got no gratitude. This girl's a...."

"Come on, Rosylyn! I'm taking you home." Dana worried that Rosylyn was going to make a public announcement that she was a lesbian. Dana's voice had a controlled anger as she stepped up and took Rosylyn's arm, saying, "Let's go, Rosylyn." The bartender winked at Dana in agreement to her purpose. Rosylyn jerked her arm back onto the bar. Dana took the arm and pulled back again. "Time to go home."

Rosylyn downed her drink and teeter-tottered to her feet. "I thought you didn't want me home?"

Dana did not answer, walking Rosylyn out to the empty street; a lonely moon hung low over it.

Back home, she tucked a reluctant childish Rosylyn in her childhood bed, and leaned over to straighten the covers out. "Yer a good little girl to bring me home," Rosylyn said. "I knew you wouldn't let me down like that." Dana felt a rubbery hand around the back of her neck, pulling her downward toward her lips. Her neck resisted. "Give me a goodnight kiss."

Confused, Dana pulled away into the dark, walking backwards. You're really drunk, she thought, shocked.

CHAPTER 29

The sliding glass door swished open. "How would you girls like some cold watermelon and iced tea?" Karen's mother wore an apron dotted with tiny red and blue flowers. She set a yellow tray down, laden with cut watermelon, long spoons, sugar, lemon wedges, and a plastic pitcher of tea.

"Thank you," Dana said, smiling pleasantly at this woman in the blonde bouffant hairdo who was like a mother to her as a teenager.

"Would you like to stay for supper, Dana? I'm fixing spareribs and cherry pie."

"I'd love to but I'm driving Rosylyn to the airport tonight," Dana said. She had made Rosylyn another airline reservation. This time she decided to drive her to meet the plane instead of trusting Rosylyn to take a taxi.

"Then promise us you'll come for breakfast tomorrow."

"I promise," Dana said, looking forward to this. Karen's mother was the best cook in Wyoming. Dana used to be invited to supper every Sunday—until Teddy entered the picture.

"You girls be careful not to burn out here. Karen, you know how easily you burn."

"Yes, mother-r-r," Karen said and gave her an exasperated but loving smile. Her mother stepped inside, closing the sliding door, and Karen turned to Dana and said, "Let's go camping tomorrow like we used to. For my last night here. It'll be good for us to get away together out of doors. Some place this side of Yellowstone."

"Rosylyn, please pack your bags. You have a flight at seven." Rosylyn didn't budge, sitting in Daddy's armchair, refusing to speak.

Rosylyn glared at Dana with eyes to kill. Dana remembered her telling that bartender how she sometimes fantasized hiring a professional killer to get her husband. It made Dana shudder. Maybe the killer had an enticing discount, two for the price of one. Rosylyn never could resist a bargain.

Rosylyn looked at her long red nails, which glinted like lethal weapons. She finally spoke. "I don't think it's good for a person to be all alone after a death. It's not good for yer mental health. I'm worried about you."

Frustration knotted up in Dana. It *would* take the National Guard to remove Rosylyn. The frustration was too much. Tears welled up in her eyes. Her heartbeat quickened like a cornered animal's. Her face reddened.

"Yer not feeling well," Rosylyn pointed out again, looking at Dana.

The tears ran down Dana's face.

"You shouldn't be left alone at a time like this."

"Please go," Dana said, feeling tortured. "If you won't pack, I will pack for you." She felt pushed to the breaking point. Finally, the tears suddenly gushed out. "I appreciate all you've done for me," Dana said, frustrated, "but I really want to have some time alone now and be on my own."

Rosylyn stared at her like she was a sorry spectacle. She still did not say she would pack or leave. She did not say a thing. She did not budge. Dana felt as if she were pushing against a thick iron wall. It angered her that Rosylyn just sat and stared at her. Threat of hired killers or not, she would have to force her to move. "Rosylyn, I'm going to have to..." The words jammed up uncomfortably in her throat. "...To call the police to get you to go."

In a low voice, Rosylyn said, "All this grieving's gotten in yer mind in an unfavorable way. You don't even sound like yerself anymore."

Dana wiped the tears out of her eyes.

Rosylyn laboriously stood up and said, "When my mama died I wanted to crawl up in a hole too. I was sick with grief too." Her hand fell to rest on Dana's shoulder.

Dana suddenly felt immensely sorry for this pathetic woman. She had such a rotten, unfulfilled, grabbing life. I don't ever want to become like her, Dana thought. I want to be totally free of her. I want to make my own life. All mine.

She felt sad as if at a funeral for Rosylyn and her. I do care for her, love her, Dana eulogized to herself. I do want her to be happy. She placed her hand on Rosylyn's hand for one brief moment. A salute to their time together. Then she took it away and slowly said, "I'll go pack your bags for you now."

"I think yer making a mistake," Rosylyn said.

Dana silently headed toward the bedroom. She tried not to listen to Rosylyn yelling, "They don't want yer kind in Cody. Yer better off in San Francisco with yer own kind. They'll run you right out of a clean little town like this." Hearing this new argument, Dana was angry and sensed the full weight of Rosylyn's desperation. She'd use anything to convince Dana to stay with her. It reminded her of how she used to feel toward Karen—desperate, afraid, obsessed, needy.

Dana set her suitcases down beside her and said in a mechanical monotone, "I'm ready to drive you to the airport."

Rosylyn finished her drink and got up and poured herself another in the kitchen.

"I'm going to call a taxi for you then if you won't go with me."

"You'll just embarrass yerself when it comes because I'll tell them I didn't call a taxi."

"Please, Rosylyn. Leave."

Rosylyn stood up. Dana grew hopeful. But no, she was just heading for the bathroom. The bathroom door shut and the lock clicked. Ten minutes passed. Damn her, Dana thought. Then suddenly the whole thing seemed ridiculous. Where did this crazy drunk woman come from anyway? What right did she have to abduct the bathroom? Was she planning to live in there now, locked inside? It could be a best seller, *The Lady in the Latrine*. No, she probably thought this was the ultimate bargaining tool, locking someone out of the sole bathroom in the house. Dana shook her head, laughing out loud. This was insane.

For the first time, stronger now and not so afraid of being alone, she saw the absurdity of her situation with Rosylyn. How could she have ever felt so dependent on Rosylyn for security? It struck her as funny suddenly that she had been afraid of herself. Was a cat afraid of itself? Or a bird? No. Dana considered it would make more sense in the future to be a bird alone than a bird who thought itself safer in the company of a feline. She could not suppress the laughter.

Rosylyn came out and huffed into the kitchen, obviously unnerved by Dana's laughter. "Do you want some cold meat loaf?" The line seemed so out of place that it added to Dana's sense of the absurdity of all of this. "How about some peas?" Dana tried not to laugh. "Jell-O?" Rosylyn's attempt at normalcy via food suddenly seemed hilarious to Dana. Next thing she knew Rosylyn would ask her to run to the store for Mop and Glow and fly strips.

"There's nothing funny about food," Rosylyn said, irritated. "If you don't stop laughing like that the men in white suits will come take you away." She poured herself another drink. "Yer not well. Now what do you want for supper?"

"I don't want anything but for you to leave."

"What's good on TV tonight? That's what this house is missing, a good subscription to *TV Guide*. You really should get some food in you," Rosylyn said as if Dana was disinterested in food because she was emotionally ill, grief stricken. "Check the local paper there on the footstool for the TV listings. A little boy came up to the house earlier today asking if I wanted a subscription to the paper."

"And what did you tell him?"

"Well, I thought we'd help him out."

This was unbelievable.

"I like having a morning paper to read after breakfast."

"You're not going to be here to read it," Dana said firmly.

Rosylyn ignored the comment.

"If you don't leave, you'll force me to have to call the police."

Rosylyn sat down alone at the kitchen table and ate her Jell-O, cold meat loaf and peas.

Dana went to the phone.

"What's the trouble?" a tall, young, black-haired policeman asked, standing under the burnt out porch light.

"I have a house guest who refuses to leave," Dana said, embarrassed. She could not ever remember feeling this nervous. Her hands trembled.

The policeman leaned in the door and looked at Rosylyn, who looked at him, the TV chattering beside her, the room laden with cigarette smoke, an empty bottle of gin beside her. She sat as silent as a live hand grenade. "Who is she?"

"Rosylyn Horstman."

"Where does she live? Is she a relative?"

"She lives in San Francisco. We're not related. I was her maid in San Francisco. She came out here to help me bury my father. I can't get her to go home."

"Why won't she leave?"

"I don't know," Dana said, not wanting to attempt to explain Rosylyn and her to him, not completely understanding it all herself yet.

"I'll talk to her," he said quietly and winked at Dana. "I'm good at talking to people."

"Ma'am, the young lady wants you to leave her house," he said in a sweet voice. "I'm sorry, ma'am, but you'll have to go. Would you like me to drive you to a motel?" Silence. "Would you like to tell me what's troubling you? Why don't you want to leave?"

"You know how I met her?" Rosylyn said as if just placed on the witness stand.

Dana stared out the front door, not wanting to be a part of this.

"She rear-ended my Mercedes Benz, smashed up the bumper. Never paid me a penny for that...."

Dana spun around, furious. "That's not true...."

But Rosylyn was like a tank without brakes. There was no stopping her. "So I told her she could work as my maid to pay off the debt seeing as she had no money, no job, no friends, no nothing and was living in a slum-hole. I thought I'd help her out. A lot of help she turned out to be staying out all night or staying in and causing just as much worry. I found her one night in a back room at my home with a...." Dana's heart nearly stopped, stunned. "With a god damned bull-dyke and she...."

That damn machine gun mouth.

The cop quickly threw up a hand like a stop sign. "Now, ma'am, I'm sorry, but...."

"She took me for what I was worth!"

Dana would have liked to blow Rosylyn up.

"She's sick. Sick with grief since her father died. What sane person would call the police on a house guest? And she's doubly sick because she's queer. You don't want...."

The cop sternly interrupted again. "How about I carry these suitcases out for you? And take you to a nice motel?" Then he added, "And I can give you the number of someone to talk this out with."

"You don't want homosexuals moving into this little town and upsetting it. I think this girl should go back to where she belongs."

"Ma'am," the cop said, reaching for her elbow. "Let me help you up." Rosylyn still wouldn't budge. "I'd hate to have to arrest you."

Rosylyn looked at Dana with an intensity of hate that astounded her. Her glare then sliced at the policeman. It was deadly quiet.

"A garden-variety terrorist..." Karen's description of Rosylyn came to mind. "...who's seized your place." Dana cracked a smile. She suddenly saw this as a scene from *A Day in the Life of Dana Wilkins*—the red-faced copy, *the terrorist and the hostage*. She painted an ammunition belt crisscross on Rosylyn's chest, plopped a beret on her head and a squirt gun in her hands. She painted a gold sheriff's badge and cowboy hat on the cop. She saw herself, the hostage, tied up to the floor lamp, her hair standing on end, and she tried unsuccessfully to muffle her laughter. *A garden-variety terrorist*. She could not control her laughter. She looked at Rosylyn quickly and was surprised to see a look of bewilderment.

"Come on, ma'am, let's go," the cop repeated sternly, glancing uneasily at Dana, impatience bursting all over his reddening face.

Rosylyn slurred, "You must be a homosexual yerself siding with her kind." Rosylyn stood up, looking defeated, and the cop grabbed her at the elbow and moved her toward the door. "I'd say you've had one too many to drink," he said. "You could use a stay at a detox center."

Rosylyn jerked her arm away from him. "Call me a cab. I aim to remove myself as far as possible from you—I ought to slap you with police brutality—and as far away as I can get from her! She's a raving lunatic, you heard that laughter. I told you she's sick. Call me a cab this instant!"

"Call her a cab," he said to Dana.

Dialing, Dana overheard, "You'll have to wait outside. This young lady obviously doesn't want you in the house."

Dana's heart beat so hard it could jump right out of her.

Rosylyn picked up her suitcases, refusing to let the policeman help, and walked indignantly to the door as if leaving of her own accord. She turned to Dana. "You're fired!"

Dana suppressed a grin over the comment.

"You won't get away with treating me like this after all I've given you," Rosylyn said and walked out. She did not look back. She stood in the darkness in front of the house next door.

A watchdog eye on Rosylyn, the policeman said, "If you have any more trouble with her, just give me a call. My name's Marty." He stepped off the porch then turned around with a curious smile. "I hope you don't mind me asking, but was all that true?"

Feeling cornered and angry at Rosylyn for causing this cop to zero in on her, Dana was queasy about the Cody Police Department knowing she was a lesbian. Cody was a small town.

"I do mind you asking."

Both his hands flashed up in the air in innocence. "Didn't mean to get personal." Then the policeman looked over at Rosylyn, at Dana, at Rosylyn, as if putting incriminating evidence together. He said leadingly, "You two both from San Francisco?"

Dana would have liked to kick him. "No, I'm from Cody. Born and raised here."

CHAPTER 30

"Serra sponda, serra sponda...," their voices sang out, accompanied by the flickering and hissing fire. A brook babbled nearby.

"What's another old girl scout song?" Karen said, after they finished the song, poking a stick into a marshmallow and roasting it in the fire. "I like them nice and burnt." Karen started singing, "There are suitors at my door," a song which referenced a father. Dana was so sensitive to any song about a father. There was such an emptiness in her where he once was. It was as if a whole organ was missing inside now. A light flickered off in the huge RV on the embankment far above them.

"Shhhh! Don't sing so loud," Dana said. "The other campers are going to sleep."

"They can't see us at all or hear us down here. Besides it's soothing to hear people sing around a camp fire in the distance while you fall asleep.... You seem sad tonight, Sweetie. Kinda distant. Are you feeling sad?"

"I'm O.K.," Dana said, melancholy, gazing off into the dark still meadow bordering them. Pine trees hemmed the meadow on the other side, flocked together below a gargantuan granite cliff that was grayish-white in the moonlight. "Daddy and Rosylyn are both in the back of my mind. I've been going through a lot lately.... I've decided not to go back to San Francisco, for sure. I don't care if I lose my deposit on that apartment. Before I flew to Cody I cleared my stuff out of the sublet because it ended this weekend, and I left it all stored at Rosylyn's because I thought I might be here a while to take care of Daddy. I'll have to call Rosylyn or see her to get my things. I'm dreading having to contact her for my things."

Karen reached over and squeezed Dana's arm sympathetically. They were silent.

Not wanting to spoil the evening with her melancholy mood, Dana said, "Teach me some constellations."

Karen lay down on their big pink-and-white squared blanket.

"Lie beside me, Sweetie. The Big Dipper's really clear tonight. See it there."

"In San Francisco," Dana said, lying next to her, "you can't really see the stars at all. They're brilliant here."

"There's the North Star." She squeezed Dana's hand. "Let's play *National Enquirer*. The subject: camping. You start."

They had a tradition of playing *National Enquirer* when they camped. Dana was momentarily quiet, thinking. Then she quickly said, "*The North Star Falls on Sleeping Campers.*"

Karen chuckled and said, "*The North Star Falls on Sleeping Campers and Two Human-shaped Holes Found in Ground.*"

"*The North Star Falls on Sleeping Campers and Two Human-shaped Holes Found in Ground and Relatives Sue Forest Service for Negligence in Wrongful Death Suit,*" Dana said and laughed.

Karen repeated the lengthy headline and before she could add on another segment, Dana went "buzzzzz," imitating a you-goofed buzzer. "One point for me. It's—and Relatives Sue Forest Service, not are sued by....!"

Karen said. "O.K., one to nothing! Round two. Remember the loser of the last round gets to pick the subject. The subject is—Rosylyn Horstman."

Dana groaned.

"Be a good sport," Karen chided. "Remember, nothing in life is all that serious. I'll start—*Hot Dog Queen Holds Wyoming Woman Hostage.*"

Dana laughed. She paused then announced like the best of news casters, "*Hot Dog Queen Holds Wyoming Woman Hostage in San Francisco Penthouse and Woman's Childhood Home.*"

"Stranger than fiction." Karen repeated the headline and added on, "*and National Guard Almost Called to Rescue.*"

Dana repeated it all perfectly and added, "*But Police Force Queen Out.*"

"*—And Now Fugitive is at Large,*" Karen said.

"*—And Sweden Offers Queen Asylum.*"

"*—But She Winds Up in Insane Asylum.*"

"*—Claiming to be Colonel Sanders.*"

They both stopped the competition to laugh.

Chuckling, Karen repeated the whole headline and Dana went "buzz" again, saying, "You goofed when you said and Sweden Grants, it's Offers."

"That was a fun round," Karen said. "You did really well!"

"I never knew my life was so, so *National Enquirer*," Dana said and laughed. She told Karen about *A Day in the Life of Dana Wilkins* and about the imagined paintings for it, and Karen was in tears from laughter.

Giggling still, Karen said, "The final painting should be something like you and me in white wedding gowns at the altar together with our maids of honors and bridesmaids in tuxedos."

The back-door proposal caught Dana by surprise and unnerved her.

They both lay quiet.

A star shot across the sky then burned itself out. "Did you make a wish?" Karen said.

"No." All her dead wishes crowded her memory. Karen would live in New Orleans with her, would let her stay in Stockton with her, would live in San Francisco with her. Jerri would truly love her. Rosylyn would buy the series she painted of her and help her become a famous painter. Rosylyn would stop drinking and be happy. Daddy would live forever. Why wish? It was not something she so readily did anymore. She was more prone now just to pray for serenity. "Did you make a wish?" she said to Karen.

"Yes." She paused. "I wished that we would be together again."

Yeah, until Teddy, Dana thought. "You know you're going back to Teddy."

"I told you I wanted to leave him for good. What I didn't tell you was that I want to because I'm in love with you and want to be with you. I didn't want to overwhelm you with my feelings when you're going through so much."

Dana's voice was bitter. "My answer to that is the same as last time. I haven't changed. I want to see divorce papers. And even then you'll need some time on your own. I don't think it's best for you to just jump from him to me." Do not make me wish for what I can never have, Dana thought, feeling very vulnerable. If I lost you again after losing Daddy, it would take a long time to recover.

"You've changed." Karen sat up suddenly. "You're different. You're not—you're not the sweet giving Dana you were before. San Francisco's changed you. You're aloof. And so clinical." She turned her back to Dana and was quiet. "You don't want me anymore, do you? Not like you used to?"

Dana was silent, remembering how she used to want Karen obsessively. Desperately in love, vulnerable, her world completely centered on her, worshipping her, giving her whatever she wanted. A real roller coaster of joy and pain. "Not like I used to. But I still love you. Very deeply. It just feels more equal now."

Karen was silent. "Just knowing you loved me has always kept me going in all the miserable moments with Teddy."

"I will always love you."

"And I will always love you," Karen said, lying back down next to Dana. "I love you in a way I've never loved Teddy. You're my best friend. My soul mate. You're family. That's how I always think of you."

Dana felt her will power giving way, weakening. She felt uncomfortably vulnerable. Stop this, Dana. Be strong. Go it alone. Be strong. Insist on those damn divorce papers first.

"I still love you much, much more deeply than him. I want to leave him for you. Do you hear me? I need you to know that I finally see that I am a lesbian and you're how I know that."

It was wonderful to hear Karen admit that she was gay again. Out of habit, an old voice spoke from her unconscious, I want you to live with me forever. A new voice rose protectively—stop it, be strong, don't set yourself up again, you need more time alone.

There was a long silence between them.

"Dana, I want to make love with you."

Dana stared up at the stars, her insides free falling with desire as if a handful of shooting stars had been thrown in her, bursting and falling. Her will power dissolved into pure desire. A weakened voice warned, don't. But she was all longing now. Longing for her loving. Longing for sweet release from Daddy, the crying and aching lately. Longing for forgetting the guilt of getting Rosylyn gone. Longing to forget herself, to become drugged by sex, sleep and stars. Karen kissed her. The campfire was splitting into flowering flames. Karen caressed her, the wind whipping the fire, which was at once wild and shy, glazing them with a star-like luster and heavenly heat.

The next afternoon, Karen slid her hand over Dana's bare chest then laid her head on her breasts. "They should make a pillow that feels this good. I wish I didn't have to go." She looked at the clock from Daddy's bed. "I only have an hour." Her hand gently stroked Dana's stomach, then playfully scooted lower. "I'm going to miss you."

Pain plummeted deep in Dana. Her hand swept through Karen's long hair and down her back, over and over in a possessive manner. She wanted to make love so thoroughly and deeply that she would be as full as a horn-of-plenty, so full she would not ache for Karen when she went again. She wanted their bodies to brand each other so brilliantly that her memory would sear endlessly with the pleasure, sustaining her through the lonely trying days to come. She felt Karen dip down in her and slide up. Dana craved for her to go deeper, so deep she would touch her heart. She consumed Karen like another life beating inside her, doubling her strength for when she was alone again.

It was so passionate the air could ignite with the friction. They could become a miracle of spontaneous combustion. A golden warmth flooded her. "I love you so much," Karen said over and over. "I love making love with you more than anyone. This could become habit forming.... I don't want to go back at all," Karen said like a pouting little girl. "I'm so happy with you.... I'm going to tell Teddy that I'm leaving him.... Do you want to live together?"

Dana wanted to say yes, but hesitation gripped her. She didn't fully trust Karen still, not after their painful history. If I say yes, am I just being a relationship addict, she wondered. Was Karen one too? Should I keep insisting on signed divorce papers? I want Karen. I always have. Is this a healthier relationship now that I'm not so obsessed and dependent on her? It's all so confusing. I don't know what's best for me. "I don't know," Dana finally replied. "I need time to think it over."

Karen looked hurt. She was very quiet. At last she spoke, simply saying, "I understand. I don't mean to rush you. You've been going through a lot lately. Take your time to decide. And pray for what's best for us."

Later that night, in the wee hours, Rosylyn rolled atop her in Daddy's bed, crushing her and suffocating her. Claustrophobia closed in upon her. Rosylynaphobia. She could not get away. Those horrid red lips were groping down for hers. Dana awakened from the nightmare, and awakened to a living nightmare: Daddy was dead, Karen had flown back to Stockton earlier, Rosylyn was loose in the universe plotting revenge, and she was totally alone.

As she recovered from the nightmare, her mind began reworking the details of Karen's departure. She had driven Karen to her mother's, then said good-bye to her at the passenger door of her mother's Oldsmobile. Around her mother, Karen acted aloof like a cordial cousin. It was almost as if Dana had dreamt up all that passion. The car motor seemed to growl impatiently as Dana looked at Karen, hoping for something like an emotional surprise party. Hoping for her to pop out of her cake of cool reserve and throw her arms around Dana joyously, lovingly. But Karen had merely kissed her on the cheek quickly and said good-bye. Finally, pulling away in the car, Karen had looked back at Dana longingly, lovingly, her eyes lingering on her until she was out of sight. Dana had suddenly felt needy for her to stay and ached for her as she drove off.

CHAPTER 31

Over the next weeks an anxious and grieving Dana, wanting to bury old ghosts, packed Daddy's things up and put them in the attic, worked on a resume, applied for a job she saw listed in the paper at the Wild Bill Gallery in town, watched TV, and quickly completed two old half-finished paintings in her closet.

One painting was of Karen, abandoned by Dana when she left to go back to Teddy after their four month affair. She enjoyed the power of painting away past pain. It was a cleansing, and it was a kind of communion with Karen. Dana felt a strange intimacy gazing into Karen's eyes in the painting. She was finding she no longer felt hurt by the past with her, but instead just felt a strong love and deep friendship, a being there for one another even though they were in different states. Karen said she had told Teddy she was divorcing him and moving back to Cody. She said that she had seen an attorney about getting a divorce, and in light of that, she was surprisingly supportive of Dana's decision to be alone for now.

Dana also finished an old painting of Lester. She painted a cowboy hat and bandanna on Lester, hoping to sell it to the Wild Bill Gallery.

The past fell away as she painted. Karen hurting her, Lester threatening. It was all past now. It was only her alone now.

Then she started a new painting, a western landscape that she hoped also to sell to a local gallery. Cody had several art galleries with a western focus.

There was a healing magic to painting and time alone, her chosen lifestyle for now. She felt herself changing, evolving as if planets were shifting in her, aligning into better positions. The change was at once exciting and scary, like standing on an alluring precipice. Being *completely* alone was a test she felt she must pass before getting involved with anyone ever again. She needed to prove to herself that she could do it. It was not easy. It was often lonely and frightening. She missed Karen and Daddy, and even Rosylyn.

One night she woke up at three a.m. gripped with anxiety, without knowing why. Her heart beat rapidly. The worry machine started up—I'm totally alone now. What if I can't make it on my own without Karen, without a lover, without Daddy? And, worse, what if I can't make it on my own without Rosylyn? What if I'm forced to go back to work for her because I can't find another job? What if I wind up as a hot dog artist? I guess there could be worse fates than that. I wonder if something could happen to me from spending too much time alone. Monks do it, but then they have each other. I have no one. I have no one. It's scary. What if I fall and am knocked unconscious and no one is here to find me? What if a burglar comes? What if I get really sick without any health insurance to pay for it? What if there's no one to pay for my funeral? What would they do with my body? At that point, Dana started to laugh at herself, suddenly seeing the absurdity of worrying over how she would pay for her funeral. You can make it alone, she told herself. Lighten up. Keep your perspective. Remember, it's only *A Day in the Life of Dana Wilkins*, one day at a time.

Near the end of her second week alone she went for a walk, deciding she needed exercise.
Several blocks from the house she glanced at one of the many motels in town catering to tourists visiting Cody or coming and going from Yellowstone National Park just fifty miles away. Her eyes ran down from a motel vacancy sign to a row of green doors along a worn red walkway to a swimming pool. Two children were fighting over an air mattress in the bright blue pool. Their faces were nondescript in the distance. A large woman was resting on an orange chaise lounge, which matched the color of her hair. Dana saw everything in terms of color these days. "It's my turn, you fucker!" one of the kids yelled.
The large woman yelled, "If I hear either one of ya'll calling the other by another filthy name I'll get yer daddy right out here to give you a whipping." The children fell silent like Dana, who was absolutely mortified. She was tempted to jump behind the nearest tree and hide before Rosylyn spotted her. Head down, she hastened her step toward the nearest side street, her heart beating rapidly.
Why was Rosylyn sitting in a motel in Cody, sunbathing, yelling at some stranger's children? It frightened her.
Back home she began painting again, whipping the brushes

around on the canvas to calm herself down. Seeing Rosylyn was like being invaded. The phone rang and she worried it was Rosylyn.

It was Karen. "Dana, Teddy and I just had a terrible fight. He stormed out of here. It's getting scary here. I told Teddy I was in love with you and that we made love and that I wanted to be with you. I told him that I'm a lesbian. Things are really scary here now. Last week he seemed to accept me saying I wanted a divorce better than hearing all that. This is all so hard."

"Don't worry. It will all be all right just as soon as you get out of there."

"I miss you so much. I wish you'd let me come live with you."

"I still need time alone."

"I know."

The line was silent.

Then Dana spoke. "I saw Rosylyn today sitting at a motel nearby like it was a sanitarium or something. I can't believe it still."

"She's crackers. I think she's having a nervous breakdown."

"I've been trying to figure out how to get my belongings out of the penthouse." Dana itemized in her mind the things of value she had left in the penthouse, caught in transition between the sublet and her new apartment. A gold heart locket heirloom of Grandma Wilkins. A diamond heart necklace from Daddy. A favorite stuffed rabbit from Karen. A couple of paintings in her studio room. Her new color TV and stereo. "I'm going to have to talk to her about getting my things back."

"You know what she'll say—that you'll have to come back to San Francisco to get them. And once she gets you trapped inside the penthouse—*Wyoming Woman Held Hostage...!*" Dana laughed. Karen continued, "Why don't you fly out here now while she's in Cody and we'll get your things and spend a few days alone together in San Francisco, the penthouse all to ourselves?"

Sometimes Karen came up with the most far-fetched ideas. "No way. If she found us there it'd be *Queen Finds Two Women in Royal Bed and Beheads Them.* And at the minimum, we'd get slapped with breaking and entering, no pun intended," Dana said with a giggle.

"No, no," Karen said with a laugh. "*It's Two Women Overthrow Monarch and Take Over Penthouse.*" She added, "*And Hot Dog Empire and Live Happily Ever After.*"

Dana laughed and said, "What's really silly is if I said yes you'd actually have us rendezvous in the penthouse."

"I know it's a wild idea. I just want to see you." Karen was quiet. "I'll call again soon."

The call left Dana with an uncomfortable intensification of missing Karen. She decided to drive deep into the calm Cody countryside to let her emotions settle down.

On the way out of town, she swung by the motel, trying to muster up courage to talk to Rosylyn about getting her belongings back. From the pickup she scanned the pool side and the windows of the motel room. There was Rosylyn sitting by an open window. She looked like a lifeless wax figure preserved in a museum. Unnerved, Dana pressed hard on the gas and escaped into the countryside.

She wondered why Rosylyn was sitting in that motel room alone like that, waiting, waiting.

She was a contaminant in Cody.

I don't want to think about her, Dana thought angrily, feeling as if Rosylyn was waiting to see if she came searching for her so she could lasso her like a little calf. Or waiting as she did at the penthouse after pulling her disappearing act on her husband, hoping it would make him give in to her terms.

"Mrs. Horstman's not in," the motel desk clerk said.

Clenching the phone tightly, Dana was partly relieved. "Could I leave a message for her? Could you please tell her Dana Wilkins wants her belongings back?"

"I'll tell her as soon as she returns. She went off with a Realtor just a bit ago to look at some ranch house."

A ranch house? My God, she's going to..., "Thank you for taking my message" ...going to live here?!

She sat still in Daddy's armchair. Damn, she thought angrily. Damn if she thinks she can buy me back. I want her out of this town. Her hand formed a fist. Why won't she leave me alone?

A week passed and the only call was from the Wild Bill Gallery; they wanted her to come in for an interview for the position of ad designer combination art salesperson. Rosylyn never replied to her message and Karen hadn't called all week. She spent the week burning off her anxious energy over them by whipping out two action paintings of wild horses, hoping to sell them at one of the local galleries.

Dana envisioned Rosylyn in her ranch house with a room all set up with Dana's abducted belongings. She dialed the desk clerk again. "Yes, I gave her the message. But she checked out of here a couple days ago."

Dana called the penthouse in San Francisco, and was alarmed to find the number disconnected. She called the front desk and learned that Rosylyn moved out, taking everything with her. She didn't leave a forwarding address. Damn her, Dana thought, taking my stuff, trying to manipulate me like this. She's always tried to manipulate me. I was so dumb to ever fall for that patron crap.

She dialed Stockton. Teddy answered. "I told you to stay away from my wife!" Teddy's voice loudened. "You're lucky you're not in Stockton or...."

Dana heard the phone hit something and then a raucous commotion. Dana could hear Karen yelling in the background. "You've succeeded in fucking up everything," Teddy said. "Don't ever call here again." The phone disconnected.

Frightened for Karen, Dana called back. Karen answered but the phone disconnected immediately.

The line was busy all night.

Finally, at two a.m., the phone rang. In a hushed voice, Karen said, "He's a jealous maniac. He broke a vase. He's been monitoring the phone like a cop every day. He's nuts! He doesn't want me to talk to you as long as I'm here still. But I'd never see him again as long as I live before giving you up in any way again. I've gotten to that point. Dana, I have to get out of here now. I want to come back to Cody now. I want to live with you."

There was a long silence.

"I've got to get out of here," Karen said again. "I'm leaving Teddy. I'm flying to Cody tomorrow. Dana, I'm coming home. I want to see you, Sweetie."

Although Dana was concerned for Karen, she did not like how desperate she was sounding. Dana understood all too well the panicky and needy state Karen was in now.

It was very hard to say, but Dana said in a gentle voice, "Please don't come see me until the divorce papers are signed and you've had some time on your own. I want you to settle things with Teddy first. We can still talk on the phone, but we should limit it to once a week if you're in Cody."

"Oh, Dana, stop it. You've gotten all these crazy ideas and rules from those groups in San Francisco. I need you now. This is no time for playing San Francisco games."

"This isn't a game," Dana said. "I thought you understood my need to be alone." She understood it until she had to face being on her own, Dana thought. "This isn't a fun and glamorous thing I'm doing. I just need to do this. I want to be sure before getting back with you. And I want you to be certain about leaving Teddy."

"Aren't you sure about us any more?"

"I need to be sure you're sure. You need time alone, too."

"I had three months alone in Cody on my last separation from Teddy. I know what I want. I want you."

"And I know what I want—for us to take time alone. I love you, Karen. But if you come to Cody, come for yourself, not for me."

The line was silent for a long time.

Dana dared to suggest, hoping to lighten things up, "Feel like playing *National Enquirer*? Subject—Us."

Karen laughed, paused, then said, "You mean something like *Woman Flees Maniac Husband to Arms of First Love?*"

"*Once Again*," Dana said without repeating the headline.

"Touche," Karen said, "and ouch!" Then she added to the headline without repeating it, "*But Divorcee-to-be Finds First Love Now a Monk Locked in Monastery.*"

"*Hiding from Maniac ex-Boss Just Escaped from Asylum.*"

"*And Threatening to Buy Ranch House by Monastery and Destroy Monk's Solitude*," Karen said and chuckled.

"*But the Pope Intervenes!*"

With sarcastic glee, Karen said, "*When Pope Finds Monk Studying Divorce Law After Contracting Strange Preoccupation with Proper Divorce Procedures.*"

"*And First Love is ex-Communicated.*"

"*By both the Pope and the Divorcee-to-be.*"

Dana retorted, "*Who Both are Stark Raving Mad from Enforced Celibacy.*"

"*Monk Found Strangled by Divorcee-to-be.*"

"Touche," Dana said and they both laughed.

Dana resolved to stick to her decision not to see Karen when Karen arrived in Cody shortly after their last phone conversation. She stuck to her resolve for the next seven weeks. During this time, she landed the job at the Wild Bill Gallery. When the opportunity arose, she showed the owners her own paintings. They were delighted with her work and selected several landscapes, the portrait of Lester as a cowboy, and three action paintings of horses to show in the gallery. The gallery job and the showing of her own artwork helped her to stay on course with her goal of building a relatively satisfying life on her own. It was not always easy, but she felt she was growing stronger and felt more able to survive the fear, grief, loneliness and pain of the past months. She was full of conflicting emotions toward Rosylyn. Feelings of anger, worry, love, guilt, relief, sadness, and even a feeling of missing her. It was bewildering.

She wanted to be with Karen, but not until she saw those divorce papers.

CHAPTER 32

It had been almost three months since they last saw each other, three months since Daddy died.

Karen gave Dana a big kiss as she stood in Dana's house. "See the signatures. I filed the papers." There was Karen's signature graciously swooping across the divorce papers. There was Teddy's, a tight, black scribble. Dana could not believe it. Karen hugged her and said, "I love you."

"I love you, too," Dana said, feeling very happy. Karen looked at her with a tender smile. For the seven weeks since she left Teddy, she had lived at her mother's. For the last four weeks, she had worked as a waitress at *Little Joe's Steak House*. Although Dana did not see Karen during this time, they did have a rich phone life. Karen continued to tease that the whole set-up was a strange San Francisco idea Dana had concocted. At first Karen was angry about it, but she adjusted to it and didn't complain.

"We're going to have a lot of lost time to make up for," Karen said. "But we'll have a lot of time in which to do it." She kissed her again.

A smile seized Dana's lips hoping to be as permanent as the green of her eyes. The divorce was being completed. That marriage, that scorpion always stinging her, was finally taking its last gasp.

A mischievous look crossed Karen's face. "Just think, I won't be committing adultery this time." She grinned playfully. "Shall I carry you over the threshold or you me? This is our honeymoon night, you know." Karen eyed the immaculately made bed and feigned a Southern accent, imitating Rosylyn, as she said, "Some say you can tell a good maid by how she makes a bed. I say you can tell by how she is in bed."

Over breakfast the next morning, Dana listened to Karen say with a sentimental flippancy, "Maybe you and me will have a baby together, maybe two."

"That's kind of impossible," Dana teased. "Unless we have an immaculate conception."

Karen giggled at the thought of a double immaculate conception. She said, "Hail Dana and Karen, full of grace, the Lord is with thee, blessed art thou amongst women."

Dana chuckled, then said, "Mary was probably a lesbian. Who but a lesbian would choose to stay a virgin after marrying a man?!"

Karen cracked a smile at Dana's comment. Then she said, "At least I won't ever have to worry about birth control again! This is the perfect birth control method." She looked out the window. "We could have a baby if we ever wanted one."

Dana asked, "What are you going to tell your Mom about us?"

"I've got to lead my own life. She won't like it." Karen stood up. "I need to get the last of my things out here from Stockton. If Teddy tries to keep any of my stuff like Rosylyn did...."

"You know, I called Rosylyn's attorney in Nashville, Simon Johnson. I told him to tell her to get me my things. He wouldn't tell me where she was. She must pay him awfully well. It makes me mad. It's the same disappearing act she played on her husband."

"Do you think she's going to show up here again?"

Dana nodded. "Just like she did at her husband's."

"I'd hate to be living her life, having nothing but a bottle of liquor to keep me company."

"Yeah," Dana said in a quiet voice. "She's really lonely.... It's odd, but I actually miss her sometimes." She wondered where Rosylyn was and what she was scheming. Where were her belongings?

A week later Dana was setting the table for dinner while Karen finished cooking. It was nice to not have to eat alone.

"There's a taxi out front," Karen said. Dana stiffened up. "Oh, my God, it's Rosylyn!" Karen said. Dana stood beside her and they looked out the window like a couple watching a swarm of locusts descending on their crops.

Rosylyn came up the walkway, her eyes aimed at the house.

Karen cracked a smile, put her hand on her hip and said, "I can just hear her now." She pronounced in her best Rosylyn accent, "The light switches and door knobs need a cleanin'. And, my God, look at the dust on the hands of that clock. Dana, yer sick, yer just sick."

Imitating Rosylyn too, Dana retorted, "I just can't function without a maid!" She laughed, for about a second, until she heard the loudest knock she had ever heard on a door.

"I'm not letting her in here," Dana said nervously. The loud rapping on the door sounded like a round of ammunition.

She opened the door slowly, but kept the screen door hooked, separating her from Rosylyn. They silently looked at one another.

Rosylyn suspiciously eyed Karen in the background and the kitchen table laden with salad bowls, rolls and spaghetti. She eyed it all as if accumulating evidence to use against Dana whose mind was quickly thinking, talk her into giving you your things. An old instinct rose to protect Karen and herself from Rosylyn, remembering how impossible it had been with Jerri and Frankie while Rosylyn was around. She knew Rosylyn would try to undermine them.

"I thought you would have been back in Stockton by now, Karen," Rosylyn said, prying but trying to sound politely curious.

"I've filed for divorce from my husband...."

"Rosylyn, I want my things I left in the penthouse. Some were things of sentimental value to me," Dana said.

"Oh, where're you living now, Karen?" Rosylyn said, ignoring Dana.

"That's Karen's business, Rosylyn. Where are my things?"

"You've got this girl living in here with you, don't you? So that's why you ran me out of here."

"Dana doesn't have me doing anything. I want to be here with her," Karen said.

Rosylyn's face recoiled into tight wrinkles when Karen said, "Why don't you just let Dana be?"

"I'm here to talk to Dana. Not you! Dana, I want to speak with you in private."

"Tell me where my things are first. You've no right to...." Dana stopped, her mind whirling with thoughts. As long as she has my things, I have to play along with her. Damn, Dana thought, feeling blackmailed. Rosylyn had hooked her in again. Forget your things. No, some are of sentimental value from Daddy and Grandma. Some are expensive, she argued to herself, but you'll never be free if you don't let go of those possessions. She'll be standing on your front porch the rest of your life manipulating you. She'll always have one scheme after another for keeping you hooked in. Let go.

"Keep my things," Dana said, surrendering. "I don't want them."

"Yer kind disgusts me," Rosylyn said.

Hearing that, Dana felt like shutting the door on her, but she maintained her poise. In an angry voice, she said, "Then why do you still want me? I know you want me to come live with you. I know what you want to talk to me about in private!"

"I want nothing to do with yer kind," Rosylyn said self-righteously.

"Then why are you here?"

"Because she's in love with you," Karen said, looking at Rosylyn. "But she'll never admit it to you or herself. It kills her to think of you loving or living with anybody but her. And you know why we disgust her? Because she's disgusted with herself for wanting and needing you so badly."

Rosylyn's face reddened, her body seemed to enlarge as if a tornado was twisting inside her, ready to blow them away. But she sank into a sullen silence.

She was silent for a long time.

A lost look was in her eyes as they reached out to Dana to please come to her defense, save her, to not leave her.

Dana looked back at her with the guilt and concern of one watching someone drown, knowing she would be pulled under too, as she once was, if she reached her hand out. I won't play the victim again, Dana thought. I'm not a victim of anyone or anything. An amusing thought crossed her mind— and certainly not the victim of a can of orange soda.

Rosylyn was so pathetic that it dissolved her anger.

"I was going to make something of you," Rosylyn said quietly, as if not understanding why Dana was abandoning her for someone who had nothing but an impending divorce to her name. She looked pleadingly at Dana, who could hear her silently saying, don't just stand there saying nothing, don't let me down, please, you know I can't be alone, I'm afraid, I'm lonely and getting old. "You know I'll always be there for you," Rosylyn said. "You can come and live with me in a nice ranch house. She's going to leave you someday, Dana."

She resented Rosylyn preying on her fears and trying to undermine her and Karen. "Karen and I plan to stay together a long, long time," Dana said. She was determined they would beat the odds and stay together forever. "I hope we will be together forever. I believe it's possible."

Dana could not clearly see Rosylyn through the screen. It was like looking at someone distanced down under murky water. Dana shook her head slowly from side to side to tell Rosylyn she was not going back with her. Her only giving now was calm silence and compassion. "I do love and care about you, Rosylyn. But not like that. Always think of me as a friend."

Rosylyn let out a sigh, a deep breath laden with worry, loneliness and giving up. "I'll have yer belongings brought here," Rosylyn said. "It's too bad you won't be there for the gallery opening of yer paintings, *A Day in the Life of Rosylyn Horstman*."

Dana stopped herself from asking if there really was a gallery show or asking where Rosylyn would go, knowing Rosylyn would not say as one last pathetic attempt to hook Dana in again. She watched silently as Rosylyn left. She knew she might never see her again, and this saddened her. There was something between them. She felt an empty spot in her formerly occupied with Rosylyn.

Still gazing out the door as if searching for something to fill the empty spot, she felt Karen's hand gently moving in circles on her back. She felt her lightly kiss the back of her neck, and rest her chin on her shoulder, her arms around her, gazing out too. Karen's presence filled her with warmth.

Love rose in her, filling her. She turned away from the door and faced Karen whose lips rested in a smile. Dana's lips formed a smile as if a rose was blooming whole in her.